ARRESTING THE Hockey Player

I0639797

WILLOW FOX

ONE

CHARLOTTE

"Do you swear this isn't a prank?" I ask Amber, my best friend. She's lying on my mattress in my apartment on campus, her chin resting on her hands and her feet kicked up from behind.

"Not a prank. Jasper has been telling me how Noah keeps going on about the hot redhead whom I hang out with. Hence, you," she says, staring at me without so much as a smirk.

I roll my lips together. "I don't have anything to wear!"

I'm not usually the frantic, nervous girl falling apart before a date. I've done my fair share of dating, although it tends to mainly consist of college boys and not professional hockey players.

I've had eyes for Noah Reece since the moment I saw him on the ice. Thankfully, Amber's love interest is Jasper Greyson, and they both play for the Ice Dragons, so there's no rivalry among friends.

"You have an entire closet of clothes I'd die for," Amber says.

"Yeah, but there's nothing *new* in there. I've worn it all before on dozens of other dates with guys I don't want to think about."

Amber quirks a grin and sits on my bed, sliding her legs around so they dangle off the mattress. "Just wear something casual. It's a coffee date with Noah Reece, not an extravagant black-tie affair."

"I don't do casual." Doesn't my friend know that about me? I like to dress sexy, but right now, every outfit in my closet is taunting me with my past, mocking me.

Amber snorts at my remark, and I reach for a pillow on the bed and toss it at her face.

"All you do is casual," she says. "You don't do boyfriends."

She's right, but I like Noah, and that thought alone sends butterflies fluttering in my stomach. Casual is easy. It keeps things from getting messy and complicated. I have enough drama to deal with between NYU and my job keeping me busy. When do I have time for a boyfriend?

I run a hand through my hair.

Who is to say Noah wants anything serious anyway? He's a professional hockey player. Maybe he's looking for a good time with a new fling? I could be that girl. That's who I'm used to being anyhow.

I glare at Amber. "You're rubbing off on me."

Her brow pinches. "What? How?"

I don't tell her that her anxiety seems to have been thrown at me and stuck like an annoying parasite, stealing my sanity.

"Find me something to wear," I say.

She pushes herself off the bed, rummages through my closet, and produces a black leather jacket, dark green shirt, and short black mini skirt. "Wear this with those hot lace-up boots."

"I thought this was casual drinks?" I ask, staring at the outfit Amber picked out. Nothing about it is quiet or friend-like; it screams *let's hook up*. At least, that's why I've worn it in the past. And do I want to hook up with Noah Reece?

Yes, of course.

I'd throw myself at him if it wouldn't get me a restraining order.

He's a ten. He's hot. A professional hockey player. And single.

Why would he be interested in me?

I'm a regular girl, nobody famous. No one interesting, at least not in his world of professional athletes and superstars. The man has dated models. Well, I'm not sure if he's dated them or just taken them to fancy events, but there's always a gorgeous blonde on his arm.

Me?

I'm a redhead, which doesn't fit his type. Fiery. Fierce. And I don't play games.

I quickly get dressed and apply a heavy dose of eyeliner and makeup. I run my fingers through my thick hair, staring back at the mirror, trying to look sexy without it being overkill. I want to be sexy without trying to be, especially knowing what I'm up against, and I'm sure it's easier for one of his model girlfriends. They probably have an entire team dressing them and doing their hair and makeup.

I love my bestie, Amber, but I wouldn't trust her with an eyeliner pen to save my life. She prefers little to no makeup. She can wear the natural look well. Sometimes I envy her. The girl can roll out of bed looking *girl-next-door-sexy*. Me? I work for it.

There's a knock at the door.

"I'll get it!" Amber chimes and jumps from the bed, hurrying out of my bedroom. It's not a far jog. I have a one-bedroom apartment. It costs a pretty penny to be near NYU, but I don't have to pay for any of it, which makes it worth it.

My dad owns the Island Bruisers, the *other* professional New York hockey team. Not even my best friend knows who my father is. She's never met him. I've made a conscious effort not to mention him, especially when we went to Ice Dragons games and she started dating a player on the Ice Dragons team.

"Hey, handsome," Amber's voice echoes through the landscape of the small one-bedroom, and I suck in a shaky breath. Why is Amber flirting with Noah?

I chance a glance out of the bedroom door, and Noah is standing beside Jasper.

Jasper, Amber's boyfriend, pulls her into his embrace and wraps his arms around her waist. "Hey, sweetheart," he whispers, and I glance away as they share a kiss.

I sneak back into the bedroom.

"Is she almost ready?" Jasper's voice carries across the hall.

"Yes," Amber says. "Let me just help her lace up her boots."

Her soft feet pitter-patter against the wood floor as she rejoins me in the bedroom. I'm seated at the edge of the bed, tying up my boots that take ages to get on.

"Ready for your hot date?"

My eyes widen. Does she realize they can hear us? "Keep your voice down," I whisper.

Amber shrugs and smiles. "I approve," she says, glancing me over. "He'll like it."

I glare at her to keep her voice down, but she doesn't seem overly concerned. I stalk out of the bedroom and pause, catching sight of Noah standing by the door with Amber's boyfriend, Jasper.

"We'll get out of your hair," Amber says and snags her purse on the way to the door. She and Jasper head out, leaving Noah and me momentarily alone in my apartment.

He smiles the boyish grin, his brown eyes, bright and speckled with amber, shining back at me. "You look nice," he says, glancing over my body.

My insides warm as his gaze rakes over me.

"As do you," I say and wrinkle my nose. Nice doesn't do his good looks justice. He's cleanly shaven, smells amazing, and is dressed to the nines, in black slacks and a dark blue dress shirt. "You look handsome."

This *just coffee* date feels a lot more formal, with him picking me up at my apartment and seeing what he's wearing. It doesn't feel as casual as I was led to believe. "Should I change?" I ask, tugging my bottom lip between my teeth.

"Whatever you feel most comfortable in for coffee," Noah says and gives me that boyish smile. "But I think you look amazing."

I'm certain that I'm blushing. "Thank you." It's rare that a guy compliments me and isn't looking to bump uglies.

"Are you ready?" he asks, and I grab my keys beside the door along with my clutch that contains my cell phone, wallet, and a few dollars cash.

I'm unsure what to expect, and we walk to the subway. There's no waiting car downstairs, no fancy transportation. It's very normal, and for a professional hockey player, I suppose I expected something more extravagant. But it is *just coffee*.

We switch trains, and I'm curious as he leads me around town through the subway system. "You do know there are good coffee places on campus?" I say with a wry smile.

"Yes, but I can't impress you at those places."

I'm unsure what he means until we exit at the next stop and realize we're at the ice arena. We exit the subway station, and he takes my hand, leading me up the stairs and to the main street. "Is there a really good coffee shop near the ice rink?" I ask.

He smiles and laughs under his breath. "Something like that." Noah leads me around the hockey arena to a back entrance, where he retrieves his identification, and we're granted access inside.

I don't ask if this is allowed.

Obviously, the security team let him in because he's one of the Ice Dragons players, but he's not here for practice or to retrieve something from the locker room.

"Come on," he says and ushers me through the hallways to a locked door. He retrieves an electronic keycard from his wallet and opens the door. The lights automatically flip on, and I take in the sight. It's not the first time that I've been behind the scenes of a locker room or the inside of a stadium. But this isn't the locker room or the equipment room.

There's a coffee bar against the wall and wooden tables set up for seating. On the wall are photographs of the players during different games, and there are press articles framed that gloat about the Ice Dragons winning the Stanley Cup two years in a row. There are signed jerseys from past players affixed behind glass cases on the opposite wall.

"The staff, agents, and sometimes the press use the coffee bar for interviews," Noah says.

"I thought this was a *coffee date*, not an interview," I say with a smirk.

Noah chuckles. "I promise, I'm not interrogating you like some of the press like to do. I just thought you might like to see where I work."

He heads straight to the coffee bar and grabs a mug. "What can I get you? Everything here is automatic. There's a cappuccino, latte, coffee, or I can make you an iced or blended ice coffee drink."

"Do you moonlight as a barista?" I tease.

"How'd you guess? What will it be?"

"A cappuccino sounds wonderful."

He prepares a cappuccino, working the machine like an expert while I head toward one of the tables to sit. Within a matter of minutes, he comes over, bringing two steaming mugs for the two of us to drink.

"I feel like I should be tipping you," I joke as he carefully places the mugs on the table.

He smiles and takes a sip of his drink, not answering me.

"When you suggested a *coffee date*, this was the furthest thought on my mind."

"Good," Noah says. "I aim to impress."

I take a sip of the piping hot drink. "Let me guess, competitive by nature."

"It goes with the sport. You're a gorgeous girl. I'd be foolish to think this was your first date. I wanted to make it clear what I have to offer."

"Backstage access to a coffee bar?" I grin, staring up at him. "You don't have to try and impress me. Just look at you." I wave my hand at him.

He's seated beside me at the small wooden table. "I could say the same about you." Noah tilts his head, staring at me. He ticks his fingers like checkboxes as he goes through the list. "Smart, ambitious, funny, gorgeous."

"That's only four things." I nod toward his thumb, that's still bent. "What do you like to do for fun? Aside from playing ice hockey?"

"Have you ever played?" he asks.

"I may have dabbled in it when I was younger." I don't mention that when I say younger, it was only a few years ago. I played ice hockey in high school, and we made it to state and won. I'm underestimating my skill level, mostly because he's a professional hockey player. With anyone else, I'd be bragging, but it doesn't feel right.

His eyes twinkle. "Finish your coffee, then you're

borrowing a pair of skates, and we're going out on the ice."

Twenty minutes later, I've got a pair of ice skates tied up and secured around my ankles. He hands me a hockey stick and takes one of his own, along with a puck.

My leather skirt is shorter than I'd like for a little ice hockey action, but I appreciate the leather jacket because it's chilly.

I'm effortlessly gliding on the ice, which I'm sure won't be appreciated come morning, but don't they have to Zamboni the ice before a game anyhow?

There are two goals, one at each end of the ice arena.

"Visitors can go first," he says, like he's doing me a favor as he tosses the puck in my direction. It glides across the ice.

I bite down on my tongue, and I skate along the ice, using the hockey stick to maneuver the puck past Noah for the goal.

He's either ill-prepared or completely stunned that I know how to play. Maybe he's letting me score, but that doesn't seem like the Noah I've watched at the Ice Dragons games.

Is he distracted?

"I thought you were competitive?" I shout at him.

He shakes his head, and his gaze tightens. "Just warming up. No sense in straining a muscle," he says, and I watch as he stretches on the ice.

I skate toward the bench, removing my leather jacket. I'm already warm, and we've just begun. I'll be sweating by the time we're knee-deep in a match between us.

"I'm ready," he says and stands. "Are you sure you don't want to stretch first?"

He's right, I should stretch before skating around and chasing his ass on the ice, but I want to start the game. "I'm good."

"Don't say I didn't warn you." He chases after the puck, and I realize he's already started the game.

I curse under my breath and hurry to catch up, but my best bet now that he has gotten the puck is to defend the goal, which is not my strength. By the time I reach the goal, he's shucked it in for a score.

"Just warming up," he says.

I shrug it off. "It's a tie score," I remind him. I started the game before he was completely ready, but he didn't exactly tell me he was going to stretch. I thought we were playing when he handed me the puck.

He doesn't argue with me, probably because he knows he can easily kick my butt in ice hockey. But

I'm not going to bend over and let him win. I'm going to give it my all.

He shoots me the puck after scoring, and I race on the ice haphazardly with it, doing everything I can to block him as he closes in on me. I keep my back to him. I'm smaller, and while it's harder with his long arms and legs as he reaches for the puck, I outmaneuver him, sneaking by as I hurry away.

But with his long strides, he chases after me, and our legs tangle, knocking us both to the ice, Noah falling first and my body landing awkwardly above him.

"Are you okay?" I ask, my body straddling his. He's breathing hard, and our hockey sticks lie beside us, abandoned.

"Yeah, just got the wind knocked out of me." Noah chuckles as his hands find my hips. "Are you okay?"

"I think you took the brunt of the fall." I should stand, untangle from his arms. But my body has other ideas. He's buried between me and the ice, and I don't dare admit aloud that the warmth of his chest and the heat he exudes makes my insides burn.

He smiles, staring at me when I brush my lips against his.

He takes my bottom lip between his teeth, eager

and hungry for more. His fingers slide against my skin, beneath my shirt at my lower back, touching me, pulling me tighter. It's impossible to miss the growing heat between us, nestled at my thighs as I straddle his hips.

He doesn't try to hide it, either. Why would he?

The lights in the ice rink flicker, and I pull back slightly, worried someone may shut off the lights, not realizing anyone is inside.

Thunder echoes overhead, reverberating through the arena, and the lights flicker again. Reluctantly, I move off of Noah and offer him a hand.

We both grab our hockey sticks, and he snatches the puck as we skate back toward the players' bench and head for the locker room.

It takes a few minutes to get my boots laced back on. I slip back on my leather jacket as we head toward the exit. Noah swings the exit door wide open and stops, grabbing me before we step outside.

It's pouring, and rain pelts the pavement. Neither of us thought to bring an umbrella. When we left, the sky was ominous, but it wasn't raining.

"I can order us a ride share," Noah offers. "We're not likely to see a cab except on game nights unless we walk a few blocks and—" He gestures to the weather outside.

"Okay, thanks." I shuffle my feet as he orders a car for us, and we wait until the driver has arrived before high-tailing it outside. We're soaked when we reach the vehicle and climb into the backseat together.

The driver glances in the rearview at us. "Noah Reece. Oh my gosh!" the woman driver squeals with delight. "I saw your picture when I accepted your ride, but I didn't think it was actually you. Can I get an autograph?" The excitement bubbles off her, and Noah smiles politely.

I can't tell if he's thrilled for the attention or just playing it up because that's part of his job, to make the fans happy. "Sure, do you have something for me to sign? I don't have a pen back here, either."

"Oh, no problem! Here, you can just sign my arm in marker."

He laughs and leans forward, using the marker she supplies. I should be relieved the woman isn't lifting her shirt and asking him to sign her boobs.

"If you plan on getting that tattooed, better keep it out of the rain," I joke.

"Good idea. I'll head straight to the tattoo parlor after I drop you guys off."

She can't be serious.

I give Noah a look, and he merely shrugs, shuffling back beside me. He stretches his arm, resting it along the back of the seat, his fingers grazing my shoulder ever so gently.

There's a pang of jealousy that sweeps through me. I can't quite explain it. Noah isn't my boyfriend —we barely know each other—but I don't want any other women fawning all over him.

He smiles, staring at me, watching me intently as he wraps an arm around my shoulder, pulling me closer. "Jealous?" he whispers into my ear.

I inhale sharply. "No. Why would I be jealous?"

He smiles and shrugs. "No reason." He opens his mouth and quickly closes it as if he were about to say something and thinks better of it.

I don't push him into telling me what's on his mind. This is new. I don't want to make a mess of a perfect evening, minus the rain and thunderstorm towering overhead.

The driver pulls up outside my apartment complex. I had been hoping the rain would have ceased or, at the very least, lightened up, but to no avail. I will get soaked when I step out from the dry confines of the vehicle.

"Wait for me," he tells the driver, "I'll be right back. I want to make sure that she gets inside."

I glance at him, surprised he's willing to get soaked for the chance at a good night kiss. Inviting him up seems a bit forward, especially since he told the driver to wait for him.

I hurry out of the vehicle onto the sidewalk and rush up the front steps, water pouring down in buckets as I shove my key into the main door to gain entrance inside.

Noah is right behind me, standing under the sky, rain cascading down him in rivulets as he squints to see me through the deluge.

"Do you want to come in?" I ask. "I have coffee." I laugh awkwardly at my offer, given that's where we came from, getting coffee.

"I do, but I shouldn't," he says, and I hear the engine roar as the vehicle no longer waits for Noah, driving off, leaving him stranded in the rain on my front stoop.

He curses, and I smile with a soft laugh. "Come on in. We can always call you a cab," I say, managing to get the key turned into the lock and yank open the door.

The hallway is bright, given the darkness outside from the dark thunderclouds overhead. We are both soaked, our feet squishing and sloshing, leaving a mess behind us on the floor as we head for the stairs. "No elevator," I say.

"I think I can handle it."

He's an athlete, a professional one. Of course, he can manage a couple of flights of stairs. I grip the handrail and climb the staircase, dripping in the process.

Noah is right on my heel, and I keep hoping that I don't slip and fall on my ass, taking him down with me. Thankfully, I make it up to the third floor and yank open the stairwell door, holding it open for Noah to follow.

He waits beside me until I lead him down the hallway, not that he isn't familiar with my apartment complex. He did pick me up a few hours earlier with Jasper. "This way," I say as I lead him down the hall as we approach my front door. I unlock the door, flip on the lights, and shiver. The heat is barely on. It's been moderate outside the past couple of days, a nice warm-up for fall.

But with the rain soaking me through, I'm chilly. I need to get out of my wet clothes. I stand at the front entrance inside my house, working tirelessly on unlacing my boots without leaning on the wall because I'm wet.

Noah watches for a beat and removes his shoes

without me asking. His socks are soaked, leaving an imprint on the wooden floorboards. He removes those next and pulls his shirt off over his head, undressing.

Glancing up at him as I'm bent forward attempting to remove my boots lands me toppling over. He catches me before I hit the floor with about as much grace and elegance as a cow tipping over. I'm a mess, and I can't imagine he has a single sexy thought running through his head while he's undressing.

However, my mind is entirely on him. His chiseled abs, wet hair, and skin that glistens in the light. My insides stir with a familiar warmth, and the shivering and chills I felt from the cold dissipate as the room is several degrees warmer.

"Careful," Noah says, his hands on my shoulders, steadying me from falling face-first onto the floor. His touch is warm and firm, and his fingers move from my shoulders down my arms. "How did you even get those boots on?" he asks at my predicament of attempting to remove them. It's an obvious struggle, and I'm grateful he's not laughing at me.

"They weren't wet." I don't intend on stalking into my bedroom with wet clothes and plopping my rear down to remove my shoes. "I swear they shrunk in the rain," I mutter to myself, but he laughs, apparently overhearing my remark.

"Let me," he says and bends down onto one knee.

I gasp softly at his position, his nose right near my crotch, my leather skirt riding up slightly from bending forward and nearly falling onto the floor.

His voice is gravelly and thick as he glances up at me. "Put your hands on my shoulders," Noah instructs.

I'm at his mercy, the top of my laces loose but not undone enough to free me. He loosens the ties and helps guide my foot from the boot, letting me lean on him for support.

"One down. One to go," he rasps, and for a moment, he's staring at my skirt, directly at my pussy, before his gaze moves up to meet my stare. "You're shivering." His eyes are dark, his voice thick, and I inhale sharply.

"I didn't notice." Heat floods my very existence as he steadies me. One foot is planted on the cold floor, the other nestled tight in the leather boot.

Noah's hands graze over my hips, keeping me in front of him, his fingers firm and warm as he guides them across my bare thigh, his touch setting me ablaze.

His eyes watch mine, his movements slow and

methodical as he moves toward his intended target, the laces of my boot.

I press my lips together, burying the moan inside me like the fire that stirs with an unwavering heat. His touch is electric, the vibration between us magnetic, and I want to pull him to my feet, kiss him, touch him, taste him.

With dark eyes, he watches me intently while undoing the lace of the leather boot, his gaze never wavering.

"I feel like Cinderella," I joke, "except you're taking off my glass slippers."

Noah smiles and chuckles while loosening the laces from the top all the way down to the bottom. My feet ache from the heels but the pain is dulled by his presence. "Hold on," he warns before tugging and gently gliding the boot down my leg and off my foot.

"Impressive."

"I'll say. How is it that women can manage to wear those and walk?"

I didn't have nearly as much trouble getting the boots off during our *coffee date* when we decided to slip into a pair of skates, but the rain worked like a vise, shrinking the cold, wet leather around my legs and feet.

"With lots of practice and training."

Noah hasn't moved off the floor, his hands on my bare legs. His touch is warm and possessive as he guides his palms up my calves to my thighs. He draws soft patterns over my bare skin, my skirt inching up slightly as he guides my legs farther apart.

He can see my panties from his position on the floor, and my tongue darts out, letting out a soft gasp as his lips move across the inside of my thighs. "I can smell your scent, sweetheart. You smell so good," he whispers, kissing and licking my thighs, moving higher toward my panties. "I want to taste you."

His tongue darts out, tasting me over my panties, and I'm sure that I'm already soaking wet as his tongue fucks my pussy through the soft cotton material.

"Noah," I whisper, and my breathing hitches as he finds that sweet, delicate spot, my tiny nub, with his tongue. My hips rock against his mouth, and his fingers press into my sides, holding me in place and guiding me as he teases me through my panties.

My heart pounds wildly against my chest, the sound all I can hear with my heavy gasps for air as he warms me to the core. I tangle my fingers through his thick dark hair, tugging him closer, deeper, wanting to feel more as I tremble against him.

"Good girl," he whispers, pulling back slightly, just enough to tug my panties to the side.

My lips part, and I gasp as his tongue grazes my swollen clit. I reach for the wall behind me, needing support, something to steady me because I feel like I am floating.

"Eyes on me, baby." Noah's words bring me back, staring down as he watches me. It's intimate and sends my heart soaring, and my insides clench, shuddering and trembling in his embrace.

He doesn't let up or slow until I've come down from the high, gasping and breathing hard.

He gently pulls back, fixing my leather skirt, letting it fall back down my thighs as he stands. "The next time we go out, I expect you not to wear panties."

My cheeks burn, and I bite my bottom lip. He traps me to the wall, his body warm and strong as he pins me, keeping me against him.

I shiver, my clothes wet from the rain and my insides aching for more. "Bedroom," I whisper, commanding him to follow, although he's the one in charge, pressing me against the wall near the front door.

We've barely made it inside the house.

A wry smile crosses his lips, and he pulls me

against him, letting me feel his cock through his pants. "Lead the way."

His hands are on my waist, my hips, grazing every inch of skin, tugging my jacket over my shoulders and disrobing me before I even make it into the bedroom.

The curtains are closed, and I flip on the light, feeling for it because Noah has me distracted. I'm in my panties and bra, and I spin around to face him, our lips clashing together as I fumble for the last layer of clothes between us. He already removed his shirt, but his pants are still damp from the rain.

I work the button free and bump against the mattress with the backs of my legs, sitting at the edge while I work his pants down. His cock is barely hidden inside his boxers, and I carefully remove them, pleased with the sight in front of me. He's gorgeous, every inch of him, and my insides ache just staring at his cock.

I suck in a tentative breath.

I've been with my share of guys but never had any of them been this well-endowed. My mouth goes dry, and I lick my lips, staring at him, unable to tear my gaze away.

"Having second thoughts?" Noah asks, his hands on my hips as he grazes the elastic on my panties, his fingers sliding along my waist, slowly inching the material down.

I shake my head, my gaze locked on his. "Never." I lean on my tiptoes, reaching his lips, pulling him down for another searing kiss as I drag him with me back onto the mattress.

He straddles my hips, pinning me under his weight. "Dominate me," I whisper, staring up at him, challenging him as he grabs my arms, lifting them above my head. He pushes them against the mattress, holding them together with one hand while the other roams over my breasts. "Did you bring a condom?" I ask, realizing where this is heading.

He grumbles and pulls back. "Let me check my wallet."

I miss the warmth of his body as I shuffle to the edge of the bed, watching as he scours through his pants pocket for his wallet. He opens it and glances inside. "I didn't exactly plan for this tonight," he admits.

"Me either," I say and bite down on my bottom lip. "I mean, I was hoping, but in a rush to get ready, I forgot to stop at the drug store down the street."

"I can run out to the store."

"In the rain?" I shake my head. Would he even

come back? "We can do other things. I can return the favor," I say, pulling him back onto the bed to lie down.

"I wasn't expecting a status quo," he says.

"A status quo? Is that what we're calling it?" I laugh and sweep my hair to the side as I straddle him.

"I have a better idea. Turn around. 69." He gestures with his finger for me to turn and face the other way.

"That's a better idea?" I ask, and the lights flicker from the storm and then go out.

I curse under my breath, not that I haven't done this in the dark, but I was enjoying the sight of Noah's cock and wanted to memorize every detail in case this is a one-time thing. While I don't usually go out with guys twice, for Noah, I could make an exception.

Especially if that exception involves condoms for our next get-together.

Thunder hammers overhead, and the room momentarily brightens with a flash of lightning.

I shuffle around on the bed, trying not to knee him in the groin, given the fact that I can't see anything. His hands are on my hips, helping me move. "Don't tell me you're scared of the dark," he says.

"Scared? No, but I was enjoying taking a mental picture of your goods."

"My goods?"

I wish the lights were on because I'm pretty sure he's smiling right now. I can hear the laughter in his words, the amusement from my little comment on his not-so-little package.

My stomach grumbles obnoxiously to the point that there's no way he didn't hear that I'm starving. We skipped dinner, and while I planned on making something when I got home after our coffee date, that plan got sidelined.

"We should eat before we continue our festivities," Noah says. He smacks my bottom, and I jump from the sudden contact. The sting is slight and feels rather pleasant, not that I'd confess that to him. "Next time, just tell me when you're hungry."

I laugh under my breath. "I'm hungry. Come on, let's order takeout, and maybe we can convince them to bring us a pack of condoms too."

Noah wrestles me around, pinning me beneath him. "I like the way you think, Red."

"Three nicknames in just under three hours," I

chide. I'm unsure how long we've been on this *coffee date,* but I can't help but tease him.

"Just trying them out to see what sticks."

Noah insists on paying for dinner, and we order Indian food and have it delivered. In under an hour, our food arrives. Noah is dressed back into his clothes and offers to grab it downstairs while I set up the living room with candles to help make it easier to see our meals and each other.

I slipped into a pair of comfy sweats and a baggy t-shirt. Maybe I should be dressing to impress Noah, but he's already seen me naked, and the lights haven't come back on yet from the storm.

It takes a few minutes before he returns, showing me the bag of delivery and the special foil packet between his fingers, sporting a single sealed condom wrapper.

"You didn't," I gasp, shocked that he asked for a condom from the delivery driver. "I order from them weekly. Oh my gosh! They're never going to look at me the same way again."

"Don't worry. I gave him a really nice tip. He even offered to bring an entire box the next time you order takeout."

"Now, I know you're joking." I glare at him and pray that the driver didn't say that. "I might need to start ordering Indian food from someplace else," I mutter.

"What fun is that?" Noah quips. "Unless you want me to send you my guy?"

"You have a guy?"

Noah removes the plastic takeout containers from the bag, placing everything on the table, while I grab two glasses from the cabinet, filling them with water.

"I've hired a chef once or twice—"

He lets the words hang in the air as we take a seat at the table and dish a serving onto each of our plates, sharing the dishes. "What's your catch?" Noah asks, staring at me, his fork in his hand.

"What do you mean?" I ask.

"I know why I'm single. Hockey is my life. I live and breathe the sport. It doesn't offer a lot of time for a partner. What I can't figure out is why you're single. You're cute, smart, and witty. Not to mention, you're sexy as hell."

I take a bite of my dinner, starving and also trying not to answer his question. His flattery makes my heart race. I avoid his intense gaze as I stab my chicken with my fork. "What are you looking for?" I ask, avoiding his question.

"Someone honest, loyal—"

I hold up my hand, stopping him before he ticks off every box that is pretty standard on a guy's list of wants.

"Do you want something serious or a fling?" I need to know what he's expecting because bringing him back to my apartment isn't exactly new for me, but if he wants a second date, that isn't something I'm accustomed to doing.

He shifts in his seat. "You go right for the tough questions," he says, and I glance up, meeting his dark gaze.

Maybe I shouldn't have looked up and met his stare, because now I can't look away, no matter how much I want to, because the butterflies take flight in my stomach the longer he watches me. It's like he's staring right through me, seeing everything inside of me, and it makes me slightly uncomfortable. Not that I'd tell him as much.

"I just want to know what your expectations are. We haven't talked about it," I say and take a bite of my dinner.

"I'd like to get the opportunity to know more about you," he says. "Not that what we did earlier wasn't fun." He's got a boyish grin that crosses his features and makes him look incredibly youthful and innocent. Although I know he is anything but that in terms of what goes on in the bedroom.

He's a professional athlete. I'm sure he's been with dozens of women.

"But my career comes first. Always," Noah says.

That bothers me far less than I thought it might, hearing the words leave his lips. "I'm okay with that," I say. "I knew what I was getting involved in when you asked me out."

He takes a bite of dinner, savoring the taste. "This is good," he says, pointing with his fork toward his plate.

I can't help but wonder if there's something else I haven't seen or don't know about him. Unlike my bestie, I didn't stalk him online before our date. "How is it you're still single? No wife. No kids. Unless you have a secret family?"

He smiles, shaking his head. "Funny. I've never been married and no kids," Noah says. "Don't get me wrong. I like children most of the time. Have you met Kyler's daughter yet? She's quite a handful." He laughs, watching me intently.

"We were introduced at one of your hockey games. Bright kid, Bristol." The little girl is my best friend's niece, so of course, I'd meet her. Amber and I are like sisters.

"The kid is smart and is always causing Kyler and Emerson trouble."

The storm begins to settle, and mid-dinner, the lights come back on in the apartment. "Do you want to watch a movie after we finish?" I ask, taking another bite of my meal.

My grumbly stomach has at least ceased embarrassing me.

"A movie sounds good," Noah agrees. "I'll even let you pick the film. Just promise me it won't be one of those girly films."

"A chick flick? No promises, handsome."

"Come on, Red." He grins, staring back at me. He tilts his head slightly, his gaze moving down over my body.

I practically feel him undressing me, and I glance away with a nervous laugh. "You are such a flirt. How many girls have you taken for a coffee date to the hockey arena?"

"You're the first," he says, and that admission steals my breath.

I tuck my hair behind my ear, trying not to fidget as I bite my bottom lip. "Never took you for a virgin," I joke.

"Trust me, *Red*, when it comes to sex, I'm not a virgin."

TWO

NOAH

Charlotte is beautiful, funny and, most of all, gives me an instant hard-on from the minute we step foot outside of her apartment for our *coffee date,* which was a fantastic idea, taking her to the arena for coffee. I never expected that the girl knew how to play ice hockey. I figured I was taking a chance if she knew how to ice skate.

She seems perfect.

Of course, so did Jasmine, until she cheated on me.

I don't get involved in relationships. Flings, yes. They're easy and far less complicated. But there's something about Charlotte that makes me want to see where this leads.

It's dangerous.

Putting my career first and foremost has molded and shaped who I am as a player for the Ice Dragons with the NHL. I didn't get this good by sitting around on my ass and taking hot chicks to movies and on long dinner dates.

Not that I don't enjoy a little flirting and foreplay, because I do, but investing my time in a relationship has never panned out well for me.

Yet here I am, situated on Charlotte's couch, my arm wrapped around her shoulders while we watch a predominately girly film that she picked out.

And for some reason, I don't mind it. I mean, the plot is pretty simple. Boy meets girl. Boy falls in love with girl. Girl breaks boy's heart. Girl apologizes, and boy eventually forgives her.

At least, I assume that's the way the story goes. But I've stopped paying much attention to the screen as I'm drawn toward Charlotte's red locks and her cute pouty bottom lip that she keeps tugging between her teeth.

Keeping my cock in my pants is trying. Not that I'd just whip it out but, damn, that hundred-dollar bill I gave to the delivery driver for his last condom in his billfold. And it doesn't look like we'll be using it, at least not for a couple of hours.

Which isn't the worst thing. Spending time with a beautiful girl is nice. There's a calmness to being around Charlotte that warms me from the inside. She heightens my senses, every one of them.

"Are you bored?" she asks, her voice soft like honey, and she methodically tilts her head toward me, staring up at me with bright blue eyes like jewels of the sea.

"I just love predictable romance movies." My voice drips with sarcasm, and she cuddles up against me, letting me pull her closer. I drag her into my lap, needing a reprieve from the film that is putting me to sleep.

At least now I know what to do the next time I have a bout of insomnia, which isn't too often. Mostly, it's after a game when I haven't quite wound down from a win.

She reaches for the remote, and I can only surmise that she's about to hand it to me when my phone buzzes in my pocket. I thought I had it completely turned off.

Charlotte's cell phone rings on the end table beside the sofa. "Sorry, I meant to put it on silent," she says, climbing off me while reaching for her phone and silencing the call.

"Let me guess, it's Amber." My phone vibrates. I

shift on the sofa and dig into my pocket to see Jasper's name on my screen as he's trying to get ahold of me.

"Jasper," she muses, glancing at my screen, coming back to sit down beside me. Already, I miss the warmth of her body nestled on my lap. "Do you think they want to ask us how our coffee date went?"

I click ignore on my phone and shrug, sliding my phone onto the coffee table. "Probably. I can't imagine he's calling to see if I made it home okay."

The laughter vibrates through her chest as she leans back on the sofa and lets me wrap my arm around her. "You're funny. I like that about you," Charlotte says. "I have an idea."

"Uh oh. Nothing good ever came from those four words."

She grabs the throw pillow and whacks me playfully in the chest with it. "We should play a prank on Amber and Jasper."

I snatch the pillow before she can smack me again with it. Grabbing it, I keep it out of her reach, holding it above my head. I'm quite a bit taller than Charlotte, and while seated, there is zero chance of her retrieving it unless she stands or climbs on all fours, which wouldn't be the worst thing in the world, having her straddle me for it.

"What kind of prank?" I pin her with my stare, wanting to get inside her head.

"We tell them we're getting married."

Her words stun me, and the throw pillow I'm holding above us falls ungraciously onto my lap. "That's a terrible idea."

She reaches for the soft blue linen pillow, grabbing it while unintentionally brushing against my crotch. At least, I don't think it's intentional, but she just suggested marriage as a prank. I'm not sure if she's crazy or brilliant. It would surprise Jasper, assuming he falls for it.

"So? Why not?" Charlotte quips, raising an eyebrow as she scoots back on the couch, guarding the pillow. She holds it against her chest and stretches her legs, resting them beside me. The gesture is intimate for two people who just met, but for some reason, I feel like I've known her my entire life.

"For starters, it's raining, and the courthouse is closed. No one would believe it."

"*Getting* married," Charlotte emphasizes. "That doesn't mean we got hitched today. We'll tell them you proposed on our date, and I said yes."

I tilt my head back, staring up at the ceiling. "I'm dating a crazy person," I mutter.

"I heard that," Charlotte says, tossing the throw pillow at my head.

I catch sight of it out of the corner of my eye, and my arm goes up, blocking the shot. "It wasn't a secret," I say.

"So, we're dating?" She stares at me, a curious look on her face. Her blue eyes are a shade darker than before, and her cheeks are a slightly rosy hue that is beginning to match her fiery locks. The longer I watch her and study her features, the more I take note.

She has a slight dusting of freckles across her face, almost invisible, like she's hiding them behind makeup.

"We're not—not dating," I say, avoiding the question. The whole marriage prank was entirely her idea. I think it's crazy, but it's tempting. I've heard the shit that Jasper has done to his brother Kyler in terms of pranks. It would be pretty funny if Jasper fell for it.

"Dating aside—" She gestures, waving her hand in front of us, getting back to her point. "Are you in?"

"Am I in on the prank?" I ask, wanting to make sure she's not serious about this marriage proposal idea. Because I'm not marrying a chick I just met a couple of hours ago. I mean, I've seen her at hockey games and whatnot, but we haven't exactly been properly acquainted until today.

It's the kind of suggestion a puck bunny would give, like Jasmine, but in her case, she'd expect me to walk her down the aisle before midnight, like a fucked up fairytale.

My cell phone buzzes again on the coffee table, and Charlotte keeps her gaze locked on me. "Are you with me?"

"Well, I'm not against you," I say and lean forward, reaching for my phone. "You're crazy, and I'm nuts for going along with it." I stare at Charlotte while answering the call.

I can hear the gasp of breath from her lips as she watches me take the call, her chest rising and falling, and her breathing growing slightly faster. Is it nerves? Her cheeks redden. She'd be a terrible poker player. I can see all her tells.

"Hey, man, I've got great news," I say.

"Yeah? Did the date go well? Amber has been trying to call Charlotte to find out how it went, but she isn't picking up."

"Oh, that's because I'm still at her place."

"You are?" Jasper says, and he chuckles. "They're still together, babe!" he calls out to Amber.

"Oh! Then leave them alone. Let them get back to their hot date," Amber says.

"Put the phone on speaker. We want to tell you both the good news at the same time," I say.

Charlotte is grinning wickedly, her eyes bright as she nods enthusiastically.

Jasper pauses for a beat. "Okay. What's going on? Good news?" I'm sure the two of them are trying to figure it out before we share it with them.

Charlotte and I meet each other's stare. "We're getting married!" Charlotte squeals excitedly and jumps up from the sofa, dancing around like the news is real.

"What?" Amber's voice is far louder and in shock, more so than Jasper, who is dead silent. "Who proposed to whom?" she asks.

"I did," I say, trying to make it sound convincing. "After one night together, I knew we were meant to be. She is the hockey stick to my puck."

"Gross," Jasper mutters. "And I think you got that analogy backward, but I'm happy for you both. And while I'm thoroughly confused—good for you, knowing what you want and having the balls to do something about it."

"You two can't be serious," Amber says. There's no mirth in her tone. I glance at the phone between us and then at Charlotte, waiting for her to break it to her friend that we're joking. "Neither of you want kids or marriage. And you're suddenly engaged after one date? I don't believe it."

Charlotte grins. "It was a really good coffee date. He brought me to the arena, and we played hockey on the ice after we shared an amazing cup of coffee."

"You're funny," Amber says. "I like that the two of you thought you could trick us. Nice try. Have a fun night, you two."

Amber ends the call, and Charlotte plops back down on the sofa beside me.

"That was fun," she says, nudging me with her arm. "Anyone else we can try to convince? Jasper was really going along with it."

"Yeah," I say and show her the emoji he just sent, flipping me his middle finger via text. "He'll probably give me crap about it at practice tomorrow, but it'll be worth it. Especially when I tell his brother he fell for it."

"Sounds like you guys are close."

"Yeah, we have to be. Part of the sport."

"True," Charlotte says with a shrug. "I suppose you guys kind of have to read each other's minds."

"Body language, signals, that sort of thing for the game."

She stands and heads for the fridge. "Can I grab you anything? Water? Wine? I think there might be some juice in the fridge."

"I'll have whatever you're having," I say.

"Wine, it is. I keep my red in the fridge. Some people freak out about it, but I prefer my wine cold."

I raise an eyebrow at her. "You monster," I joke as she brings the bottle of unopened wine to the living room along with the corkscrew.

"Think you can open this for me?" she asks, depositing the corkscrew in one hand and the wine bottle in the other. She saunters back to the kitchen, and I can't help but watch her walk as she goes to retrieve two wine glasses.

She's like fire with her bright red hair and mesmerizing gaze. I've spent more time with her tonight than I do most girls in an evening.

"I think I can manage," I say as she returns with the wine glasses, placing them on the coffee table. In a matter of seconds, I have the wine bottle opened, and I'm pouring us each a glass, handing one to Charlotte.

I lift my glass, prepared to make a simple toast, and my cell phone lights up even though it's on silent. I glance at the screen and wince.

Jasmine.

When I don't answer quickly enough and the call goes to voicemail, she calls back.

She's always been persistent.

I take a swig of the wine and pour more from the bottle.

Charlotte tilts her head, staring at me. "Everything okay?" Her voice is calm, peaceful, and she has no idea I'm about to be swept up by a hurricane.

I don't want to take the call. If Jasmine is reaching out to me, it's some new drama she's involved in and needs help. I flip the phone over, the screen face down. I'm done with her. Done with the drama.

"It's nothing. Just an *old friend*." The bitter taste stains my lips at the words that leave my mouth.

"Ex-girlfriend?" she muses.

"Yeah, but we're over. Been over for years. She's married, so I'm unsure why she's calling me." I run a hand through my hair, grab the wine bottle, and refill my glass.

"Sounds complicated." Charlotte smiles, not jealous or unnerved by what I tell her. It's nice to see that she's got a strong sense of self-confidence. Honestly, that's hot. "First love?" she guesses.

I'm easy to read when it comes to Jasmine. It's a

short story, simple, and doesn't have a happy ending, which isn't entirely bad since I have a beautiful woman sitting across from me on the sofa.

"You don't want to hear it," I say, sparing her the details.

"Sure, I do," Charlotte says and scoots closer. She rests a hand on my lap. "We all have a past. Lay it on me. What's your baggage?"

She has the power to calm me in a way I never knew possible. I exhale a soft breath. "I fell for her when the NHL drafted me. We hooked up. Hung out. Dated exclusively, or what I thought was exclusively, and then she ghosted me. I assumed she couldn't handle the pressure of the spotlight until I saw on the news that she married another hockey player. It's a pretty short story."

"Damn. Does he still play hockey?" Charlotte asks. She gives me that slight head tilt which I find absolutely adorable. Her gaze is on me, never wavering.

"Yeah, he's with the Island Bruisers."

"What's his name?" she asks, raising an inquisitive eyebrow.

"Grant Brass. You've probably never heard of him. He's always in the penalty box or benched for shady shit that he does on the ice."

There's a flicker in her gaze. The name clearly does mean something to her, but as quickly as I see the recognition, the flash of familiarity, it vanishes.

"And you haven't spoken with your ex-girlfriend since?" she asks.

"No, I certainly wasn't invited to the wedding three months after we broke up."

"Ouch. Not that you'd want to attend the event, but three months sounds like a shotgun wedding," Charlotte says.

"Enough about her." I reach for Charlotte's hands and place our wine glasses on the table before dragging her into my lap. "What about you?"

"What about me?" she asks, her voice soft and musing while she straddles my hips. Her fingers comb through my hair, caressing my scalp and neck. "I'm an open book. Ask me anything."

"Anything," I repeat, the words momentarily lost on me. I wouldn't even know what to ask her.

There's a stillness, a quiet from the night that surrounds us. The storm has passed.

"Have you ever been in love?" I ask. It's an easy question but a difficult answer to hear. I'm not sure why I want to hear about her past. Maybe she doesn't feel any stroke of jealousy, but I can't say the same.

Charlotte smiles and shakes her head, carefree. "Never. I'm saving my heart for the right person."

I chuckle at her words. "Saving your heart?"

"Well, I'm not a virgin," Charlotte muses.

I try not to choke on my wine at her admission. She's bold and outspoken. I like that about her. That's not the only thing I like. I am a man, and my cock keeps reminding me that she's the most gorgeous woman I've ever laid eyes on.

"Do you want to watch the rest of the movie?" she asks, reaching for the remote.

For a moment, I think I might get a reprieve until she starts the flick back up, and I inwardly groan.

"I swear if you're trying to friend zone me—"

"I'm not. We can pick something else to watch," she says and hands me the remote control. The gesture feels domestic, and I take a second to shake the cobwebs from my head.

I don't do domestic.

I don't date women. Well, I grab drinks, sleep with them, and then generally move on to the next one. Long-term commitment is not a part of my vocabulary after Jasmine. Neither is spending the night or staying over. I've already stayed longer with Charlotte than any other girl, except for my ex.

"Or we could do something else," Charlotte says,

shifting on the sofa, resting her hand on my chest as she gazes at me suggestively.

A wry smile crosses my features. "Something else," I say, pondering her words. "What did you have in mind?" I'd bet my life savings that *something else* is code for sex, but I like dragging it out with her.

The teasing and flirting is a new kind of foreplay that I find entertaining. I'm used to the ladies coming up to me, making it known they want to fuck, and then leaving after a wild romp in the sheets.

She finishes the last of her glass of wine. Her cheeks are rosy, but I'm not concerned about her being too drunk or inebriated in her decision-making process. It was one glass of wine, the open bottle on the table still unfinished.

Charlotte bites down on her bottom lip, scrunches her nose in the most adorable way possible, and then straddles me. Her fingers caress the back of my neck as she leans her forehead against mine.

"Do I need to spell it out for you?" she asks in a breathy voice that makes me instantly harden. It could also be her womanly scent, with floral notes of lavender and something much muskier and earthy.

Her fingers trail over my neck in soft patterns,

and I imagine her spelling the words, but it could be just the pads of her fingers dancing over my skin.

I don't wait to hear more from her, the desire overwhelming as she grinds against me, making it clear she wants me to fuck her. Our lips crash together, and whether she kissed me first or I leaned in and started the roaring fire between us, I'm not sure, nor does it matter.

Heat licks us like wild flames as my fingers steady her hips and lift her slightly off me only to undress her. She's gorgeous naked, more perfect than any painting or piece of artwork I've ever seen.

Our clothes are quickly discarded on the floor in a heap. I carry her to the bedroom, our lips tangled like our bodies, intertwined, as I trip over her discarded shirt on the floor from earlier, my feet managing to twist unceremoniously.

Cursing, I attempt to regain my balance. I'm just a few feet shy of the bed and manage to place her on the bed before I lose all footing and have to catch myself from landing face-first into the mattress with my feet still on the floor.

Charlotte giggles. "Sorry, I know it's not funny." She's still laughing like she can't help herself, and I grumble, shuffling my feet and tossing the discarded shirt across the room.

Her purse is still on the floor. Turns out both items tripped me up.

"Trying to kill me before my next game? Maybe you *really* are an Island Bruisers fan." I cast an ornery glance at her.

She purses her lips and shuffles to sit up at the edge of the bed. Her arms reach out for me, bringing me to sit with her. I'd rather be doing a dozen other things had I not just made a near-ass out of myself.

It could have been worse. I could have ended up face-first on the floor with a broken nose. Although I'd have liked to have thought I have a little more grace, given all my time on the ice. But I've fallen before and hard.

For some reason, I feel I'm falling again, but this time it's not my feet tangled in her discarded clothes.

"Your friend, Jasper, told you about that?" she asks. Her teeth capture her bottom lip. I reach out, my thumb grazing her lip, willing her to release it.

"I saw it with my own eyes," I say. "And I heard you're the encouraging factor behind her supporting the opposing team."

A smirk grazes her features. "Do you like it when I do that?"

I laugh under my breath. "No, sweetheart. I like it

when you cheer for *my* team. You should wear *my* jersey when you go to a hockey game."

"Even if it's not an Ice Dragons game?" she asks with a knowing smirk.

"Yes. Even if you're at a game with two other teams, you show your loyalty to the Ice Dragons."

She purses her lips together, pondering my statement. "That seems a little—*possessive*," she says. There's a twinkle in her eye, a spark that roars the warmth and fire inside my belly straight to my groin.

Damn right.

The smirk doesn't leave my face. Right now, nothing could wipe it off. The glee that resonates through me is impossible to mask.

"Good, because I don't sleep with Island Bruiser fans," I say, glancing her over, memorizing every detail of her body in case she breaks my heart and tells me she isn't an Ice Dragons supporter.

A laugh reverberates through her body as she shuffles back and lies against the mattress. "What if I told you that I hated hockey?"

I study her, the rouge of her cheeks, the blush that spreads across her breasts as she makes herself comfortable. "Is this your idea of pillow talk?" I ask, "Because I don't like it."

Charlotte reaches for my hand, and I easily

follow as she tugs me to join her. I lie on my side, one hand on her hip, keeping her close as our foreheads are nearly touching. "I'm just asking, what if I hated hockey?"

"But you don't," I say. I'm confident that she doesn't hate the sport. I've seen her with her best friend, Amber, cheering on the Island Bruisers. She even owns one of *their* jerseys. There's no way that she hates hockey. "Is this hypothetical? Would I sleep with someone who doesn't like my job? Would you sleep with a guy who doesn't like the college you're at?" I turn the question onto her.

"That's a moot point," she counters, leaning on her elbow to face me as she shifts onto her side. "I'm not in college forever."

"I may not be playing for the Ice Dragons forever," I say. I'm under a three-year contract from when I was drafted. After that, anything could happen.

"Okay, so I don't *hate* hockey," Charlotte says, tugging me closer, her arms around me.

I pull her tighter, rolling us around so I'm lying above her, straddling her hips. My gaze tightens, trying to figure her out. She's a mystery to me, one I want to unravel but concerned that if the threads aren't tight enough, it might just come undone.

"Do you secretly love it?" I ask, suspecting there's more than she's telling me. She knows how to play hockey and is pretty good at it, which doesn't fit the profile of someone who hates ice hockey.

She kisses me, and whether it's to silence or quietly tell me she's done talking, I'm all for it. We roll around on the bed, her fighting to be on top, and as much as I love to dominate in the bedroom, it's a turn-on when a girl knows what she likes and isn't afraid to command it.

"Have you ever been tied up?" she asks, a growing smile on her face.

I laugh under my breath. "That depends," I say, my hands on her hips, tracing a soft trail up to her breasts and then back down to her navel.

She shifts her hips, the smile growing on her face as she enjoys my touch. I'm distracting her.

Good.

I may like being in control more than I let on.

I roll her around, my hands pinning hers against the mattress at her side. Our lips tangle together like our legs, wrestling for control.

"Do you always have to be in control?" she asks between kisses and bites my bottom lip.

I groan from the pain, but there's also pleasure

behind the superficial degree of hurt, which is vanishing with each passing second.

Damn, she knows what she's doing.

I like it. I should let her take the reins if she wants to lead, but fuck it. I don't know how much control I'll have tonight if she retrieves any type of restraints.

"Most women don't fight me when I dominate them in the bedroom." I pin her with my stare, and her breath catches in her throat. She glances away, a sheepish smile on her face. "Eyes on me, baby," I say.

The flush spreads from her cheeks down her throat as she turns slowly, meeting my stare. "I'm not like the other women you bring home," she says, and this time there's more certainty in her voice.

Charlotte pushes me onto my back and crawls down my body, straddling me.

"Maybe you should find the restraints," I mutter.

"What's that?" she asks, glancing up at me, her mouth hovering just over my cock as it begs to be sucked.

I'm throbbing, the ache tormenting me as she stares up at me, teasing and waiting for my reply.

Did she really not hear me?

I exhale a breath, but my heart is hammering in my chest. "You will be the death of me," I say.

She quirks a grin. "Good. Just don't die tonight. Okay?"

Before I have time to respond, her luscious lips form the perfect 'O' as she brings them against the head of my cock. Her tongue teases me, tastes me, and all further thoughts vanish on instinct.

Charlotte knows what she's doing. She doesn't need instruction, and the way her hands tease my balls while her lips move over my shaft is tantalizing.

My breath catches in my throat. I haven't had a blow job in months, well, not a decent one. Right now, her mouth, lips, tongue, and everything she does brings me closer to the edge.

I run my fingers through her hair, wanting her to take me deeper.

She understands, and I feel the soft hum from the back of her throat as I'm fucking her mouth. It feels animalistic, raw, and savage. There's nothing sweet or pretty except for her form, down on her knees, bent over, sucking my cock.

"Fuck," I grunt as I feel myself closing in, and I won't last much longer. I tap at her shoulder, gently trying to push her back and warn her.

She releases my cock from her lips, the doe-eyed smile follows with a giggle. "How was that?"

I'm panting hard, trying to catch my breath. "Do you really have to ask?"

Charlotte shakes her head, and I pull her to lie with me, rolling her onto her back and straddling her hips.

Gosh, how much I've wanted her since I saw her in the stands, shouting for the opposing team, cheering *them* on. She's like this perfect little challenge I want to ruin and make her mine.

The grip of possessiveness, like a skeleton hold on my heart, pains me in ways I've never felt, never quite experienced before.

She's not like the puck bunnies, the girls I'm used to hooking up with after a game to burn off adrenaline and get another shot of endorphins flowing through me.

There's a mystery to her, the red ringlets cascading down her shoulders and back, falling around her like a halo. "Are you a screamer?" I ask, grinning as I trail warm kisses down her torso.

She writhes beneath my touch, and I haven't even licked her yet. I plan to devour her, every breath stolen from her body.

Her legs part, willingly opening up to me as my lips warm her navel and press soft, warm kisses across her stomach and down to her thighs. But I don't greet her with the desire she seeks. My lips tease as I kiss her inner thighs and down her leg, my fingers trailing soft patterns as I hold her to me.

Already, she's breathless and antsy, a sight to be seen and treasured. The paleness of her skin against her red hair glows with a blush spreading across her chest.

"You're staring," she rasps, panting, and I've only just begun making her ache with want. I can see the neediness in her gaze and the squinty stare as she struggles to maintain her composure.

I desire her to get lost in the feeling, forget everything for a moment, and let the want envelop her.

She keeps her gaze on me, making my cock ache to be inside of her, but I won't give in to my temptations and needs until hers have been met. She's glistening and swollen, her desire obvious as I slowly crawl up between her thighs, my fingers trailing a soft, featherlight path along her folds.

Her head tosses back, and her breathing grows louder, quicker.

I tsk. "Not yet," I say with a devious smile. Oh, I want her to break free, fall into oblivion, but not before I've tasted her while on my knees and watched her gaze trained on me.

There's something primal in keeping her staring at me, watching her come undone under my tongue.

I lick at her slowly, methodically, tasting and teasing her bud as she whimpers and her fingers bunch at the bedsheets beside her.

She's restless, and I imagine her insides are throbbing much like mine as I enjoy the sight of her trembling and needy.

Charlotte moans, her gasps growing louder, more insistent with urgency as she struggles to maintain her composure.

The smile merely grows on my lips as I continue licking and sucking, sliding one, then two fingers inside of her warmth, stretching her.

I'm rewarded with a moan, her breathing quicker as she trembles against the mattress. Her back arches, and I feel her teetering on the edge. Her insides quiver, clenching onto my fingers as she chases her orgasm, moaning through the intense riveting ecstasy that courses through her.

She curses as she collapses onto the bed, glistening and glowing as I climb up her body. "That was amazing," she says.

I chuckle and press my lips against hers, needing a taste, hungry for more. "I wasn't sure," I say, only mildly joking based on her expletive at the end of her orgasm. I've heard women thank the deities and myself, but usually, cursing is saved for when I tease them and don't let them get off.

Charlotte continues to bewilder me. I'm enchanted with her, mesmerized by both her complexity and beauty.

Her fingers are on me as I break our lips apart long enough to catch my own breath. She pushes me onto my back, her hand stroking my cock, teasing me at her entrance.

"Wait," I choke out, the words barely leave my lips. "Condom."

"Fuck," she curses again, and her eyes widen, realizing what almost happened.

It takes me a minute to retrieve the condom and sheath it on my length. This time, I'm on top, in command, as I guide my length inside her. I move slowly, taking my time, inch by inch, to let her adjust to my size.

Her lips are parted, slightly swollen from kissing, and I lean down, covering them, needing another taste of her mouth as I move deeper.

She moans as I fill her. "Okay?" I ask, staring down, concentrating on taking my time and not letting my desires win out. I need to know if she's still on board.

Charlotte nods and expels a heavy breath before wrapping her legs around me.

She's tight and warm, but it feels amazing. Her fingers graze my back, and her nails scratch at my bottom, tugging me closer, tighter. "Harder," she whispers into my ear.

Every breath and gasp encourages me, making me want to satisfy her again. I know she's close, her insides clench onto me, but I'm not ready for this to be over nearly so soon.

Aggressively, she rolls me onto my back, riding me, her hands on my chest as she tosses her head back.

Fuck, she looks hot. Her hair is tossed, her cheeks rosy. Her eyes are half-glazed, struggling to stare at me, but she doesn't look away.

My fingers caress her breasts, playing with her nipples. Her lips part, forming a perfect little 'o' that makes my cock twitch, and she clenches down, which is all it takes for me to brace the edge.

"Come with me," she says, and her hands are on my chest and then my arms, attempting to pin me down as she rides me.

"I'm right there," I say, tinkering on the edge and waiting to fall.

Seconds stretch on as she trembles and tightens,

her walls like a vise around my cock. She moans my name, and the sound is like honey dripping from her lips.

"Noah," she chants, and that's all it takes to come crashing down, like waves on the beach, pounding us into shore.

She collapses against me, my heart pounding mercilessly against my chest, and I swear I can feel hers. Charlotte gasps for breath, attempting to roll off me when I guide her onto her back and climb off to dispose of the condom.

I swear the room spins, and I hold the edge of the bed for a moment before regaining my strength.

———

She falls asleep, the room perfectly quiet and peaceful.

I can't stay the night. I climb out of bed, retrieve my clothes, and sneak away. I wouldn't know how to handle tomorrow morning if I did stay. It might be awkward, and besides, I have to be up early for practice.

Going home makes sense.

Why do I feel like such a dick about leaving?

I grab my wallet and keys, and the slight

shuffling sound around her bedroom stirs Charlotte. "You don't have to go," she murmurs.

I sigh heavily and lean down, pressing a firm kiss to her lips. "Maybe I'll see you at a game this week?"

A lazy smile spreads across her face. "Wearing the enemy's jersey? Then, yes, I'll be there." A yawn escapes her lips.

I growl, capturing her lips with another searing kiss to remind her of what we just did. "You'll wear my jersey, *Red*, and scream my name from the stands just like you screamed my name tonight."

A blush spreads across her cheeks as her eyes lazily close. She's drifting back toward slumber.

"Sweet dreams," I whisper before heading out of her apartment.

The rain has stopped, and while it's chilly and cloudy outside, it's nicer than it had been hours ago when we got drenched. I order a rideshare service, waiting outside, the streets dark and empty, for it to arrive.

It doesn't take long, and I'm across town in record time, heading into my building.

"Mr. Reece," the doorman greets me. "You have a visitor in the lobby."

At this hour? I can't fathom who would have shown up and didn't call, trying to get a hold of me. I head inside the building and glance toward the lobby seats. Her cold blue eyes stare back at me.

Jasmine.

She's bundled up in a winter parka with little arms wrapped around her frame. Since when did she have a kid?

Not that I've kept tabs on Jasmine. She's married and my past.

Jasmine stands, cradling the sleeping toddler against her chest. As she steps closer, I see the darkening skin and fresh bruises forming on her pale cheek.

"Who did this to you?" The bitter taste, like cold, metallic blood, stains my tongue. I don't even want to say *his* name.

She nods ever so slowly, cautiously. "My husband."

"For fucks' sake!" I growl and bunch my hands into fists.

"I need a place to stay. Somewhere he can't find us," Jasmine says.

I glance her over. She looks to be telling the truth. Not something Jasmine was great with. I can't help but wonder if she cheated on me with *him*, but none of that matters.

"And you thought I'd help you." There's disdain

in my voice. I try to keep it down, not wanting the lobby attendant to overhear the conversation. "Come upstairs." The words leave my lips, but the moment I voice them, I'm reluctant to follow through.

"Thank you," Jasmine whispers, her hand finding my arm. Whether it's gratitude or something more, I can't say.

I shake off her arm. This is strictly platonic. A friend helping another friend in need. And she's right. Her husband won't come looking for her and their child with me.

"I promise, it's just for tonight." Jasmine follows me to the elevator, and the little bundle in her arms begins to stir. His eyelids flutter open and then close just as quickly. He's got rosy cheeks and matching red lips.

The elevator doors open, and Jasmine steps in first. The little boy wiggles against Jasmine, burying his arms and face in her chest. I can't tell if he's trying to hide or go back to sleep. I'm not around kids much.

"Did he touch the child?" I ask, my jaw tight, teeth grinding together. I'm afraid to hear the answer, but at first glance, the little boy doesn't show any sights of abuse or neglect.

"No, he didn't touch Zayn," Jasmine says.

"Zayn," I whisper, punching the button on the elevator, his name falling from my lips. I don't try to do the math. The boy looks old enough that he could be mine. But she would have told me if she got pregnant. She wouldn't have run off and married Grant. "How old is he?" I ask. Because the sinking pit in my stomach tells me what she isn't. "Is he mine?"

Jasmine laughs nervously, and that sound tears me apart from the inside.

Why didn't she dispel my fear and say no?

"Jasmine?" My voice raises an octave, and the elevator doors open. I unlock the front door to my apartment and let her inside.

I shouldn't let her in. I shouldn't help her. Not if she's been lying to me. "Is he my son?" I ask again, this time, my voice louder. I can't help the anger from surfacing any more than I can keep the sun from rising.

"Maybe," Jasmine says, her voice soft, tentative. "I'm not one hundred percent sure."

Fuck it! I knew she'd cheated. My stomach sinks at the thought that the little boy in her arms might be mine.

I gesture at her cheek. "Is that why Grant did this?"

"No, he hit me because he's an asshole." Jasmine

follows me inside, and I flip on the lights. I'm tired and want to go to bed, but this news also has pumped more adrenaline through me than when I score a goal during a game.

"You can stay tonight, but tomorrow morning, you need to file a police report, and you have to do a paternity test."

She exhales a soft breath. "About that—"

"You don't have room to negotiate, Jasmine." My blood is boiling, and I pace the length of the kitchen and grab a bottle of beer, needing something to help the massive throbbing in my head. I doubt the beer will help, but she's getting to me.

Could she be lying about the kid? Trying to make me feel sorry for her. Who would do that?

Jasmine.

She's always been manipulative. I never wanted to see the red flags staring me blatantly in the face.

"I can't file a police report because his brother is a police officer. He's just as bad as Grant, if not worse," she whispers. "I'd run and hide, but Grant will accuse me of kidnapping my son and have the entire police force looking for me."

"Fuck it!" I can't help but let the anger get to me. I try controlling the rage. At least when I'm on the ice, it gets channeled into the game.

I'd never hit a woman, but damn if I'm going to let Grant beat on Jasmine. There are some lines never to be crossed.

"I just need a place to crash tonight. I'll drive to my sister's place in the morning."

A dark laugh is forced from my chest. "Your sister? You don't think he'll look for you there?"

"We're not that close," Jasmine says. "He doesn't know where she lives. He's never met her."

Her idea is ludicrous. "You said it yourself. Your brother-in-law is a police officer. You don't think he can find that information? And you just said you weren't going to run and hide."

"I don't have a lot of options," Jasmine says. She cradles Zayn to her chest and rubs his back. "Maybe the paternity test is a good idea. If he's not Grant's son, then no court in their right mind would give him custody."

"No court would give him custody if they knew he was abusive," I challenge.

"I already told you, his brother—"

"I heard you." I can't just let it go. Whether the little boy is mine or not, he doesn't deserve to be raised by a monster.

She exhales a heavy sigh. "Can we just... continue this tomorrow?"

"Yeah, fine. You and the little one can share the guest bedroom. I don't have a crib. Does he need one?"

"We'll manage for tonight," Jasmine says. "Thank you."

———

By the time morning rolls around, I'm not in the best of moods. It's early, I barely slept, and when I stalk out of my bedroom, the guest door is wide open.

She's gone.

I shouldn't care.

Except that Jasmine might have had my son and hid it from me. I run a hand through my hair, put on a pot of coffee, and head to the bathroom to shower.

She didn't leave a note. Not that I anticipated she'd write me a letter, but some acknowledgment after last night's bombshell would have been great.

Will she follow through on the paternity test? Maybe she left early to avoid facing me and the fact that the kid is mine, and she knows it.

I'm in and out of the shower in minutes, dressed, standing by the counter, pouring myself a cup of coffee.

The math in my head, the little boy's age, lines

up to about the last time I slept with Jasmine. Shit. He could be mine.

He also could be that dirtbag's son, in which case, I'd still help Jasmine and the boy, but my responsibility would end with getting them away from Grant.

It shouldn't even be my burden, but I can't just turn my back on her. Even if there were days I hated her for what she did, running off to marry Grant. Had she done it knowing she was pregnant but not knowing who the father was?

The coffee is bitter, and I swallow it without a drop of cream or sugar. I don't deserve anything sweet today, nor could I stomach it.

I head out for practice. I need to burn off some of this restless energy on the ice. I need to do something to make sure that my head is in the game tomorrow. At least it's a home game. I won't have to worry about traveling out of town.

Although, right now, that might be nice to get away from the shit show that has suddenly blown through my life.

————

"How was your night?" Jasper asks, wagging his eyebrows suggestively at me with a grin.

"Just fucking fine," I mutter. I should be in a better mood, considering I had the perfect evening with Charlotte, but that memory feels a million miles away, like it happened in another lifetime.

"Damn," Jasper says, sitting across from me in the locker room as we get dressed for another day of practice and training. "Did she tell you she just wants to be friends?"

"No." I don't elaborate. I change rather quickly and lace up my skates, wanting to get away from this line of questioning. At least on the ice, even doing drills, I can let my mind clear and feel free.

"Late night?" Kyler asks, glancing at me. "You look like shit."

"Thanks, man. Appreciate it." I head out of the locker room, doing my best not to pound the shit out of my team before we get on the ice. However, fighting with them is traditionally frowned upon. We don't need an injury before the game.

Kyler is probably the one person on the team whom I could talk to about the situation, at least regarding Zayn. He's got a kid of his own, a daughter he's raised as a single father until Emerson came around. They're engaged now.

That's not going to happen with Jasmine.

The thought of her name on my lips sours my stomach.

And thinking about Charlotte feels wrong and dirty. She even said it herself that she didn't want kids. Suddenly, me maybe having a kid throws us in a tandem. I won't do that to her. She's still in college. She has her entire life ahead of her.

Me?

I can afford a nanny if it turns out Zayn is, in fact, my son. One step at a time. Jasmine still needs to do the paternity test on the kid, and don't they need a sample from me to compare the DNA?

―――――

I don't hear from Jasmine all day. Not that I expect a phone call or text, but it's silent. Which I find more troubling because what if she went back to Grant and forgave him?

After I get dressed, I grab my phone from my locker and text Jasmine. It's been a while, but I assume her number hasn't changed. If it has, then I have no easy way to reach her.

Don't you need my DNA for the test?

Three dots appear as she types and then

disappear. She's slow to answer, and then, finally, she responds.

Yes. I will send you the address of the lab.

"Everything good?" Kyler asks, glancing at me as I'm seated on the wooden bench, bent over my phone, giving it my undivided attention. Not exactly my standard, since there aren't too many people I care enough to text that aren't in the room with me.

"Yeah, just girl trouble," I mutter.

"Not a great night with Charlotte?" Jasper quips, overhearing my conversation with his older brother.

"Charlotte was great—" The words hang in the air because I'd nearly forgotten all about our fun little romp last night. I exhale a sigh. She doesn't need my baggage. From what I'd heard, she was a bit of a free spirit, which is even more reason to shut that door and let her live her life.

"But?" Kyler asks, waiting for me to continue. "Not your type?"

"She's got great legs and a nice ass, of course, he's her type," Jasper says and laughs.

I glare at him. Yes, I have a reputation for banging a lot of chicks, but that doesn't mean that I don't have standards. "She's more than just her looks," I say, glaring at Jasper. I grab the sweaty jersey that I just wore and toss it at his face.

Jasper catches it before it lands in his face. He drops it to the floor, grimacing in disgust. "What's the problem? Too clingy?" Jasper asks, trying to figure out why I wouldn't want to see her again.

"No, I don't think so," I say. She didn't seem distraught when I left last night. I probably should have stayed, we had a great time, and it would have saved me from running into Jasmine when I got home.

"Does she hate hockey?" Kyler quips. "Because, believe it or not, that can be fixed. Unless, of course, she's a huge fan of another team. Then you can't see her again. Write her off and tell her that unless she converts to the Church of Ice Dragons, she's a sinner."

I snort at his joke. "She does tend to wear Island Bruisers jerseys to our games," I say, glaring at Jasper.

"Hey! Don't look at me. Your girlfriend is the one who convinced Amber to wear that monstrosity," Jasper quips.

"She's not my girlfriend," I correct him a little too quickly.

He holds up his hands in mock surrender. "Fine. Your lady friend. Whatever. Same difference. I've never even known you to have friends who are girls you're not hooking up with."

I'm silent, hating the fact that he is right. I make it a habit of sleeping with the girls I hang out with, but only because they're beautiful and they hit on me. I don't even have to make the first move because they typically throw themselves at me.

Kyler clears his throat. Maybe he can sense the tension between us. Jasper and I have been friends since we were both drafted into the NHL. It happened to be the same year, so we had something in common, not knowing anyone and being the rookies on the team.

"It's just..." I rub the back of my neck. Can I tell them about Jasmine and the little boy? I shift uncomfortably on the bench. Maybe I can tell them a little and leave out the part about the kid.

They both stare at me, waiting for me to elaborate.

"Jasmine showed up at my door last night."

"Why the fuck did you go home?" Jasper asks. He holds up a finger. "Don't answer that—what did Jasmine want?" He gets right to the point.

The words feel heavy, like I betrayed Charlotte even though we're not dating. We're not exactly anything, no label, yet I still feel like shit over it.

"Her husband was beating on her. She wanted a safe place to crash for the night."

Kyler growls. "What the fuck, man? There are shelters and shit for that. You don't need Jasmine dragging her trash into your house."

Those words burn more than I care to admit. "She was desperate," I say as if that is enough of an explanation. "And her brother-in-law is a cop. You don't think they know where all the shelters are located?"

Jasper curses and shares a glance at Kyler. "Does her husband know about her past? About you? You don't need trouble following you home."

I hang my head in my hands. "Tell me about it," I mutter. I've done well to avoid the tabloids and media. There's the press after a game, when we're required to answer questions, but I try to keep my personal life private. And thus far, there's been no juicy gossip. Nothing to encourage the paparazzi to hound me.

But now, with the news of Zayn, it's like a stormy thundercloud hanging overhead, waiting to unleash its torrential downpour.

And the range of emotions, a mixture of anger for not knowing that I might have a son and Jasmine hiding it, to sadness because I've potentially missed out on so much already, is unsettling.

My stomach flops thinking about me being a dad.

It's not something I ever contemplated happening. I've always been careful when having sex, because kids and a career as a star athlete don't exactly mix. Maybe some people can pull it off, but I'm not the guy who has a family.

That's not me.

It's not my dream.

And certainly not with Jasmine.

My mouth is as sour as my stomach, the nausea sweeping over me.

Kyler pats me on the back, oblivious to the baby problem because I haven't told them yet. No sense in bringing it up until it's a sure thing. If I'm lucky, it won't be. Jasmine very well could have another baby daddy out there, one who isn't an abusive dick.

"Do you want to come over? We can have drinks tonight and get your mind off Jasmine," Kyler offers. "Jasper and Amber can tag along."

"Gee, thanks," Jasper says, flipping Kyler his middle finger at the roundabout invitation.

"What?" Kyler deadpans. "I was serious. You and your girlfriend are welcome over."

Jasper snorts. "That invitation sounded about as welcoming as your—"

I interrupt the two of them, keeping them from bickering. "Save it for the ice and our game tomorrow," I scold them like children.

"Okay, Mom," Jasper says, and I growl, doing everything I can to bite back the feelings surfacing.

"Shut up before I take my hockey stick and shove it—"

"Reece!" Coach Malone shouts at me.

I grumble under my breath, shut my lips, and snap around to face the coach who has decided to grace us with his presence in the locker room.

"A word," Coach says and nods for me to join him.

"Good luck," Kyler says with a wry grin. "I'll see you tonight?" he asks.

It might be good to stay away from my place for a few hours, especially if Jasmine decides to show up. I can't turn her away, I don't have it in me to be cruel, but I also don't want to face her. Not until I go to the lab, do the test, and get the results.

I need to know what I'm dealing with and not be played by her again.

I follow Coach to the front entrance of our locker

room. He glances me over. Am I that much of an open book?

"You didn't play like yourself during practice," Malone says.

"Just an off day," I excuse. "I'll have my head in the game tomorrow when it counts."

Malone huffs. "You better, kid." He doesn't press the issue, and I'm grateful for the reprieve.

I head out, and Kyler is right on my heel. He throws an arm around my shoulder. "So, are you coming over tonight for drinks and dinner?"

It feels like an invitation that I can't refuse.

THREE

CHARLOTTE

He didn't call or message me after last night. I feel like a creepy, obsessed girl who is constantly checking her phone for a text. For the record, he hasn't sent one. I've glanced at my phone every few minutes since I woke up this morning.

Not a single text or emoji.

He's busy. I'm sure that's the only reason I'm receiving silence. I could text him. Maybe I will, tonight, if I still don't hear anything and he's done practicing.

Could he be blowing me off?

He did tell me he puts his career first, and I thought I was okay with it.

I chew my lip raw, confused by the stalkerish

feeling that has washed over me since the minute that he left.

I'm not *that* girl.

I've done my share of hookups with no strings attached.

Is that what last night was with Noah? It didn't feel like it, but we barely know one another. His focus is on his career. Mine should be on school and my job.

But I keep staring at my phone instead of my homework, which is boring and complicated.

I finally text Amber because at least she helps keep me grounded.

How long from a hookup to the first text?

My phone lights up, and Amber doesn't bother answering via text. She's calling me.

"You hooked up with Noah?" Amber squeals, and the excited giddiness bleeds off her with excessiveness.

"I don't kiss and tell. But hypothetically, if a girl hooks up with a hot guy, at what point should he text her?" I ask. I'm well-versed in hookups and fun times in the sheets. But I don't usually expect a guy to reach back out because it's always pretty clear it's one night. I never give them my phone number.

"You're asking me for dating advice?" she squeals,

and this time I can't tell if it's delight or trepidation. I'm aware she doesn't have much experience in the boyfriend department other than Jasper, who is one hell of a catch.

"I'm asking you to find out from Jasper how long a typical hookup to text message takes."

Amber giggles. "I don't know that there's a specific time frame, but I'll ask him tonight. We were invited over to dinner at his brother, Kyler's, place. Do you want to come?"

I'm quiet for a second, considering my options for tonight. "I'm not invited. Isn't it rude for me to show up to Kyler's house?"

"Well, it's my sister's place too," Amber says. "They're talking about wedding stuff. I'm sure Emerson would love another girl's opinion on all the planning."

I scrunch my nose. I've never been super girly. I wear makeup and love short skirts, but the thought of wedding planning makes my stomach roil.

"Only if I'm not imposing." I climb off my bed, shut my school books, and yank open my closet. I'm donning a pair of sweats and a t-shirt, something I'd never be caught dead wearing out in public. Some girls can pull it off. Not me.

"You're not. It's fine. You're my plus one," Amber says.

"Dress code?" I ask. I'm not expecting a black-tie event this evening, but I don't want to be overdressed.

"Casual? The last time I was over, they had a bonfire in the backyard after dinner. Bring a sweater or something warm for that. It was chilly."

"That sounds good," I say. I get the rest of the details from her before hanging up and staring at my closet, finding nothing to wear.

Three hours later, I'm stalking up to the mansion, which isn't the easiest task with a giant gate entrance. I press the buzzer and wait to be let inside. There's an ominous feeling. Maybe it's the dreary sky and the threat of rain overhead. I shiver, pull my leather jacket tighter and hurry up to the front steps.

Before I knock, the front door swings open, and Amber tosses her arms around me. "I'm sorry," she whispers into my ear, and I don't know what to make of her apology.

Am I not invited inside?

Are the evening plans canceled because something has come up?

"Who is at the door—" Jasper asks, raising an

eyebrow when he sees me. He curses under his breath and hurries down the hallway.

"Come on inside," Amber says.

"Are you sure? That wasn't the warmest greeting from your boyfriend."

Amber rolls her eyes and shrugs it off. "He's just preoccupied. The guys are already standing around the fire pit in the backyard while Kyler is grilling up dinner. I'll let them know you're here."

I slip out of my heels, leaving them by the front door.

Amber's eyes widen. "So, maybe we should start in the kitchen. Grab a bottle of wine before we join the guys outside, where it's chilly."

"Wine sounds good," I agree quite easily. My hands are a bit cold from being outdoors. I took the train from my apartment to Kyler and Emerson's house, which really is more of a mansion. I try not to gawk at how lavish it is.

I follow Amber into the kitchen, my footsteps light and silent as we cross the hallway.

A little girl, all of maybe five or six, comes barreling through the entranceway past us. She's wearing a paint smock. Her fingers are covered in red, blue, and purple and she looks a bit like a hurricane.

"Have you seen Emmie?" Bristol, the little girl asks.

She's Kyler's daughter. I met her at one of the hockey games a few weeks ago. The kid really is a hurricane, and I'm surprised she hasn't stained the walls with her painted fingers and frilly smock.

"She's outside," Amber says, "but you probably shouldn't be running through the house."

"It's okay," Bristol says. "My hands are dry." She wipes them along the once-white smock, showing us that most of the paint doesn't come off her hands.

Before Amber can answer, Bristol sprints down the hallway and presumably outside. From the kitchen window, I can glimpse the backyard, the roaring fire, and the crowd of guys hanging out with drinks.

"Kids," I say with a laugh, shaking my head.

Amber grabs the bottle of white wine and pours us each a hefty glass. I just turned twenty-one. She, however, still has a couple of months to go. Not that it's ever stopped us from indulging in a little fun.

"I feel like I probably should have brought something over tonight, a bottle of wine, a dessert," I say, realizing how empty-handed I was when I showed up. Most parties I attend are on campus and don't fit the same vibe.

"It's fine. Don't worry about it."

I take a swig of wine, and she tips her neck back, finishing her glass in a matter of seconds. "Worried your sister will see you drinking?" It's been a thing between them. Emerson is not on board with Amber consuming alcohol before her twenty-first birthday. I'm not sure why. It's not something I asked about. I just noticed her hiding it and not wanting to be seen at the bar when she used her fake I.D.

Amber exhales a heavy breath. "Any word from your date?" she asks.

"Noah?" I shake my head. "Radio silent. I swear I thought he was interested, that he wanted more than a hookup. I spent hours hanging out with him. Am I that bad of a judge of character? Or is it that guys don't find me appealing for anything more than a quick lay?"

It's only been a day. You shouldn't be this love-struck over one night with a guy.

"I swear. I'm done with guys. With dating. I'm never sleeping with a guy because he's hot again. Because you know what, the hottest guys are the worst! They know they're good-looking and can get any girl they want. And don't even get me started on hockey players and athletes. Ugh!" I toss my drink back, swallowing the contents of the glass, and reach for the bottle.

There are footsteps and movement, and I glance back, seeing a shadow cross the hallway.

Someone is lurking outside the kitchen. "Hello?" I shout, not the least bit ladylike. I swear I'm not inebriated. One drink doesn't do it for me, but the rising anger that's from all the pent-up frustration of today, waiting for Noah Reece to call me. And what? Why should I sit around and wait?

Why does he have me in such a tailspin?

I've never felt like this for any guy in my life.

Why him?

What makes Noah different?

I bring the wine bottle to my lips, tip my head back and drink.

"Sorry," Amber says again, but this time her apology is softer, and her bottom lip juts out.

"Wait. Why are you apologizing?" I ask, bewildered that she's said that now twice in one day. The first time, I nearly forgot about it, but I can't stop wondering what she's referring to.

Noah Reece turns the corner of the hallway, where he's presumably been hiding, and steps into the daylight.

"How much of that did you hear?" I glare at him,

pulling back the liquor bottle for a moment, awaiting his answer.

"Just the part where you thought I'm hot," Noah says.

I huff. "You wish. You think you're hot. You didn't call or text," I say as if that explains my behavior. I take another swig from the wine bottle.

Noah closes the gap between us, and Amber takes a step backward, hurrying out of the kitchen.

"Traitor," I mutter as she leaves me alone with Noah.

"How much of that did you have to drink?" he asks, nodding at the bottle of wine.

"You can pry it from my cold, dead fingers."

He raises an eyebrow. "Isn't that a tad dramatic?" Noah asks.

"Bad day, and I'm not liking who I'm becoming," I admit. "Sue me." I take another swig of the wine, letting the taste glide down my throat. It isn't cheap, certainly not like the stuff that we buy.

Noah watches me with bewilderment. "I like you plenty," he says.

I laugh darkly, the bitterness biting me. "Yeah, enough to sleep with me. Not enough to text or call me the next morning." I grimace, hating the anger in my tone, the sound of my own voice making me more irritated. "Sorry," I say, quick to apologize.

"I told you I put my career first. You said you were okay with it."

I can admit when I'm being a bit of a bitch. I exhale a heavy breath and finally relinquish the bottle of wine, offering it to him. That's my way of silently apologizing.

Noah takes it, brings the bottle to his lips, and drinks. "Bad night," he confesses.

"Ouch," I say and stumble one step backward into the cabinets. I rub the back of my neck, his words tearing me apart. "I didn't realize our date was that bad for you. I guess that's why you—"

"Stop right there," he demands, glaring at me. "You don't get a pity party because I didn't call you. I was busy. And the bad night is what happened after I left your place."

A shudder courses through me, and I feel guilty for the accusation. "Oh." My eyes widen as I glance up from the bottle of wine to him. "Did something happen on your way home?" I study him, his face, his tense jaw. He doesn't look like anyone tried mugging him, but it could have been at gunpoint.

"You could say that," he says with a sigh. "It's fine. I'd rather not talk about it."

I shake my head. "You don't get to do that. Tell me something horrible happened, and then say how you don't want to talk about it."

"Why not?" Noah asks, staring at the cabinets, his vision far from me.

"Because I care about you!" I wince at my words and my tone. We barely know one another, but spending the evening together, not just tangled in my sheets, made me feel more toward him than any other guy I've met.

"We had one date," he reminds me, and I glance away, folding my arms across my chest.

"Yeah, so?" I try not to let him belittle what we had, what we did together. I enjoyed his company, even when we were watching a movie or eating dinner.

"It was good," Noah says, his voice calmer, softer, more rational.

The silence hangs in the air like a fog between us.

"What happened last night?" I whisper.

"My ex showed up. She was at my apartment, waiting for me."

"So, you're getting back together with your ex," I say, finishing his thought. I can't do this. Pretend not to care. Yes, it was one night, but I wasn't expecting to be a rebound. "Excuse me," I mutter, moving away from the kitchen and heading for the hallway.

"Wait," Noah says and grabs my wrist, pulling me to turn around and face him.

My lips part, and I stare at him, waiting for him to say something else. To give me a reason to stay, to talk to him, to figure this out.

"I'm not getting back together with my ex," Noah says. "But it's more complicated than that."

"More complicated?" I repeat, and my eyes widen. "Is she pregnant?" I blurt the question out before really thinking it through. Noah hadn't mentioned a girlfriend or a recent break-up. But maybe he didn't want to talk about it last night. It wouldn't be a great conversation on a first date.

"No, she's not pregnant," he says, stoic, refusing to give anything away. "But I've got to deal with her shit. It's why I didn't text you. I didn't want to drag you into her drama."

Okay, not pregnant.

"Were you two married?" I ask, trying to guess what the big deal is. What could possibly have him so uneasy?

He quirks a grin. "Thankfully, no. She's married to a real creeper. I'm just trying to help her out.

That's it. But I don't want to drag you into her mess. I like you, Charlotte. I'd like to keep seeing you."

"But?" I ask, waiting for him to let me down, tell me he's not interested, that he'd rather reconcile with his ex.

"No but," Noah says. He offers a faint smile. "You're a real catch, and I don't want you to get snatched up by another guy."

I chuckle at his remark. There aren't any guys at NYU that I have even the slightest desire to get to know further. It's always been about sex with them, never anything more.

"I don't have any intention of dating anyone else," I say. "Trust me, after our date last night at the ice arena, I don't think anyone else can even compare."

"Good," he says, the smile growing on his face. His eyes shine as he stares at me, his fingers falling to my hips, holding me steady and keeping me close against him. "I hope you'll be at my game tomorrow. Cheering for me."

"I wouldn't miss it."

He's smiling, staring at me, making the butterflies surface. "Afterwards, you're welcome to come to the Blue Line, when we celebrate our victory."

I don't ask what the plan is if they lose.

"I'll be there," I say. I've been to the Blue Line with Amber when she was flirting with Jasper, and I was abandoned at the bar. Not that I minded, but this arrangement will be far better.

"Good. And I expect you to wear my jersey."

I laugh under my breath. "That's a tall order, Reece."

He smirks. "I don't even know your last name."

I tilt my head, thinking it over. Should I tell him? "I suppose you don't." I'd rather keep him on his toes. I like a little mystery in our relationship.

Noah pulls me tighter against his firm body. "You're not going to tell me?"

I shake my head. "What fun is that?"

His gaze tightens. "Fine. You tell me your last name, and I'll answer any question that you have."

"Oh, tit for tat," I say, my eyes lighting up. "Sounds fun and a little dangerous."

"So, last name?" he asks again.

"Grace," I say.

"Charlotte Grace," he says, repeating my full name. "I like it."

"Thanks. I mean I'm stuck with it," I say and shrug. I never really gave it much thought. "Now, my turn." I rub my hands together with a laugh, excited to ask him anything.

"What do you want to know, Grace?" he asks.

It feels strange hearing my last name on his lips, but it's not a bad feeling, just unusual, like a pet name or a secret meant only for us.

"Would you have called me after we slept together if I hadn't run into you today?"

He sucks in a sharp breath. "Honestly, no."

I press my lips together and take a small step back. I shouldn't be surprised, but the truth stings.

"Can I explain, though?" he asks, and I let him continue, choosing not to interrupt him. "I wanted to call you, but I didn't think it was fair to drag you into the drama with Jasmine."

I wince at her name on his tongue, hoping that he doesn't notice.

"Until I get my shit together and Jasmine out of my life, you deserve better."

"That's for me to decide, not you," I say. "And I still don't get why your ex is suddenly showing up in your life."

"Like I said, she needs help. I'm just trying to help."

"And she can't go to anyone else?" I ask. I don't want to sound like the jealous girlfriend, but I can't fathom why she's showing up unless she's after something, like his money. He's a professional NHL player. She probably got wind of his success and wants part of it.

"It's more complicated than that," he says. "And it's not my story to share."

"Okay," I say, letting it go. The first step in a relationship is trust. And I trust Noah. "Am I going to meet this elusive ex-girlfriend of yours? Does she come to your games?"

He laughs under his breath. "No, her husband was traded last year. He plays for the Island Bruisers."

Noah winces, his eyes flickering, holding something back.

She's not after Noah's money if she's married to an NHL player. That's at least a good sign. But I'd be lying if I said I wasn't disappointed they weren't on the other side of the country.

"So, she attends his games." I frown. "Don't the Ice Dragons play the Bruisers later this month?"

"You've been studying my schedule?"

FOUR

NOAH

That was one hell of an awkward encounter with Charlotte earlier in the week. We've been casually texting back and forth since running into each other at Kyler's place.

I'm still waiting on the test results for the DNA sample to find out if the little boy is, in fact, my son. I stopped by the clinic to give my DNA sample to the lab and told them to contact me with the results.

Waiting is the hardest part.

No, keeping it a secret is harder.

There's no point in telling anyone if it turns out to be nothing. Which, knowing Jasmine, could very well be the case.

I haven't seen Jasmine or the little boy since the

night she showed up unannounced and uninvited. She's just been gone, which is unsettling.

Did she get back with her husband?

Did she run off to hide from him, in which case, where is she, and will she return if the boy is mine?

My head isn't quite in the game when we play the Island Bruisers. I'm even more distracted when I notice Charlotte in the stands with Amber, seated behind the glass and our team's bench.

Charlotte is wearing *my* jersey, and my heart swells with pride.

Damn, she looks good.

Her eyes meet mine, and she smiles and waves excitedly.

I give a brief nod. It's all I can do while on the ice. My attention should be on the puck and the game.

I've never worried about a girl being a distraction before, but now I can't keep my gaze from finding her, especially after I stop the Bruisers from scoring a goal and manage to pass the puck to Jasper who scores.

She stands, clapping and cheering. I can't help but imagine it's entirely for me.

In her defense, the entire crowd is roaring with excitement, but she's the one I notice among the sea of spectators.

We win by two goals in the final period, and I head to the locker room with the guys at the end of the game.

"I noticed your girlfriend was in the stands," Jasper says as we head into the locker room together.

I laugh under my breath. I'm not sure Charlotte is technically my girlfriend. It's not like we put a label on it.

"I could say the same for you. Amber was with her tonight."

We stalk through the locker room entrance. There's a long, wide hallway ahead before we round the corner to change out of our gear.

Kyler throws his arm around our shoulders. "And was this the first time they both cooperated and wore *your* jerseys?"

He had to notice.

Although most of the team noticed a few weeks ago when Amber and Charlotte were donning Island Bruisers gear. I thought it was funny when I didn't know either of the girls.

If Charlotte pulled that crap now, I'd be pissed.

"Says the man who had his fiancé wear a dick jersey to the game," Jasper quips.

Kyler releases his grip on me and roughs up his

younger brother, grabbing his neck and yanking him down, putting him in a headlock.

Jasper doesn't willingly take his crap and manages to land a couple of blows to Kyler's chest.

"Boys!" Coach Malone intervenes, like a father scolding his sons.

Kyler releases his hold, and Jasper shoves him to get one final hit in before we head to the bench to remove our skates and gear.

After we get cleaned up, showered, and dressed, a few of us have to deal with the press interviews. Thankfully, Kyler, Aiden, and Chase take the helm.

I escape without having to do a press junket which I'm relieved for because I hate the press. They like to twist our words around for the ultimate headline.

"You coming to Blue Line?" Jasper asks as we head out of the locker room.

"When don't I enjoy a few victory drinks?" I'm hoping that Charlotte stays after the game. "Is Amber coming tonight?" The girls were together at the game, which makes me hope that if Amber is joining us, then Charlotte will as well.

Not that the girls live together. They used to live near each other, and both attend NYU, but Amber lives with Jasper.

I almost feel stalkerish knowing what I do, but it's because Jasper yammers on about his girlfriend, and I have a good ear, taking it all in.

Jasper quirks a grin. "You're asking because you want to know if Charlotte is coming to Blue Line. Did you invite her?"

I snort. "When has that stopped Amber from showing up?" And while I did mention it to Charlotte and was hoping she'd come hang out with us, I wasn't exactly sure where we stand after a few nights ago.

"She's my girlfriend," Jasper says and knocks into me. "Don't forget that."

"How can I when you're saying lines of poetry to her and writing her love letters?"

Jasper glares at me. "I do *not* do that."

"Right," I say and smack him on the back. "Too manly to do that chivalrous stuff, I get it."

"Whoa, now! I never said I didn't know how to woo a girl. I got Amber, didn't I?"

Seriously? Does he think he won Amber over, because that girl was chasing after him for months before they finally hooked up, or so I've been told?

Jasper didn't tell me when they hooked up, but the sexual tension between them had been palpable for months. And then, one day, it wasn't nearly so bad.

Hence, they had sex.

Not that it's any of my business. But the point remains, he didn't have to woo her. She was already into him for a long time. Hell, I was the one trying to convince him not to hook up with her, but that had more to do with bro code than anything else.

I don't answer his question. If I point out that they were roommates and that's what landed her in his bed, he might jump my ass, and I'd prefer to keep the physical brutality to the ice.

"Fair enough," I say with a tight smile. We head out together, making our way to the back exit where the girls are waiting for us. I glance at my phone, and my stomach somersaults.

The paternity results are in.

I shove my phone into my back pocket. I'm not ready to see the news. I'm not sure how I even feel about all of it.

There's no sign of Charlotte. She isn't standing beside Amber. I force a smile, trying not to look dejected when it's clear to me that she didn't care enough to stick around. And maybe that's for the best. If I'm the little boy's father, can I really drag Charlotte into my mess?

As it is, my career has always come first. If I have to put a kid at the top of my priority list, a girlfriend will fall even lower on that list.

Exhaling a sigh, I rub the back of my neck, my fingers itching to reach for my cell phone.

No.

That's the last thing I need to see, the results tonight in front of the guys. There would be too many questions from them, and until I know what the results state, I'm not telling a soul.

Jasper pulls Amber into his arms, their lips locked in a searing kiss. I glance away, not needing to watch them play tonsil hockey.

Irritation sets in my veins.

I can't explain the discomfort, the rawness of their glee hitting me in the face.

"Ready to hit the bar?" I ask, interrupting their make out session. Can't they wait until we grab our table at Blue Line before they go at it?

Amber pulls back, grinning at Jasper before glancing in my direction. "We should wait for Charlotte. She's in the bathroom."

I exhale a breath, relieved that she didn't leave. "Oh. She could have used ours," I say and shuffle my feet, glancing down the hallway. Being around her makes me happy, and right now, I could use a dose of Charlotte Grace.

Her name clicks on my tongue, a familiarity that swirls around me like a misty fog. But I can't place it. I've heard that name before. I'm sure of it. Somewhere.

"Gross," Amber says and pulls me from my thoughts. She scrunches her nose. "It probably smells like jock strap or something."

"That's not a thing," I say, glaring at her.

I'm relieved when I see Charlotte stalking down the hallway, heading toward us. Her red hair cascades down her back, slightly wavy, and she is looking completely fuckable.

I clear my throat and shift uncomfortably. I'm going to need to keep my thoughts clean if I'm not going to ravish her before we get out of the arena.

That's one way to put the shit from my past behind me, but not the best option. Kind of what got me into my current predicament in the first place. Well, not exactly. Jasmine wasn't a one-night stand. She was before my professional hockey player days when I thought a relationship was what I wanted. After her, I was one hundred percent a bachelor, hooking up with whomever showed the most interest.

Because she hurt me, and that was how I dealt with it.

And now I don't know what it is that I'm after. Other than Charlotte.

I want her.

Tonight. Tomorrow.

I want her for more than another fun night in the sheets at her place. Not that I'd turn that opportunity down because it was amazing. But I want more. And yet I'm plagued by the knot in my stomach, the worry that the paternity results will forever fuck up my life.

I'm being selfish.

I should be thinking about the little boy, the one who could use a father as a role model as opposed to the abusive asshole whose roof he's been living under.

Charlotte's eyes shine, and all worry seeps out of me.

"Hey, good game tonight," Charlotte says with a warm smile.

I pull her into my arms, embracing her in a hug. "Glad you stuck around for drinks," I say. I don't admit that I worried she bailed. Not that I'd blame her; we haven't put a label on this new thing between us.

"We have to celebrate. That was a great play you made on the ice tonight."

I'm thrilled she noticed. "Just one great play?" I grin, nudging her as we all head for the back exit.

"You were great all night," Charlotte says, and then her eyes widen, realizing her words. "I'm talking about hockey."

I chuckle. "Sure, if you say so, *Red*."

She wrinkles her nose with an adorable smile and brushes against me as we walk to the bar. It's not far, and the others will catch up with us when they've done the press interviews that they're required to do.

"How was your week?" I ask.

"You're asking about me?" her voice squeaks in surprise. It's adorable how the question flusters her. "It was uneventful. Lots of schoolwork, regular work, and whatnot. What about you?"

I refrain from admitting that I missed her and that the sweet texts were almost torture when I'd fall asleep in bed dreaming about her.

Not exactly a second-date discussion.

Although this doesn't classify as a date when the entire team is hanging out with us.

I try to hide the grin from my face. The last thing I need is my teammates giving me hell over a girl.

"Busy," I say, brushing up against her as we walk to the bar. "Lots of practice and working out." I leave off the bit about Jasmine and the paternity test.

When we head inside Blue Line, our reserved table is waiting for us in the back. There's already a crowd and I'm getting the feeling that maybe some fans have figured out our local afterparty hangout.

Not that it's been a secret, but we don't advertise it, either.

Quite a few girls are wearing our jerseys, huddled together by the bar. When we step inside, it's impossible not to miss their heated stares as they sip their girly drinks by the bar.

"Fans?" Charlotte says, noticing the girls. She doesn't appear the least bit intimidated, but they also haven't brazenly stalked over and asked for our numbers yet.

Give it five minutes, tops.

Jasper chuckles, overhearing Charlotte's question. "More like puck bunnies."

Amber swats him on the arm. "They could just really like hockey," she says. "Just because they're wearing a jersey, doesn't mean they'd sleep with every hockey player on the team."

"Yeah, zero chance of that happening since I'm taken," Jasper says, pulling Amber tighter into his arms. Their lips meet, and I glance away, gesturing for the waitress to bring us a bucket of beers as we grab our seats at the table.

Usually, their displays of affection don't typically irritate me, but right now, I don't want to watch them making out at the bar. I shift in my seat, turning my back to the two of them and giving my undivided attention to Charlotte.

She grins. "You two lovebirds are gross. Get a room!" she jokes. "I feel like I need popcorn. Something I can throw at them to interrupt their little love session."

At least we're on the same page.

"I can give you my shoe," I say with a straight face.

Laughter bubbles up from her chest, her cheeks red. "Tempting, Reece."

I quirk a smile, liking the sound of my name on her lips, even if it's my surname. "Not into big public displays of affection?" I ask.

"Yes and no. Not for making out," she explains, "but proposals, yes."

"Proposals," I repeat. "Are you like an expert in that or something? Have a lot of guys proposing to you?" I'm teasing her, but I can't help but feel the pit of my stomach churn at the hint of jealousy brewing to the surface.

Charlotte laughs. "No, but I do tend to be the friend guys go to, to help arrange their girlfriend's proposals."

"Seriously, that's a thing?" Jasper asks.

"Yeah, my cousin and her best friend, both of their husbands came to me before they got engaged. The girls wanted big proposals, with their names and pictures on the jumbotron at a hockey game."

"And you have the connections to do that?" I ask.

"Something like that." She shrugs and reaches for a beer when the waitress brings over a bucket. "Have either of you ever proposed to a girl?" Charlotte asks us.

Amber raises a curious eye. "Yeah, Jasper, have you ever proposed to a girl?"

I laugh, sensing that he could easily be in for a world of trouble tonight if he answers wrongly.

"Never," Jasper says, "I only have eyes for you, baby." He's staring at Amber and pulls her to sit on his lap. There's not much room on the chairs, but they make do.

"And what about you?" Charlotte asks, waiting for me to answer her question.

I laugh and grab a beer. "Can't say that I have." Although the thought of proposing to Jasmine had been fleeting, it certainly crossed my mind. It's for the best that I didn't, given the fact that she cheated on me.

Charlotte looks dynamite wearing my jersey. It's hard for me to tear my gaze away from her for even an instant.

"See something you like?" she asks cheekily, tilting her head and smiling up at me.

I like that she isn't shy. There's a brazenness to her that's hot as hades, and I can't wait to tear off her clothes and bring her back to my place.

Growling, I stand, grabbing her hips and pulling her against me.

"I'm going to lose my seat," she whines, but there's a smile on her lips, and somehow, I don't think that she cares about her seat.

I lean my lips against her ear, my voice thick as I whisper, "If that happens, you can have mine."

"Promises, promises." Her tongue darts out and licks the top of her lip.

It takes everything in me not to ravish her in the bar. She's my saving grace, my distraction from the one thing tearing me up inside. I don't want to use her while I'm feeling this way, but the fleeting moments of happiness that Charlotte brings me overflow me with joy.

"Go out on a second date with me," I say, taking her hands in mine. We've only been together a week, and I'm not sure what we are qualifies as together.

"Tonight isn't a date?" Charlotte asks, smoothing down her jersey that looks absolutely sexy on her. "I dressed up for you." There's a warm smile grazing her lips, her eyes shine, and she sucks in a sharp breath as I study her features, taking all of it in.

I want to memorize every detail as she's making it known that she wore my number for me.

Damn right.

"I wouldn't classify drinks with the team as a date," I say, clarifying that when I wine and dine her, she'll know it's a date. Like the coffee date where I took her to the ice arena. I don't do anything half-assed. When I like a girl, I want her to know it.

"What about if we dance?" she asks, swaying her hips as she stands in front of me. She gestures for me to join her on the dance floor as she takes a small step backward, waiting for me to accompany her.

I groan but find myself drawn to her. My hands fall gently at her hips as I lean in, brushing my mouth over her ear. "You should know I don't dance."

"You don't know how?" she asks, staring up at me with wide, curious eyes.

I know how, but when you're over six feet, you lose quite a bit of grace when it comes to dancing. "You don't want to see me on that dance floor."

"Now, I really do," she says, like it's a challenge.

She grabs my hand and drags me to follow her.

"Where are you two off to?" Jasper asks, watching Charlotte pull me away from our reserved VIP table in the back of the bar.

"Dancing!" she shouts.

Jasper doesn't even attempt to hide the grin on his face. "Good luck with that! Noah is great on the ice, but have you seen him on the dance floor?"

Amber elbows him. "Be nice!" she scolds and whispers something into his ear.

"Why don't you two join us?" I shout at them before she tugs me farther from the guys, and I can't see them around one of the pillars in the room.

Her hips sway to the music, and she turns with her back to me, bumping and grinding up against me. She pulls her hair to one side, holding the long red locks as she wiggles her hips into my crotch.

For fucks' sake, how am I supposed to survive a night of this and behave?

I'm trying desperately not to rush our new

budding romance, but she just lit the match for the sparks to fly.

"You dance like a goddess," I whisper into her ear, certain she can feel the bump in my pants.

She spins around to face me, and her arms wrap instantly around my neck. "Does that line work on all the girls?"

"I told you, I don't dance."

She's wearing a perfect smile while her eyes shine up at me. "You've got some good moves. I've seen them," she says. "Felt them."

Damn, the bar just got a hell of a lot hotter.

Her cheeks are red, not as fiery as her hair, but a close second. I rest my hands on her hips, my fingers holding her tight, possessively against me.

There's a camera flash from across the bar, probably some asshat taking a photo of us for their social media page. I'm used to it. Don't particularly like it, but it's nothing new.

She raises a hand to cover her face from the amateur photographer. It could be worse. The paparazzi could be stalking us at Blue Line. The club does a decent job of keeping them out; the bouncers and owner are good about letting us attempt to have some privacy.

But you can't stop everyone with a cell phone camera.

Charlotte's eyes widen, and she sucks in a nervous breath. "I have to—" She untangles from around me and hightails it through the crowd toward the back of the bar. She grabs her purse from the booth.

"You two looked awfully cozy," Amber says, grinning as she sees us return to the table. Her brow pinches, glancing from me to Charlotte, sensing something amuck. "What's going on?"

"I have to go," Charlotte says, snatching her purse. She heads for the back exit.

I don't know what happened. Is she worried about being seen with me? Her reputation?

I let her go. I'm not one to chase a girl. I'm usually the one being pursued, and for the moment, if she can't handle being in the spotlight, then she isn't the right girl for me.

FIVE

CHARLOTTE

Holy hell, that was close! I escape Blue Line through the back exit and hope my face isn't plastered on the news or the tabloids. The last thing I need is for Noah to discover who I am, because right now, he thinks I'm just a girl who goes to NYU.

And he's right.

That's part of who I am. But that's not the only part. I'm also the daughter of the owner of the Island Bruisers.

And my father has made it quite clear that he doesn't appreciate it when I steal the spotlight.

I'm sure he'll be even less delighted when he discovers my interest in Noah Reece. I hurry for the subway, my feet aching as I walk as fast as possible, alone in the dark.

There's an ache in the pit of my stomach, like an anvil sits there, and I exhale a shaky breath. I'm sure that no one noticed me. The photographer was probably taking a shot of Noah. After all, the bar was packed with hockey players.

I should be a nobody to them.

A fancy black sports car slows beside the sidewalk, and the passenger window rolls down.

"Charlotte?"

I stop walking and glance at the open window, trudging toward the vehicle. "Shouldn't you be celebrating your win?" I ask.

"I'd rather celebrate with you," Noah says.

My breath catches in my throat, and I reach for the door handle, sliding into the passenger seat. "Nice car," I say, glancing anywhere but at him. The tension is thick, but maybe it's only from my side, because I can feel his piercing gaze right through me.

His fingers tap against the steering wheel, drumming with anxious energy.

Okay, I'm not the only one feeling the tension.

"Do you mind dropping me off at home?" I ask,

not like there's anywhere else I was expecting that he'd take me.

I haven't seen his place.

I'm not sure if I will. I mean, what the hell are we? Friends? Dating? There's a grey line, and then there's whatever we've settled ourselves into.

He's famous.

Noah Reece doesn't date. At least from what I've seen and read. Plus, he told me he puts his career first, which sounds like solid confirmation. He sleeps around. He's the team's hotshot playboy, and for good reason. I try not to glance at him because once I do, it's hard to tear my gaze away.

"Sure," Noah says and gives me that smile that goes right from my heart straight into giving me butterfly tingles, and not in my stomach.

I'm silent, and he rolls up the window before he pulls out into traffic.

It's New York. The city is still bursting with life even at this hour. The bars and clubs are open. That's about it. Nightlife is booming, and we inch through the city until he makes his way toward NYU.

"Do you want to talk about what happened back there?" Noah asks.

His fingers are once again tapping against the steering wheel.

"Me leaving?" I ask and chance a glance in his direction.

The traffic light turns red, and he slows to a stop and glances at me.

My breath catches in my throat. The air is thick and heavy. I inhale sharply and bite down on my bottom lip. "It was getting too crowded."

His gaze flinches, and I can't tell if he knows I'm lying or is unconvinced. "Crowded," Noah repeats.

The word sounds flimsy on his lips. He's not buying my story.

And I refuse to tell him who my father is because that would make a mess of things. Plus, I can't expect him to hide our relationship from the world, not when I'm showing up at his games wearing *his* jersey.

I don't want that to change, either.

"And here I thought you were just unimpressed by the company." There's a smile that adorns his face. It's simple. Sweet. Boyish.

It's hard not to fall for him, even if it's a bad idea.

But the problem is that I've already fallen hard. It was one date. One passionate night. And now I've become obsessed with the man like a crazy stalker.

I mean, except that I'm not physically stalking him. Save that job for someone like Amber, who, yes,

I know, was stalking her crush online. The girl can't keep a secret from me.

"I like your company," I say and smile weakly before he returns his attention to the road as the light turns green. "I just, sometimes, prefer a less crowded space."

"Yeah, I'm not buying that, Charlotte." He shifts, the tension growing thicker, like ropes in his muscles as he tightens his grip on the steering wheel.

The tension before was palpable. Now, it's suffocating.

I open my mouth to ask *what do you mean* when he continues speaking.

"I've seen you go out with Amber. I've heard stories." He grimaces and shakes his head, "I don't care about the past, but I know there's a wild side. So, telling me that you don't like crowds or it was too busy a night is absolute and utter bullshit. And I don't like to be lied to."

My voice is soft and calm, trying not to worsen the situation. "What stories have you heard?" I ask.

"I know you party. Like to have fun. Cut loose. Whatever," he says with a dismissive wave. "Jasper mentioned having to pick Amber up one time, because you disappeared at a party."

"Oh my gosh," I gasp. I know the party he's

referring to, and my cheeks burn remembering that torrid night. "You were talking about my sex life?" The car is a million degrees. How are the windows not fogging up? I open the window, needing a blast of cold air because my stomach is like a sailboat in the middle of a hurricane.

"Well, not specifically." He chuckles, and I'm relieved he's not trying to humiliate me.

However, it doesn't mean I'm any less embarrassed to discuss the topic with him. "Anyways," I say with a bit of forcefulness, wanting to change the topic to anything else. "I needed to get out of there. I was heading for the subway when you showed up."

"I figured as much." He glances at me, perhaps realizing that I don't intend to answer his question on why I left.

He lets it go. And I hope that's the last of it.

The remainder of the ride is in silence, mostly listening to music on the radio, but not much is said between us. As he approaches my apartment complex, I unbuckle my belt while he pulls over to park the car.

"Thanks for the ride."

He shuts off the engine and opens the car door. I wasn't expecting him to walk me to my door.

Honestly, I'm not sure what I'm expecting. Tonight wasn't a date, but I still feel out of sorts. I like him, but I'm not sure he's good for me.

He's made it clear he puts his career first. I thought I was okay with that, but the feeling of being emotionally crushed doesn't exactly scream *okay*.

And then there's the photographer tonight.

I should end this before either of us gets hurt.

But I don't want to.

His hand falls to my lower back, the gesture protective and utterly romantic. I try not to swoon, but my heart balloons out with longing.

"Thanks for the ride tonight. And good game," I say, grabbing the key and unlocking the main entrance to the apartment complex.

I'm not letting him inside, not again.

He seems to get the message without me having to spell it out. At least he's not a dumb jock. "Have a good night," Noah says, as I head into the building, leaving him standing outside on the front stoop.

————

I love my job. I love my job. I love my job.

I keep chanting the phrase in my head, trying to

make it true. Because if I keep saying it, maybe I'll believe it.

I work for the park district of a small town outside of the city. When I'm not in charge of the phones and the front desk, I teach kids on the ice how to ice skate or play hockey, which is ninety percent of my schedule.

There are two classes that I teach, both of which are in the late afternoon. I barely make it on time this afternoon with the snow blanketing the city and the trains delayed.

But at least I'm not the only one behind schedule. I'm sure the kids will be late if they show up at all.

And when I finally get to the station, I hurry up the escalator and attempt to jog the three blocks to the rink. Although my footing is more along the lines of sliding through the slush and it's hell on my ankles.

While I might be mean on the ice in skates, slushy snow and sneakers are not the same thing. Especially with pedestrians in business suits and coats packing the pathway.

Grumbling under my breath, I finally make it to the arena, toss open the door, and while the place is chilly, it's warmer without the assault from the cold wind whipping my cheeks.

"Ms. Grace," Lotti shouts and waves at me with one hand while holding her hockey stick in the other. She's already on the ice, apparently not waiting for class to start, along with a half dozen other kids.

It's a beginner's hockey drills and thrills basics class for elementary-aged kids, which always surprises me when their parents drop them off and are nowhere to be seen. I get my skates on and work on drills with the kids. Sadie, the intern assistant, shows up twenty minutes into class to help with the kids. She's usually timely, so I chalk her delay to the trains and weather.

"Okay, pair off into two teams," I shout at the kids, letting them pick which team they want to be on. Sadie hands out red and blue jerseys to the kids while they get set up.

She stays on one side of the rink with me on the opposite while we let the little rascals practice their hockey skills in a game.

The kids are cute. That's about all they have going for them. Well, that, and they seem to be having fun.

Talent? I don't see much of it. But none of them care, and that's what matters.

As a team, they're a hot mess. And it would be fun to watch if I wasn't trying to teach them how to play. Everything they've learned in their drills is completely obliterated, and they're in survive or die mode.

One of the girls skates in the wrong direction with the puck.

"Jennie!" I shout at her, pointing at the opposite side of the ice, trying to grab her attention.

The young girl, Jennie, breezes past another girl with fiery red hair who stands there watching while holding her hockey stick. She's always great when we run drills, but the minute the game starts, she seems to forget what she's supposed to do.

Sadie and I glance at one another, trying not to laugh.

My watch buzzes, alerting me to a phone call. I thought I'd put my phone on silent but maybe I got distracted in my rush to work.

It's my father.

The last person I want to talk to.

I hit ignore on my device.

He's persistent, calling immediately back. I hit

ignore again and wrap up the game with the kids before the next class piles into the rink.

Unfortunately, it's not just the kids with their parents.

"Charlotte, a word." My father nods at me, and I grind my teeth together, my jaw tight.

He has impeccable timing. I don't know how he knew I'd be between classes and have a ten-minute break. It could be a coincidence, but knowing him, doubtful.

I refrain from asking him why he's here and what he wants.

He only ever comes around when he needs a favor. "It's good to see you, Char."

I purse my lips, fold my arms across my chest, and glance at the clock affixed to the wall. "I only have a few minutes until the next class starts."

"Yes, my assistant told me."

So, that's how he knew when to drop by uninvited. He made his assistant look into my schedule. I shouldn't be surprised, but it still fills me with disgust.

"What can I do for you?" I ask, because he's not here for chit-chat or to see me teach a bunch of kids to play ice hockey.

"There's a charity event that I need you to attend. It's for a good cause."

"Aren't they all?" I ask. My fingernails dig into my arm.

"I need you there in a show of support, Charlotte. I'll have my assistant text you the details."

"Of course, you will," I say a bit harshly.

He ignores my remark like he always does. Probably chalking it off to moodiness, which he swears I get from my mother.

"One other thing," he says, his jaw terse. "I've volunteered you to be part of the auction."

I'm sure that I'm scowling at him. "Am I showing off the prizes or something?" I ask, unsure what he's offered me to do without even asking me.

"You'll be the prize, dear. A date with my daughter."

I choke on his words. "No."

His eyes are frigid, making the arena feel even colder. "I'm not asking, Charlotte. It's just one date. It's not like you don't do plenty of that in college."

I scoff at his suggestion. "My own father pimping me out," I mutter under my breath. I don't need the mothers overhearing the conversation as they're helping their four and five-year-olds get their gear on for the next class.

He doesn't so much as blink or flinch at my words. "Just a tad dramatic, are we? It's one date. I'm not asking the world of you. Besides, it's for charity."

"Are you even going to tell me what charity this benefits?"

"It's a fundraiser to build a new wing at the children's hospital. Are you going to tell me you don't support kids with cancer?"

I growl under my breath. He seriously had to play the kids with cancer card? How am I supposed to say no, I don't support *that* cause?

"Fine, but I'm bringing my boyfriend."

"Boyfriend?"

SIX

NOAH

After dropping Charlotte off, I haven't heard from her in days. Not that I've exactly reached out to her, either.

There's been an envelope burning me, sealed, with the paternity results. I can't bring myself to open it.

I have mixed feelings. And it's starting to show in games and practice.

"Everything okay?" Jasper asks, smacking me on the back after practice as we head into the locker room. "You don't seem like yourself."

He's right. But how do I tell him without him and the other guys freaking out? Because they will make a big deal out of the whole situation, and I'm already walking a tightrope. I don't need to fall.

"Just have a lot on my mind," I say with a heavy sigh. I strip out of my gear and head for the showers, wanting to get cleaned up and some hot water to erase the day's events. The shower stalls offer a modicum of privacy from mid-chest down.

"We're all going over to Kyler's tonight," Jasper says from his shower stall. "Bonfire and beer. You should come and unwind."

I hesitate, inhaling a sharp breath. "Who else is attending?" I turn the shower on and let the hot water bead over me.

Knowing Kyler, he isn't just having the team at his place. He's also letting Emerson invite a few friends over, girls. One of them could possibly be Charlotte.

"Are you asking because you want to know if Charlotte is coming?" Jasper asks. "Do you want to see her, or are you avoiding her? Ever since Blue Line, I can't tell what is going on with you."

"Me either," I say and let the water pour over my face. It keeps me from having to answer Jasper's question.

"Is she a bit too much for you?" Jasper can't let it go.

I know he's got good intentions, but I'm in over my head with the fact I might be a father.

I also might not be.

I should open that damn envelope and just rip the band-aid off.

Kyler shuts off the water in his shower stall and grabs his towel. "Drinks tonight at my place. Who's in?"

"How about who's not in?" Parker quips as he heads for an empty shower.

"Bonfire and beer," Kyler insists, trying to remind the guys he's a responsible parent. He's not throwing a kegger.

Maybe a couple of beers would be good, to take my mind off that damn letter I've avoided opening. And with enough alcohol, I'll even find the courage to tear open the envelope and read the results.

My stomach churns just thinking about what it could mean.

I've avoided dealing with it because the weight of what it could mean is heavy, and I don't have time to fixate on it.

I haven't heard a word from Jasmine or seen her. Which, again, makes me relieved but also concerned.

Did she go back to her husband? Is she on the run? Are they even still alive?

After the way Jasmine treated me when we were together, I shouldn't care, but if the boy is mine, then I can't just walk away. I won't.

I finish shutting off the shower, dry off with a towel, and get dressed in front of my locker. I grab my jacket and phone, about ready to head out.

"You dropped something," Kyler says, bending down and picking up the folded envelope I've been carrying everywhere as if it holds the secrets to the universe.

No, only my future.

He flips it over, glancing at the return address, and raises an inquisitive eye.

"Yeah, it's nothing," I say, snatching it from his grip.

He studies me, silent and brooding as I fold the envelope in half and shove it into the back pocket of my jeans, where it fell out.

"I'll see you tonight," Kyler says, nodding at me, letting the discussion drop, and I'm immensely grateful.

———

After a couple of beers, I can finally relax outside, the fire roaring in the backyard of Kyler's estate.

Amber is curled up on Jasper's lap, the two of them practically sucking face.

I stand, needing to get away from their romantic encounter. If I weren't in such a foul mood regarding relationships, I'd find it endearing.

But right now, it makes me want to vomit.

Correction. The thought of Jasmine and the letter makes my stomach churn, but any inkling of a relationship right now can get tossed into that bonfire and be doused with gasoline.

Romance is dead.

Charlotte stalks outside, head held high, a glass of wine in her hand. She gives me a nod and smiles. "Hey, stranger," she says, staring at me.

She's sunshine, and I'm rain.

I don't deserve her kindness.

Her gaze doesn't so much as glance away, and when she approaches and climbs onto my lap, it takes every ounce of energy not to fall under her spell.

Too late.

My hand immediately wraps around her waist, pulling her closer, tighter, wanting to feel her body above mine. She's warm, and there's something about feeling her weight above me that stirs something inside of me, and, well, yes, that too.

She sits casually on my lap. One arm falls around my shoulders, and the other holds onto her wine glass as she brings the dark red liquid to her lips for a taste.

Her head dips back, exposing the perfect creamy complexion of her neck, and I stifle a growl.

This woman does things to me without even trying.

It's hard not to imagine her lips wrapped around my cock, sucking me. She dips her head down, her cheeks are slightly rosy, and she quirks a smile when she pulls the glass back from her mouth.

"See something you like?" she whispers, teasing me.

Maybe she is trying, and I've just been oblivious tonight. Her hips shift slightly against my groin, and, oh my gosh, she's going to kill me.

My breathing is heavy and thick, and it takes everything in my power not to let my fingers wander up her skirt and discover if she's as wet as I think she is for me.

"You're being a *very* bad girl," I say, keeping my voice low and quiet, not letting anyone else overhear us. Although most of the team and the couples are enthralled in their own conversations.

Her lips curve upwards, and my cock twitches.

Damn, she looks hot tonight, in her fiery red lipstick and those dark eyeliner-rimmed eyes. Her mouth looks delectable. And I'd love to see her lips wrapped around my cock, my fingers fisting her hair, seeing how deep she'd take me.

"I'll bet that turns you on," Charlotte says.

She lifts her hips as if she's going to get up, but I refuse to let her bail on me. The minute she moves, anyone who glances over will see my hard-on. I don't need the guys giving me shit for the rest of the season over it.

Besides, it's nice to have a distraction, and that is precisely what Charlotte is for me. A welcoming distraction that I want to surround myself in and allow the world around me to disappear, if only for a little while.

I don't even know what the hell it is that we are. She's not my girlfriend, but she's more to me than some fling that I've one and done. Just the mere fact I'm fantasizing about her is not typical for me. And the girl has gotten under my skin.

Pressing my lips together, my fingers grip her hips, unwilling to let her go. I need her, and I have a feeling she'd be happy to oblige. "Where do you think you're going?" I whisper, making sure she feels the bump where she's seated.

Charlotte raises an eyebrow.

She may have pretended not to notice it before, but I'm not letting her act like she's unaware of my desire for her any longer.

Charlotte gestures to the empty wine glass in her hand. "I was going to grab a refill." She pauses and smiles, her cheeks turning a pink hue before she glances down at my lips, studying them for a long moment. "Good game today," she says.

"Just doing my job." I try not to brag. Hockey is a team sport, and I'm not the only one who has reason to celebrate. I kept the other team from scoring.

It's almost as though she's flustered in the way she compliments me, like she's not sure if I knew she was at the game.

I knew.

It was impossible not to notice her screaming my name, cheering for me as I made a goal. Okay, well, actually hearing her wasn't possible on the ice, but I felt her presence, and when I glanced in her direction on the bench behind the team, I saw her on her feet, clapping and shouting.

Another reason I'm torn.

She's perfection, and I'm spiraling out of control.

The letter burns a hole in my back pocket. I can't bring myself to face the truth, the consequences of my actions, with a woman I thought I loved.

There's a bitter taste in my mouth every time my thoughts swim back to the woman who cheated on me.

While I know Charlotte isn't *her*, it doesn't matter. It's still challenging to find myself capable of trusting again, which is why when *Red* ran off the night at Blue Line, I couldn't stop myself from chasing her down.

She brings her hand up into my hair, her fingernails dragging along my scalp, bringing my lips closer to hers.

I inhale sharply. The warmth from her breath tickles my lips and sends electricity straight to my cock, the way she stares at me. My heart hammers inside of my chest, banging to come out like it's locked inside a prison, begging for release.

"You didn't return any of my texts," Charlotte says.

"Texts?" I lift my hips slightly, digging my hand into my pocket to retrieve my phone. "I didn't get anything from you. Are you sure you weren't texting your other boyfriend?" I prod with a wry smile.

She chuckles. "Right. I can't keep all my hockey hotties straight."

"You think I'm hot."

She opens her mouth and quickly shuts it. The slight pink hue from earlier has now turned bright red. "Did I say hot? I meant—"

Before I let her continue, I brush my lips against hers. She tastes like cherries and vanilla, and I lean in to steal another kiss because the first is a temptation, a tease for more.

"So, did you open it?" Kyler interrupts the heated moment, standing over us while holding a beer.

"Open what?" Charlotte asks, giving me the sexy little head tilt that makes me want to go back right to kissing her and ignoring the guys.

"Do you mind if I steal him for a couple of minutes?" Kyler asks.

Charlotte climbs off my lap, giving me that wanton look that goes straight to my cock.

Fuck me.

Can't we get a room and let my cock have the time of his life? I mean, it would help me forget my current dilemma, which is burning a hole in my back pocket.

"No problem. I should visit with Amber since she's the reason I'm here."

Charlotte stands, and I reach for her hand, intertwining our fingers together. "I'm not the reason?" I ask, staring up at her, and she gives me a grin, scrunching her nose in the most adorable fashion.

"You come in second, my love," she teases and squeezes my hand before untangling and sauntering off to steal away Amber from Jasper.

"Are you two officially a thing?" Kyler asks.

I stand, stretching my legs, and follow him inside to grab another beer. Besides, if he's intending to bring up the letter, I don't want to do it around anyone else.

"We haven't put a label on it," I say. "We're just... having fun?"

While we've only hooked up once, there's chemistry between us. Plus, we keep running into each other, being in the same social circle and all.

Which is reason enough not to tangle in the sheets with her again, but my cock thinks otherwise, and I happen to agree with him. He should get to make all the decisions. I'd be a hell of a lot happier right now.

"You haven't opened the paternity test results yet, have you?" Kyler jumps straight to the point.

I cringe, grab his arm, and pull him into the

house, shutting the door behind us. No one needs to hear this conversation.

"How do you know it's for a paternity test?" I ask. "I mean, it could be checking to see if I have the cancer gene."

"*The* cancer gene?" He laughs and runs a hand through his hair. "There's more than one gene that relates to cancer, and besides, the clinic you went to specializes in paternity tests. Trust me, I know." Kyler doesn't elaborate.

He has a daughter who is six, and while I never thought there was a question regarding his paternity, maybe he had doubts.

"What did the results say?" Kyler gets right to the point.

I shuffle my feet and turn my back, opening the fridge to grab another beer. Honestly, I want something a bit harder. But while I might want to get wasted, I won't be doing the team any favors tomorrow.

I grab a beer and pop the cap off. "I haven't opened it," I say, avoiding his heated stare.

He huffs under his breath. "I never took you for a coward."

"Excuse me?" I spin around on my feet, staring at him.

"You heard me," Kyler says, challenging me. "If you're too chicken shit to open up the test results, give it to me. I'll read it for you."

"I'm not chicken shit or afraid of anything." I yank the folded and battered white envelope from my back pocket.

I don't back down from a dare. Not now. Not ever.

Tearing open the envelope, I pull out the crinkled paper and inhale sharply.

"So?" Kyler says, waiting for my answer.

"It says there's a 99.8% probability that I'm that kid's father."

Fuck.

SEVEN

CHARLOTTE

The air outside is chilly, and I stand by the fire with my arms wrapped around myself. I nod toward Amber, giving her *the look* to silently shout at her to get off her boyfriend's lap and come chat with me.

She invited me to the bonfire to hang out, and all she's been doing since I arrived is suck face with her boyfriend.

Not that I'm upset. But I need a friend to confide in about the whole *I lied to my father, and he thinks I have a boyfriend* fiasco.

Noah and I haven't had that talk yet. The one that defines what we are or aren't. We slept together once.

He made it eternally clear that he puts his career

first, always. I don't fault him for that. He made his intentions crystal from day one.

I, on the other hand, thought I was okay with that, but my insides are twisted, and I hate when I'm waiting for him to text me back, and he doesn't. I feel like a crazy mess, and I wouldn't be surprised if he never wanted to see me again. Which is why I've made sure not to jump into bed with him, again.

I'm protecting my heart. It's weird, it's not something I've ever had to do before, but I've never been this head over heels for a guy, either.

And what we have, this more than friends but not quite with benefits thing between us, seems to be working, mostly. This past week, he's been a bit harder to reach.

I've tried chalking it up to his schedule with the Ice Dragons has been busy. He probably doesn't have time for friends, but then seeing him tonight at the party, he could have texted me once this week.

Here I go again, feeling something that I shouldn't for a guy I'm *not* dating. And I throw all that insecurity and fear aside the moment I laid eyes on him. I sauntered up, pretended like none of it mattered, because when I'm around him, all I feel is complete and utter bliss.

With his hands on me, it's like we have found our

own ebb and flow. Nothing else matters, we're just Charlotte and Noah.

And that's when his teammate, Kyler, dragged him away.

I shouldn't care. Noah is not my boyfriend.

We haven't gone out on a single date.

And we've only hooked up once. The first night that we met.

Which puts me in a precarious position because I fibbed to my father, and it's about to bite me in the ass. Oh, I could invite Noah to the event to accompany me, but there will be lots of cameras and press.

If I know my father as well as I do, he'll be livid when he sees who I bring as my *boyfriend*. A knot forms in the pit of my stomach just thinking about it, but who is he to try to auction a night off with his daughter?

I grumble inwardly just recanting the story in my head, fuming inside.

Amber climbs off Jasper and throws her arms around my shoulder, pulling me away from the boys. "You seem tense," Amber says.

"I royally screwed the pooch."

Amber's nose wrinkles at the analogy. "Gross, and what did you do?" she asks. "Did Noah catch you making hearts with your initials in the center on your notebook?" There's a teasing note in her voice, and I elbow her in the ribcage.

"Brat."

Amber shrugs. "Tell me something I don't know." She smiles and steps closer to the flames to keep warm. Rubbing her hands together, she glances over at me, waiting for me to elaborate on how I screwed up.

"Are you going to give it to me?" she asks.

"That's what she said," I joke, trying anything that I can to avoid the discussion, but the truth is that I need her opinion. I mean, I'm not normally nervous around Noah, or any man, for that matter. But asking him to pretend to be my boyfriend has my stomach in a flurry of butterflies.

"You're stalling." Amber stares pointedly at me and steps closer. The boys are engrossed in their hockey talk and don't pay us any attention.

"My dad is forcing me to do this charity auction next month, and he's volunteered me as a prize for the evening. One lucky winner gets to go out with me for an evening."

Amber's brow pinches. "I'm guessing by the words *my dad is forcing* that he didn't ask you."

"He never asks."

"You're an adult. You could tell him no." Amber glances me over. "Unless you want to go out on a blind date with a stranger."

"It's not a blind date. I mean, I'll be at the auction," I say.

"Still sounds creepy and gross for your dad to do that."

I exhale a heavy breath. "That's not the worst part." I bite down on my bottom lip and wince from the onset of pain. "I told him that I'm bringing my boyfriend."

Amber's eyes widen, and she coughs, trying to contain her amusement. "Sorry, what?" The bubbly laughter continues spilling out, and she's bent over with her hand out, telling me to hold on a second.

I shuffle my feet and wait for her to stand upright.

Amber's cheeks are rosy, and after she finally manages to catch her breath, she says, "You got yourself into this mess. Have fun getting out of it." She points at the back door of the house.

Inside, through the open window blinds, I can see Noah and Kyler having some type of discussion, probably about today's game.

"No sage advice?" I ask, hoping for a few pearls of wisdom. I may have more experience with dating, but Amber has been in a relationship longer than I ever have.

I do hookups, not boyfriends.

At least, I did.

Noah turned me into the girl who wants a boyfriend, and I want to hate him for it, but he's sweet and cute. Not to mention, easy on the eyes, and that body, oh my gosh.

She pushes me toward the house.

"Now?" I squeak.

"Well, I mean, you could wait, but then you'll have to find someone else if he says no."

"Maybe he'll be out of town for a game," I say.

"Are you seriously talking yourself out of bringing him?" Amber asks.

I don't answer her because if I don't bring him, then my father wins. And the only thing worse than having to do what I'm told is doing it and bringing the enemy.

Dad is going to hate Noah Reece.

Solely due to the fact that he plays for the Ice Dragons, and Dad is an Island Bruisers fan. After all, he owns and manages the Bruisers. He ought to be their biggest fan.

Noah doesn't have any inkling about my family or my father. I haven't told him. There hasn't been reason to bring it up, well, except for that night at the bar with the photographer.

And I shied away from telling him because it would complicate things between us.

Not that I think Noah will care. But I can't deal with the drama and my father. My father is the drama.

My schoolwork and studies should be my focus. Not the paparazzi and press hounding me with questions and following me to class.

I dealt with that in high school after getting caught kissing one of the younger brothers of an Island Bruisers player. Charlie Hayes wasn't on the team yet. But he played hockey and had a promising career ahead of him. The press caught us playing tonsil hockey behind the bleachers, and Dad forbade me from seeing the boy again.

Which was impossible since we were attending the same school.

So, he pulled me out of the local private school he had me enrolled in and sent me to a boarding school in London.

I'm still sour about the whole ordeal. Not that Dad had any say in who I dated or kissed in London, but I liked the boy he tore me away from.

But it's neither here nor there.

Charlie and I haven't spoken since the night I left for London. And that says a lot since he plays for my father's team.

Dad won that battle.

But he won't win the war.

I head inside, out of the cold and through the entrance, stalking my way in a rush toward Noah. "We need to talk," I say, interrupting his conversation with Kyler.

He glances back at me, his gaze moving over my body and lingering a little too long on my breasts.

I cross my arms over my chest and notice what he sees. My nipples are standing at attention from the cold.

Whatever. It's not like he hasn't seen them before, naked.

He bites his bottom lip and nods. "We do," he says, and my stomach flops.

I know what I have to tell him, but what does he think that we need to speak about?

I glance over my shoulder at Amber, who followed me into the house, and she gives me a nod and gestures for me to go with Noah.

Noah leads me down the hallway and opens a pocket door, leading me inside. He flips on the light as I enter, and he closes the door after him.

"I need a favor," I say. The words stumble out before I can even catch my breath. My heart pounds wildly as I wait for his answer. Not that I've elaborated on the request.

And why would he agree to do me a solid if I haven't told him what I need?

"That depends," he says, taking a step closer.

"On?" My mouth is dry, and I lick my parched lips, staring up at him. I feel the heat of his breath, the warmth of his body inches from me.

We are like lightning during a storm. The energy between us sizzles and sparks, waiting to crash down and catch fire.

"There's a charity auction coming up in a couple of weeks, and I need a date. Actually," I exhale a sharp breath, "I need a date who pretends to be my boyfriend because I may have accidentally told my dad a little white lie."

"Accidentally?" Noah laughs, and his shoulders relax at my embarrassment. "You really do need a favor," he muses, considering my request.

"Are you in town on the sixth, next month? I mean, if you have an away game, it's a moot point." I didn't check the schedule for the team. I could have saved myself the humiliation of him saying no and laughing at me. Amber certainly thought it was funny. Noah is smiling, but he's not making fun of me, at least not yet.

"I'm pretty sure I'm in town," Noah says. "How does one accidentally tell their father they have a boyfriend?" He steps closer, his hand brushing a strand behind my ear as he stares straight into my soul.

My stomach flutters, and the heat seeps lower. "That's a funny story," I say and force a laugh.

He waits for me to elaborate, staring at me as if I'm the most important thing in the world. His attention is captivating. Noah tilts his head just slightly, luring me to continue, to give him the details that he's so patiently waiting to hear.

"My dad decided that I would be part of the charity auction as a date for the evening. You know, the highest bidder gets to go out with the pretty girl-type scenario," I say in a rush. "To piss him off, I told him I'd attend the charity ball if I could bring my boyfriend."

"Wait, your dad is auctioning you off at a charity event? That's a bit backward. I mean, you should be choosing if you want to support the charity and if you want to go out on a date. If your dad wants to donate to the event, he can offer up himself for a night!" Noah is a bit testier and more heated over the whole situation than I am.

I rest a hand on his arm. "It's fine."

"It's not fine," Noah seethes. "He didn't even ask your permission, did he?"

I shake my head. He's right. I didn't get much of a say in the situation. I was told to attend and what to expect, typical of my father.

"I'll attend, as your boyfriend, but I can't promise that I won't say something to him about selling his own daughter."

I squeeze his arm. "He's not selling me, per se. Besides, it's for charity."

Noah's jaw is tight. "I don't see why he can't offer himself as a date."

"Because no one would agree to go out with him." It's obvious why he elected me, his only daughter, to be one of the girls at the event. "Besides, he's doing it for the publicity."

"The auction?" Noah's brow pinches. "There will be press at the event," he surmises.

"Well, yes, but he isn't just doing it for himself. He thinks showing off his daughter and having an Island Bruisers player take her out on a date is good for his career."

"Your father's career, or the Island Bruisers

player?" Noah's fuming. "And why would you date an Island Bruisers player when this Ice Dragons star is willing to attend the function?"

I shift uncomfortably as I avoid the question.

"Charlotte?" Noah doesn't like my silence.

"My father owns the Island Bruisers. Their entire team will be at the charity event. It's a requirement, one of the events they're required to attend yearly."

He curses under his breath. "Wait, your last name is Grace. You're *the* Charlotte Grace."

I wince at the way he says my name. "So, I guess you've seen the tabloids."

"Heiress gone wild. You were kicked out of private school and sent to some posh boarding school overseas. London, is it?"

"Were you stalking me?" I can't believe he remembers those details.

"I just kept thinking that you got lucky to escape your asshole father. Turns out, I was right."

"Seriously? That was what crossed your mind when you read the article?"

"Read it? It was all over the news. The papers. You couldn't escape it if you were a hockey fan. It made you into a puck bunny."

I grimace, not realizing it was *that* bad. It was awful for me, but my new peers in London made it out to be like I was embellishing how terrible the situation was. The news didn't make it international.

"For the record, I wasn't kicked out of that private school," I say proudly. "I had decent grades. Dad didn't want me living at home anymore. I brought too much negative attention on him."

Noah's hands are at his sides, bunched into fists. "And he didn't defend you against any of the press's accusations."

He didn't, but I've moved on past all of it. I don't necessarily forgive my father for what he did, but I try to consider his actions as a way of protecting me.

"Can we not talk about the past?" I ask. I certainly don't want Noah bringing it up at the charity event, or ever, if it were up to me.

"Text me the details. I assume it's black tie?"

"It is," I say with a resigned sigh.

I haven't even thought about what I'd wear to the gala, but at least I have my father's credit card. And I fully intend on going on a little shopping spree with Amber this weekend if she's free.

EIGHT

NOAH

I haven't seen or heard from Jasmine. And with the paternity results revealing that I'm, in fact, that little boy's father, I can't ignore it.

Oh, believe me, I've tried.

But I can't ignore that she's married to an abusive asshole, and I don't want him anywhere near *my* son.

Jasmine hasn't answered her phone or returned any of my messages, and I don't have time to play games, not the kind she's up to. I hired a lawyer to discuss paternity options and my rights. He suggested I use his private investigator to locate and track down Jasmine, and we go from there.

One step at a time.

I'm not the most patient person, either, and finding Jasmine and *my son* doesn't come cheap. Not that money is an issue. I'm fortunate to have a steady stream of income from my career, but I don't enjoy throwing my money at the law firm and the private investigator. I'd rather be spending it on my son's needs or buying him toys to play with.

My stomach churns at the thought of having a kid.

What the hell do I know about raising a son?

Not that I want to fight for full custody, but if she's still with that asshole, I'll do everything in my power to make sure my child is safe.

My phone buzzes as I head down the hallway to the locker room. We have a game tonight against the Island Bruisers.

There's a certain amount of pent-up frustration before every game. Tonight is different, going up against the Bruisers and coming face-to-face with the man raising my son as his own.

According to Jasmine, he doesn't know he's not the father, but her silence worries me.

I grab my cell phone from my pocket, reading the notification of a new text message.

I open the app, smiling when I see who it's from.

Charlotte: Knock 'em dead.

I chuckle under my breath and type back to her.

Noah: Oh, I will.

She has no idea how much I want that tonight, not just figuratively. I stalk into the locker room and shove my phone into my jacket pocket before changing into my uniform.

"Any updates?" Kyler asks, coming to stand beside me, keeping his voice low.

"Updates on what?" Jasper asks, glancing between us.

Kyler and I have never been that close, not like Jasper and me. It was inevitable that someone would overhear the news.

"Turns out I'm a dad," I say.

"Congrats!" Jasper smacks me on the back, grinning proudly. "I knew you two were hooking up. When's Charlotte due?"

I cough, surprised by the assumption. "It's not Charlotte's."

Jasper takes a step back and folds his arms across his chest. "One of the puck bunnies?" He doesn't look pleased. "You should get a paternity test if one of those girls claims you're the dad."

I bite my tongue at his remark regarding the fan girls who throw themselves at us. It doesn't take much to find an easy hook-up after a game, that's for sure. "Do you remember Jasmine?"

I swear the entire team is staring at me, gathering around for the news. Although it's just a couple of the guys, the rest are getting ready, glancing over their shoulder. They're listening in, though, because, otherwise, you could hear a pin drop in an otherwise noisy locker room.

"Yeah, the last girl you dated," Jasper says. He's familiar with Jasmine and our history together. He wasn't too fond of her, but he waited to tell me that until after she ghosted me and we broke up. I had been pretty confident that she'd cheated, and Jasper had told me that he wasn't surprised.

She's also why I swore off dating and girlfriends and stuck to puck bunnies. I didn't want another relationship.

"Shit." Jasper's eyes widen, the realization dawning on him. "Are you sure it's not that Bruisers player's kid? I mean, she hooked up with him when you were dating."

"I'm sure. I had a paternity test done, and Zayn is my son."

Owen curses under his breath, overhearing the entire conversation a few feet away.

Jasper raises an eyebrow. "Congrats?" This time, he's asking, unsure if it's something to be celebrated.

That is exactly how I feel.

Uncertain about the whole situation.

I always thought I'd be a dad someday, but I didn't expect it to happen like this, where I'd be hiring a lawyer or a private investigator in order to protect my kid.

I turn toward my locker, indicating the conversation is over as I start gearing up for the game.

"What'd Charlotte say when you told her?" Kyler asks, stepping toward his locker and yanking his shirt over his head, undressing. He may have been in the locker room before me, but he's the last to start getting ready.

"I haven't."

"Hell of a secret to keep," Jasper says.

"What are you boys going on about?" Coach Malone asks, stepping into the locker room. "You ought to be ready by now. Hurry the hell up! The other team isn't going to wait for you."

————

I try to keep my head in the game, but my mind is on other things. It doesn't help that the man I despise, Grant Brass, is on the opposing team.

He knows the history that I have with Jasmine, but she told me he didn't know that I was Zayn's father.

Has that changed?

Brass has a few scratches on his face. They could be fingernail marks if you examine them close enough. It's hard to tell under the helmet covering his face.

Are they from Jasmine, or did they transpire during another game or at practice? Maybe he makes it a habit of roughing up pretty girls. I wouldn't put it past the douche.

The puck slides across the ice as Brass and I battle for control. He's a few inches taller and has fifty pounds on me. He uses it to his advantage, knocking me into the wall and drawing his stick up with a high swing, hitting me in the jaw.

The pain sears and burns. I curse under my breath.

"Want to say that to my face?" Brass taunts.

The referees don't seem to notice the dirty shot. It's either retaliate or ignore his pompous ass and focus on the game.

I choose the latter. "You're an asshole," I growl.

"My wife says the same thing about you. You used to like to eat hers out. You can eat mine all night if you want." He winks at me, laughing, amused with his joke.

Heat floods me even though the air is chilly. "Fuck you, Grant."

"No, thanks. But I'll take you up on that offer of that cute little redhead."

How the hell does he know about Charlotte?

My eyes flicker, and he snickers at me with a wicked grin as we fight for the puck, shoving each other back and forth against the wall. The battle seems unending between us.

"You can thank your buddy for that invite," he taunts.

Who the hell on the Ice Dragons is friends with *him*? I ignore his comment. I'm not about to get thrown into the penalty box or ejected from a game because of a few choice words that he makes.

I refuse to let it get to me.

"And have you seen her sex tape? She'd look great with her mouth wrapped around my dick."

My brain fires with expletives. I can't listen to this crap from him, talking shit about Charlotte.

I charge at Brass, the puck at his feet as I slam

him back into the boards. My hockey stick remains in my grip, battling for the puck before I drop it in favor of my fists. Blow after blow land on his chest and his face.

He's laughing, clearly pleased with riling me up, but he doesn't just stand there and take it. Grant pounds his fists into my chest, but I don't feel it.

It's not until his helmet flies off and my brothers on the team drag me away as the referees attempt to break us apart.

We're both thrown into our respective penalty boxes, the sin bin.

Hell, it was worth it.

But his words keep drifting through my head.

Sex tape.

————

How did we manage a win? My head wasn't in the game, and the guys played like they were distracted.

But a win is a win. It doesn't matter that we took the lead at the end and managed to scrape by with 3-2.

We shower and dress. A few guys handle the press junket while Jasper and I step out of the locker rooms to head to Blue Line to celebrate.

"That was a great game!" Charlotte is waiting with Amber and Emerson by the doors.

A smug grin tugs at my lips. "I didn't know you were at the game," I say, staring at Charlotte.

She blushes, her cheeks not quite as red as her fiery hair, but she takes a step toward me and leans up on her tiptoes, dropping a kiss on my cheek.

"Congrats on the win," she says, her voice soft and tentative.

The girl has sexy black boots with a heel that gives her a couple of extra inches. They're the same sexy pumps she wore on our date. She's taller than usual, and I dare admit that I like the added height. I pull her toward me. My arms instantly wrap around her waist.

"Want to get out of here?" I whisper into her ear.

"Blue Line?" she asks, licking her lips.

It's where the Ice Dragons always go after a win to celebrate. We have our own VIP section with a table in the back reserved for us, even on nights when we don't win and want to drown our sorrows.

"Yes, the guys will meet us there," I say.

I want to take her back to my place and ravage her, but my conscience keeps reminding me that I have too much going on in my personal life to complicate hers.

We agreed on keeping things casual and fun. No commitments. She's well aware that I put hockey first. Pretty soon, I'll be putting my son, Zayn, first.

I don't think Charlotte or any other girl will be keen on being number three.

And Jasper is right. I have to tell Charlotte about my son, the lawyers, and the investigator. It's just a lot to process, and we're still quite new at whatever this thing is between us.

One hot night, and we've been building a friendship since. Turns out, I do things ass-backward with Charlotte.

"I'm going to wait for Kyler," Emerson says, giving her sister a wave. "I'll catch you guys at the bar."

"Sounds good," Charlotte says with a grin.

We head down the hallway for the back exit. "I bet you never thought you'd hear the day when your sister said those words!" Charlotte quips, glancing at Amber.

"Well, I'm six days away from twenty-one." Amber chirps, "Hopefully, one of the newer bartenders is on staff tonight."

I chuckle under my breath. The regulars know that Amber isn't twenty-one yet. But the Blue Line hired three new bartenders over the past few months. During the hockey season, the place gets packed because we frequent there, and they always need more help.

"Don't worry, babe. I've got you covered," Jasper says, wrapping an arm around Amber's waist while nuzzling her neck.

"That's right!" Charlotte squeals. "We need to plan a birthday bash for your twenty-first."

"I'd be content with just going to a bar and being able to drink legally," Amber says. "Do you think they'll notice that my I.D. has changed and has a different name?"

I chuckle under my breath. "I doubt it. They see so many different I.D.'s. You're probably fine."

"Probably," Amber says. "Yeah, that's the part that worries me. The probably."

Jasper pulls her tighter to him. "Relax, babe. I've got you covered. I don't think they're going to call the cops on something that you did in the past. It would only look bad on them. And if they did, you know I'd bail your ass out of prison."

"Cute," Charlotte says, nudging me as we walk toward the bar. "Would you bail my butt out of jail?" She stares up at me with sparkling eyes and an eager smile.

I snort at her question. "Depends on what you're in the slammer for," I tease.

Her jaw drops in mock astonishment. "Seriously?"

I shrug, pulling her closer, my arm snaking around her waist. "Well, I mean, if you're being arrested for murder, I don't think bail would cover it. But even if it did, I don't need you murdering me and chopping me up into tiny pieces when I'm asleep."

Jasper glances at me. "You've been watching too much murder porn, bro."

"I'm just saying, I'm not letting a murderer loose on the streets."

"First of all, it's innocent until proven guilty," Charlotte quips. "And second of all, seriously. Do you think I'd murder you in your sleep? I'd do it to your face." She sticks her tongue out at me playfully.

"Duly noted."

Jasper shakes his head. "You two have a twisted sense of humor."

"That's why they're perfect together," Amber says with a sly grin, like she knows something I don't. Those two girls are always up to mischief.

I can't stop thinking about the Grant's words earlier, *sex tape*. It was just a taunt to get into my head, right? But I can't let it go.

"Can I ask you something?" I keep my voice low,

not wanting anyone else to overhear the conversation between us.

"Anything," Charlotte says, giving me that smile that eases all worries.

"Have you ever made a sex tape?"

She raises an eyebrow, staring at me curiously. "That's a bit out of the blue," she says. She doesn't appear the least bit tense or flustered by the question. "No. What about you?"

I smile and wink. "Once."

We stalk into the bar, head for the VIP table in the back, and the waitress immediately brings over a bucket of beers. We don't even have to ask.

My phone buzzes in my pocket, and I grab it and exhale a heavy breath when I see the caller's name on the screen.

Charlotte glances at me and doesn't say a word, but I'm pretty sure that she saw the name *Jasmine* pop up on my phone screen.

"I have to take this," I say and answer the call while heading outside into the icy-cold air for some privacy.

"Where the hell are you?" I'm stewing after the news of my son and having no way to get ahold of her.

"I'll explain tonight. Can I come by your place?" Jasmine asks.

I refrain from telling her that I'm not home. She should know that since her husband's team played my team tonight. "If you bring my son, Zayn," I say. He's the only reason I want to see Jasmine.

Her words are like an anvil on my chest, weighing me down when I speak with her. I've never felt so stressed and frustrated, not even during one of our hockey games.

"Of course," she says, like she hasn't been keeping him a secret for the past few years and lying to me.

I don't even know why she asks permission to drop by. She didn't ask me the last time. She just showed up and waited for me.

"I'm on my way."

I bite down hard on my bottom lip. I don't want to leave Charlotte or the guys. I want to celebrate the win we just had. But I can't do that knowing my son is in the lobby with his mother, waiting for me back at my place.

I growl angrily and end the call, storming back into the bar hastily.

"Everything okay?" Jasper asks, raising an eyebrow.

"I have to go," I say. I force a smile at Charlotte. I want to kiss her and show her that she means the world to me, and this is just a bump along the way, but the bump is my son. And it's not a little obstacle that's going to disappear.

He'd better not.

Charlotte's brow is pinched as she stares at me. Is she waiting for me to elaborate? I don't say anything further. I turn, leaving her in the dust, but at least she's with her friend. I'm not abandoning her.

This isn't a date.

I don't date or do relationships. Jasmine is my ever-present reminder of why.

Relationships blow up in my face.

The betrayal cuts deep, like a knife to my back. I head home, and even though I'd rather be out, I have to do the responsible adult thing, which is to deal with the fact that I have a kid.

Tomorrow, I'll call the lawyer and the private investigator after I gather whatever information I can from Jasmine.

But I'm not looking forward to going home, and that thought is painfully burning a hole in my chest and heart.

My phone pings from the back of the cab, and I glance at the message from Charlotte.

Charlotte: I hope everything is okay. You left in a rush.

I don't answer her text.

I don't know what I'd say. Besides, what needs to be conveyed to her shouldn't come as a text: I'm a dad. Apparently, I have a kid whom I never knew about until recently.

That would be the coward's way out. I refuse to do that with Charlotte.

And I will tell her. I've just been waiting for the right time.

She sends me one more text after a couple of minutes. It's a red heart emoji.

I wince and start to type a reply and then erase my message. I don't want to break her heart. And anything I say tonight might do that.

NINE

I can't believe he just up and left without an explanation.

And I saw a woman's name pop up on his phone.

Who the hell is Jasmine?

Maybe I don't have a right to be jealous since Noah and I aren't officially dating. We haven't spoken about being exclusive, but my stomach is in knots just thinking about him jumping and running for some other girl.

When the hell did I get so wrapped up in Noah?

Oh, right, the night that we slept together. Which I swore I was fine with it being a fun night and no strings attached, since he doesn't do relationships and, well, neither do I.

At least, I didn't.

But from the moment that he left, I've been a bumbling mess. And I hate myself for it.

I'm the girl I despise. The one who waits by her phone or sends a dozen text messages, waiting to hear back.

I've refrained from sending all the texts that I want, but I still shoot him a message, hoping he'll answer.

I don't get why he ran off to be with *her*.

Maybe he's looking for a hookup and she's the booty call.

I grab a beer from the bucket and pop the cap off.

"What's going on with Noah?" I ask, glaring at Jasper, expecting him or Amber to tell me the truth. Someone has to know something. And I hate being left in the dark or the last to know things.

"He is acting weird," Amber says, glancing at her boyfriend.

Jasper shrugs, his eyes wide as he grabs his drink to keep from having to answer.

"Spill it!" I say and knock his arm.

He grumbles as his beer sloshes, and he puts the glass bottle down on the table. "It's not my place to say. You should talk to Noah," Jasper says.

"That's cryptic."

Kyler and Emerson join us at the table along with a couple of other players and their significant others, whom I'm not as familiar with.

"Where'd Noah go?" Kyler asks. "Grabbing more drinks?"

Jasper wordlessly shakes his head, and I swear they're sharing some unspoken message between them.

"He up and bailed after getting a call from Jasmine. Is she his booty call?" I try not to sound jealous, but I know I'm failing miserably.

I bite my bottom lip to keep from letting the green monster bring tears to my eyes. This is stupid. I shouldn't even care. But the truth is that I do.

"He's with Jasmine?" Kyler asks and runs a hand through his hair.

"Who is Jasmine?" Emerson asks, apparently just as clueless as I am about the mystery caller. I feel a little better that she doesn't know since she's been dating Kyler for a while, and they're engaged.

"Just an old girlfriend," Kyler says and shrugs it off. "It's nothing to worry about."

How can he easily dismiss the fact that Noah's old girlfriend just called, and he ran off to be with her?

I open my mouth but quickly shut it. I'm not going to convince Kyler of anything. He's friends with Noah. I'm sure that he's just defending his teammate and buddy.

"Right, because we're not dating," I say and exhale a huff. I shift on my chair, the seat is uncomfortable, and my stomach is tense. I can't just sit idly by and wonder what is going on.

Do I grab a cab and head to his place?

What if they're hooking up at her house? Or worse, what if they're hooking up at his condo, and I show up uninvited?

I'll look desperate.

Amber nudges me as I peel at the label on my beer bottle. I'm fidgety and restless.

"He likes you," she says matter of factly. "I'm sure this Jasmine girl, it's nothing. Maybe it's all a misunderstanding, and he also has a cousin named Jasmine?"

I wish her words were convincing, but I can't recall him ever mentioning any family nearby. "Yeah, maybe," I say and chance a glance up at Jasper.

His jaw is tense.

She's definitely not his sister or cousin based solely on his look. He knows something, and he shifts to face Kyler, changing the topic to the game they played tonight.

An hour passes before I get hit on twice by the same guy, who happens to be a huge hockey fan. I can't help but wonder if his hitting on me is trying to get into the guy's inner circle.

I politely decline his invitation to dance and again the drink that he carries over. He's cute enough, but I have zero interest in him. There's no chemistry and not even so much as a spark.

I drop some cash on the table to cover my drinks and tip.

"Are you heading home?" Amber asks.

"I'm leaving," I say and pull her aside. "Do you have Noah's address?" I ask.

She stalls for a minute and then nods. "I think I saved it in my phone. We went to a party at his penthouse a couple of months ago."

She gives me his address and I plug it into my phone. "Thanks."

"You didn't get it from me," she says and winks. We exchange hugs and pleasantries before I request a rideshare. When the vehicle arrives, I head outside into the brisk night and climb into the back of the vehicle. I'm more awake than I should be, my hands sweaty as I wipe them on my pants.

The address that I gave is Noah's penthouse suite. I just hope I'm not making a huge mistake.

TEN

NOAH

I'd be angry that Jasmine called me after the game if it weren't for the fact that I've been trying to get ahold of her, and she hasn't been returning my calls or answering my texts.

Even the private investigator hadn't found much, but it had only been a few days since the paternity results.

I head inside the building, through the main doors, when I catch sight of Jasmine. She's got one hell of a black eye, and the little boy has a matching one too.

I curse as I lead her to the elevator and upstairs.

"I thought you were leaving town?"

"I was going to," Jasmine says, "but I wanted to wait for the paternity results."

I hit the button for the penthouse suite, my jaw tight as I stare at the little boy in her arms. I don't have to ask who gave them the black eye.

"You should have been at a hotel or a shelter. Somewhere safe."

"I know. That's why I called you."

She follows me through the front door and places Zayn on the couch, making herself at home. She unzips his coat and slides off his shoes before dropping a kiss on his cheek. "Stay here, okay?"

He wordlessly nods, and she grabs my arm, pulling me down the hallway out of earshot.

"I'm leaving town."

"What?" My voice raises an octave. "You can't keep my son from me."

"I'm not. I want him to stay with you, where it's safe," Jasmine says. "You have the resources to protect him. I don't." Her eyes glisten and I exhale a heavy breath.

"What about your ex?"

"He won't be a problem. He doesn't care about Zayn, now that he knows the boy isn't his."

"You told him?" I'm steaming as I pace the length of the hallway. The little boy is still seated on the couch but he's several feet away, mostly out of earshot.

"He saw the paternity results. All he knows is that he's not the father, and he told me he was glad because then he didn't have to take care of the *little one*."

How she says *little one* makes me think those weren't his exact words. They were likely more colorful and expletives. I wince and nod. "It won't take long until he realizes I'm the father. He'll put two and two together. He knows we were dating before the two of you got hitched."

He hadn't mentioned it tonight on the ice, but maybe he found out after the game.

"Even if he attempts to fight for custody, he's not biologically related to Zayn. And I have legal documentation that signs over my rights to you. It's all with my lawyer." She slides her hand into her coat pocket and retrieves a business card.

"If you have a lawyer, why aren't you requesting a divorce and an order of protection?" I can't believe she'd walk away from her child, our child.

"I told you, Grant has a brother in law enforcement. Besides, isn't this what you want? Me out of your life and custody of your son?" Jasmine stares at me, her eyes glistening.

I bite down on my tongue. "I assumed that you'd want to share custody." But it had crossed my mind that if she went anywhere near Grant Brass, I'd fight to protect my child.

"I should go."

"Where?" I ask, staring at her. "If you need money or a place to stay, I can get you a hotel and help you—"

"I don't want your handouts," Jasmine says.

I wince. It wasn't intended as a handout or charity. She is the mother of my child, even if I don't particularly like her after how she hurt me.

I exhale a sigh. "You can't go back to him."

"Why not?" she asks, staring up at me. Her bottom lip juts out, and I glance away toward the large windowpane that overlooks the New York skyline. It's gorgeous at night, but at the moment feels chaotic and overwhelming right now.

"He'll beat you to death. Is that not reason enough? Look at what he did to our son!" My voice booms and a shiver courses through her.

I should apologize for raising my voice, but I'm angry with Jasmine and even more so with Grant for what he did, for laying a hand on Zayn.

"And that's why I'm leaving him with you. I need

to make sure Grant will leave you and Zayn alone before I leave."

"What you're saying doesn't make any sense." She's bound to get herself killed if she stays with the monster. "You already said he doesn't care about *him*." I nod toward the living room.

"Yeah, that's what he's said, but I have to make sure that his actions follow through with that promise. That he doesn't care."

"What you're doing isn't noble or bold. It's stupid. Going back to your abusive husband is only going to get you knocked around, and you're lucky if he doesn't kill you."

"You wouldn't understand."

"I understand plenty," I seethe, taking a step closer toward Jasmine.

She fumbles backward and away from me, bumping into the wall.

The flash of fear flitters across her features as she tries to flee. Does she honestly believe that I would hurt her? "I should go." Her voice catches in her throat, and she hurries to the sofa. "Be good for Noah, okay?" she tells Zayn.

My heart aches that the little one doesn't know me as his father but as Noah.

Zayn nods with wide, curious eyes.

She kisses his cheek and hugs him before exhaling a sharp breath. "I should go."

"Mama!" Zayn wails as she heads for the door.

"You don't have to leave," I say. There has to be another way. "Stay in the spare bedroom. In the morning, we'll get ahold of my lawyer. He'll be able to help you. I'm sure of it."

"Grant will come looking for me." She shakes her head. "My job as his mother is to protect Zayn at all costs. I couldn't do that today." She exhales a shaky breath.

"What that monster did isn't your fault."

"I have to go." Jasmine hurries for the door. There's pain in her eyes, agony.

Zayn continues to cry, his tears coming down like two rivers as his sobs become hysterical, and he climbs off the sofa, chasing after his mother as she slips out the front door.

ELEVEN

CHARLOTTE

I hadn't entirely thought this through, showing up uninvited to Noah Reece's home. For starters, there's security and a private elevator. I can't just waltz in like at a hotel without being noticed.

"Can I help you?"

"Yes, I'm here to see Noah Reece," I say.

He glances me over and nods. "Let me call him. He didn't mention any other visitors this evening."

Other visitors? My stomach tumbles. At least he's home.

The attendant on duty picks up the phone, and I glance around the lobby. It's quite extravagant, with high ceilings and a crystal chandelier, not to mention the stained-glass window in the back past the elevators.

After a moment, he hangs up the phone. "You may head on back for the elevator."

A security guard is waiting by the elevator, and he uses his key to unlock access to the penthouse. He offers me a warm smile and a brief greeting, "How are you this evening?" Which sounds more like he's asking because he has to and less because he wants to.

After he unlocks access, he steps out, allowing me to ride up the elevator alone. The doors close, but I don't feel relieved.

I'm more nervous because Noah wasn't expecting me, and I'm showing up invited. I'm unsure how he'll feel about that after ditching us at the Blue Line for *Jasmine*. Whoever she is, I don't like her.

The elevator doors open, and Noah stands at the front door, staring at me pointedly. "What are you doing here?"

So much for pleasantries.

"You left in a rush. I wanted to make sure you were okay."

There's crying from a child behind him somewhere in the house. Unless he has the television on, but I doubt it. It sounds pretty damn real.

"I'm fine. Did the guys give you my address?" There's no sparkle in his gaze, no smile. He doesn't seem happy to see me.

But he hasn't pushed me away or told me to leave, either.

"Mama!" the little boy wails, and I push past Noah, inviting myself inside his home. The little boy, who is all of two years old, is lying on the kitchen floor, crying and screaming for his mommy.

My heart aches for the kid. "Do you make it a habit of kidnapping little kids?" I wince at my question. It came out harsher than intended, but he told me he never wanted kids, and finding one screaming on his kitchen floor makes the whole situation befuddling.

"He's my son," Noah snaps at me.

I didn't honestly believe he kidnapped the little boy. Noah doesn't seem the type. But he clearly lied to me about wanting kids, because he has a son. Does that mean that he didn't want him?

I bend down, crouching at the little one's level. "Hey," I whisper, my voice soft and warm.

The little boy glances up and sniffles. My heart

breaks into a million tiny pieces when I see the toddler's black and blue eye.

"Who did this to you?" I ask, my voice catching in my throat.

"Daddy," the little boy whispers, and more tears pour like its monsoon season.

I sweep the child off the floor and into my arms protectively. "You're a monster!" I shout at Noah, grab my phone from my pocket, and immediately call 9-1-1.

"Charlotte, what the hell are you doing!" Noah shouts at me, his voice livid as he stomps toward me to grab the phone. "Give me the damn phone!"

The 9-1-1 operator hears the exchange before I can say anything further. "Is this a domestic situation, ma'am?"

"Yes," I say. "My boyfriend, Noah Reece, beat his son." I shout the address for the condo complex over the phone.

"Charlotte, that's not what happened!" He yanks the phone from me and slams it across the wall, breaking it.

"Really? You didn't hit him?" I wrap my arms around the child, protecting him as I turn my back to Noah. "Are you going to hit me too, coward?"

"I didn't fucking hit my son!"

"Daddy hit me," the little boy sobs.

"You're a fucking liar!" I shout at Noah, heading for the door.

Noah blocks me from leaving. His hand presses against the door as he refuses to let us leave.

"Seriously?" I can't believe the nerve of him. "Are you going to hold us both as hostages? Because I am walking out that door, and you're never seeing your son again!"

"You can't do that. Listen to me, Charlotte, you're not seeing the whole picture."

"Oh, I see it pretty damn clearly!"

"Daddy hit me!" the little boy shouts between tears.

"Let me explain."

"Explain how you hit your son?" I refuse to listen to any excuse that he gives. I know he's rough on the ice. It's not unusual for the players to get into a fight, but to hit a child, there's no excuse. No explanation that would make up for what he did.

There's a pounding at the front door, and Noah's resolve crumbles. He takes a step back, and I use the opportunity to flee.

I yank the door open, and one police officer pulls us out of the way and practically pushes us down the hallway toward the elevator while two more officers rush inside to apprehend Noah.

A moment later, Noah is in handcuffs. All the air is sucked from my lungs. My stomach is in my throat. I manage to keep down the beer that I had earlier, but I'm not sure how.

I'm shaking, the little boy is crying, and I don't know how any of this happened.

"Are you the boy's mother?" the male officer asks.

"No, I'm a friend of Noah's."

"When you called 9-1-1, you mentioned that you were his girlfriend?" he asks. He flips open his notepad, jotting something down. "What's the little boy's name?"

I shake my head. "I don't... I didn't even know he had a son until tonight."

"I think it would be good if you came down to the station and gave your statement while we work on locating the boy's mother."

TWELVE

NOAH

"I need to be with my son! You don't understand what's happened."

"Daddy hit me," Zayn repeats like it's the only sentence the kid knows how to say. It's also fucking incriminating because I just told Charlotte I'm the little boy's father.

I get how it looks, but she ought to know me well enough to realize that I wouldn't hurt a child.

"Where are you taking my son?" I shout at the officers who escort Charlotte and Zayn to the elevator outside.

Meanwhile, I'm in handcuffs and being forced to watch the two of them leave.

"So, you admit you're the boy's father?" the officer with a funny mustache asks, glancing me over.

"I only found out about Zayn less than a week ago."

"Where's the mother?" the other officer asks. Thankfully, her gun is in its holster because she looks ready to shoot me.

"I would guess she went home to her abusive husband, Grant Brass."

"Quite an allegation coming from a child abuser," the female officer says, reading me my Miranda Rights as she escorts me to the elevator.

"I didn't hit my son."

"Sure, it was his other daddy." The officer laughs as he grabs my arm and yanks me to follow.

"The kid doesn't even know me. He's referring to Grant Brass." I try further explaining, but it's like talking to a brick wall.

As I'm escorted out of the building, past security and the concierge, there are a few guests in the lobby taking photos or videos with their phones.

Wonderful, this is going to be all over the news by morning. My hockey career will be dust before I even get to tell my side of the story.

Good ole' Charlotte Grace, the girl who ruined me in more ways than one.

There's no sign of Zayn or Charlotte. "Where is my son?" I ask.

The officers refuse to answer as I'm escorted to the back of a squad car. It's humiliating. But none of that matters.

I'm seated in the back, my hands in metal cuffs.

I've done everything by the book, kept out of trouble, and I've had my share of opportunities, given my professional hockey player status.

Getting arrested was never part of the plan.

"Listen to me. You can't send Zayn back to his mother, Jasmine." I try to reason with the officers as they drive me toward the stations.

"Yeah, why's that?" one of them finally answers me.

"She's living with Grant Brass. He's the one who did this to Zayn. Jasmine brought him to my house to protect him. She can corroborate my story."

"M'hmm," the officer says, sounding unconvinced.

————

The officers book me, then drag me to the holding cell, tossing me inside and removing my handcuffs before shutting the door.

"Don't I get one phone call? What about bail?" There's no way I'm spending another minute behind bars.

"You can go before a judge in the morning to see if you make bail," the officer says, a smarmy grin on his face. "That's what you get for hitting an innocent little boy."

"I didn't fucking hit him!" I shout.

I'm not alone in the cell. It seems more like a drunk tank than anything tonight. One man is lying on the floor, staring up at the ceiling. He might be high. I'm not entirely sure what he's on, but being here doesn't seem to faze him.

The other guy glances me over. He's got a beard, scruffy-looking fellow, but doesn't look wasted or high. There's an air about him like he's dark and rough around the edges. Regal but not royalty.

I do my best to keep my head down. The man could be mafia for all I know. He looks like an ad campaign for *how not to end up in jail but get away with shady shenanigans.* His luck ran out.

"Hey, child abuser," he says in his thick Russian accent, attempting to get my attention.

Great.

"I didn't fucking touch that kid," I say, glancing up at him.

"You look familiar," he says. His eyes are dark, but they shine with mirth as he stares at me. His jaw twitches as the realization dawns on him of who I am.

He laughs under his breath. It's throaty and deep. Gravelly.

"You're a sports guy. Hockey." He points at me as the recognition hits him, but maybe he's not great with names.

"Dragons team."

"Ice Dragons." There's no sense in denying it. I'll be all over the news with that stony mugshot of me looking straight into the camera, perturbed.

"Right. Right," he says and gestures for the seat beside him. "Mikhail Barinov," he says, introducing himself.

I'm not sure if that name is supposed to mean anything, but Barinov sounds Russian, as does his accent.

Did I land in a prison cell with the Russian Mafia?

That's not a question that I choose to ask aloud. Best to keep that one to myself if I want to survive the night in hell.

"Noah Reece." I sigh heavily and take the bench beside Mikhail. I'd prefer not to sit on the filthy cement floor that looks not just uncomfortable but is sticky. I don't want to know how many men have vomited or pissed on that floor.

"That's right. You play left defenseman on the team."

"You're a fan?"

Mikhail shrugs. "I've never been to a game, but when we both get out of here, maybe I'll get tickets to see you play."

"Maybe?" I shouldn't even question it. The guy is bad news. Befriending him isn't in my best interests.

"Depends on if you're getting out, hotshot," he says, sizing me up.

I laugh under my breath. "Maybe I'll see you there, assuming you get out," I say, trying to turn the tables on him. I don't even know what he's accused of doing.

"I have good lawyers." There's a smugness to him, and he folds his arms across his chest, pleased with himself.

"What are you in for?" I ask.

He chuckles. "Rule of advice. You don't ask a fellow prisoner that unless you *really* want to know."

My mouth goes momentarily dry.

The officer wouldn't have thrown a murderer in

the drunk tank with someone accused of hurting a child, would they?

My hands ball into fists at my side. Every breath becomes louder, more labored, and pronounced. I try to keep my cool, pretend I'm not the least bit intimidated, because I fight guys on the ice nearly every damn day.

But this is different.

It feels different.

"Attempted murder," he says, staring at me, keeping his cool. His voice is even and low, unwavering. "This guy touched a hair on my daughter's head. Thought he could lure her into his van with the promise of a new puppy and lollipops. Do you think I let him walk away after that?"

My voice catches in my throat.

Attempted murder may be one of the charges, but the guy is clearly guilty as sin. He doesn't look apologetic about it, either.

Although, if someone tried to lure Zayn into a van, I can't say that I wouldn't lose my cool and go rogue. Who knows what I'd be capable of doing in that exact moment to protect my son?

"How old's your daughter?" I ask, trying to hide the stampede of my heart pounding wildly in my chest.

"She's four," he says. He unfolds his arms and glances down at his hands, revealing the name *Kira* inked in cursive on his skin between his index finger and thumb.

THIRTEEN

CHARLOTTE

The little boy is seated on my lap as I'm left waiting by an officer's desk to give my statement.

It's been an hour since Noah's arrest, and every second feels slow and painful, like there's an elephant on my chest.

But I know that I did the right thing. I needed to get the little boy away from his abuser. That's all that mattered, relationship be damned.

"What's your name?" I ask the little boy, and he finally gives me a weak smile.

"Zayn," he whispers and points at me, "Your name?" The words run together and sound more like one syllable coming out of his lips.

His words are difficult to decipher, but I try to make sense of them. "I'm Charlotte," I say.

He cuddles into me. "Want Mama," he says, and I wrap my arms around him protectively.

"I know, little man. We're trying to find her for you."

A female officer who had been on the scene but whom I hadn't met comes over to us and takes a seat at the desk. "I'm Officer Bradley," she says.

She has a notebook in one hand and flips the page back, reading over her notes briefly while opening her desk drawer. She hands Zayn a lollipop, removing the wrapper for him.

"And you are Charlotte, and this is Zayn," the officer states, making sure she has the information correct.

"That's right," I say, exhaling a shaky breath. "I'm Charlotte Grace. I don't know Zayn's last name."

"It's Brass," she answers, already knowing more about the little boy than I do, and I've spent more time with him. Not by a lot, of course. Just waiting for the officer to take my statement.

"Why don't you walk me through what happened?" Officer Bradley asks.

I explain what happened, what Zayn said, and gesture at his black eye.

"Did you witness Noah Reece hit the little boy?" Officer Bradley asks.

"Well, no," I say. "But he has a black eye."

"Yes, I can see that," she says.

"The little boy told me that his father did it," I say, gesturing toward Zayn, who is seated on my lap. He wiggles his little bum and stares at Officer Bradley curiously while sucking on his orange-flavored sucker.

The officer smiles warmly at Zayn. "Can you tell me who gave you that?" She points at his face but doesn't touch the fresh bruise.

He scrunches his face as her finger nears but relaxes when she doesn't hurt him. "Daddy hit me."

"Do you know your daddy's name?" Officer Bradley asks.

"Daddy," Zayn says, but it comes out a bit garbled from the lolli he's gripping as though his life depends on it.

"Okay, this isn't working," Bradley says. She puts her notebook down and taps away at the computer screen at the desk in front of her.

"I'm sorry, I don't really know much else," I say.

The officer keeps tapping away at her keyboard for another minute before sitting back.

"I managed to track down the address and phone

number of his mother. I'm going to give her a call, let her pick up the child so that we won't need to get social services involved."

"Good," I say, rubbing Zayn's back. I'd hate for him to get put into the system, even for one night.

———

I remain seated at the officer's desk when a couple enters the police station. From my seat, I get a nice long look at the woman, and Zayn does too.

"Mama!" Zayn squeals in delight.

"Oh, good, there he is," she says, forcing a smile. As she approaches, the lighting is harsh under fluorescent and the concealer that the woman has dabbed on her cheek and beneath her eye shines through just enough to reveal that Zayn isn't the only one with a shiner.

Behind her, a stocky fellow follows close on her heels. He's got a hat on and sunglasses, like he's trying to be inconspicuous. It's dark outside, and he hasn't taken the shades off indoors, either.

Even with his so-called disguise, I know his face. Grant Brass. He plays for the Island Bruisers.

"Mama!" Zayn climbs out of my lap and throws his arms in the air for the woman to pick him up.

"I just have a few questions," Office Bradley says, staring at Jasmine and Grant.

"Daddy," Zayn points at Grant and cuddles farther into Jasmine's arms.

Grant glances at his watch and shifts from one foot to the other. "Are the questions really necessary?" he asks. "You found our son. I want to get him and my wife home. I have a busy day tomorrow."

"Yes, I'm sure that may be the case, but I have an investigation that needs to be handled, given the allegations of abuse."

"Abuse at the hands of that psychopath hockey player, Noah Reece. You better keep his ass behind bars and throw away the key," Grant says smugly.

"Sir, if you wouldn't mind following me so that we could talk—" Officer Bradley says, trying to gain control of the situation.

"I do mind," Grant says. "I have my family, I'm done. It's time for us to head home."

"You can't leave yet," Officer Bradley says. "I need to get your statement along with your wife's."

"Can't I? Unless we're being detained and charged with a crime, you can't keep us here." He wraps an arm around Jasmine's shoulders and forcefully leads her and Zayn out of the police station.

My stomach drops as I realize my mistake, handing the little boy straight back into the arms of his abuser. "I'd like to drop the charges against Noah Reece," I say, staring at Officer Bradley.

She expels a heavy sigh. "That was a big fuck up tonight," she mutters, shaking her head in dismay. "Next time you make an accusation, be sure you're on the right side of it," she warns me.

Like I don't already know I screwed up. I'm nauseous and dizzy from the realization that I not only potentially screwed up Noah's life but the danger I put Zayn into.

"What happens now?" I ask. "You saw the black eye Jasmine had on her face."

"I need to get social services involved and have them begin an investigation. In the meantime, let me find out about getting the charges dropped and your boyfriend released. Just sit tight."

Easier said than done. I feel like hell, and I can only imagine Noah hates me after what I've done.

FOURTEEN

NOAH

I exit the police station, and there's a wrath of reporters swarming with their cameras out and film rolling.

"Noah, what do you have to say about the child abuse allegations brought on you by your girlfriend?" a reporter asks.

She shoves the microphone into my face, and I take a deep breath, refraining from shoving it up her ass.

This isn't her fight. She's just doing her job.

Even if I hate the press and the paparazzi, they spin the version of events into the story that will make sales. It's never about the truth.

"No comment," I say, heeding my lawyer's advice

when I called him inside the station after the charges were dropped. I needed to know the next steps to get Zayn away from Grant and back home with me.

It's a lengthy process, according to him, fighting for custody. And everything I do in front of the cameras can be welded into a good campaign or bad one for their lawyers.

The only satisfaction I get is that Grant will be under the same scrutiny. And he's bound to slip up.

The cold, brisk air is even chillier when I lay eyes on Charlotte. She's lurking in the shadows on the sidewalk. Her bottom lip tugged between her teeth as she glances from her cell phone back up to me.

"I'm so sorry, Noah," she says, stepping toward me under the streetlamp. "I feel sick about the whole thing, if I had known—"

I hold up a hand to stop her. I don't want to hear her lame excuses. Anger doesn't even begin to cover the surface for the rage building inside me. And I have no choice but to tame it, given the reporters filming our conversation.

"My son is with that monster because of *you*," I growl at her. What she did is unforgivable. The cab pulls up just in the nick of time. I don't think I could stand another second of Charlotte or be in her proximity without screaming at her. "I never want to see you again."

I yank the back door of the cab open and climb in, giving the driver my lawyer's address.

I don't look back at Charlotte. She doesn't deserve another second of my time. What we had is over.

In the back of the cab, my phone buzzes with a text. I half expect it to be Charlotte with another apology which reminds me I need to block her number, but her phone is broken, so I doubt I'll hear from her tonight at least.

The message is from Coach.

Malone: My office 9 am.

I grumble and shift uncomfortably in the back of the cab. "You're that hockey player, aren't you?" the driver asks. His gaze meets mine in his rearview mirror before he focuses again on the road.

"I am." I don't elaborate.

"Can I get an autograph for my kid?"

"Of course," I say. "Although I don't have anything to sign, or a pen."

When we pull up at a traffic light, he hands me a pad of paper and a pen. "Maybe we could take a picture when we get to your stop?" the cabbie asks. "My son would love that."

"Sure." I force a smile.

The radio in the cab, a local news station, rattles off the weather report. Another cold and bitter day tomorrow, followed by a chance of snow.

"What were you doing at the police station?" he asks, glancing at me again in the rearview. "Helping out a friend? I heard you guys did a food drive last winter at the police station on the north side."

The radio station's reporter gives an updated newscast featuring yours truly.

In other news, Noah Reece, a professional hockey player for the Ice Dragons, was arrested and released after child abuse allegations from his newly acquainted girlfriend. More on the story up next after these messages.

"You were arrested?" the cabbie asks and shifts uncomfortably in the driver's seat. His hands remain on the steering wheel, his grip tight.

"I didn't hit my son, his stepdad did that, but no one gives a shit about my side of the story. Can you change the radio station?" I grumble and fold my arms across my chest.

When the cabbie drops me off, he doesn't get out for that picture that he requested, and I'm pretty sure I saw him ball up that autograph I did for his son and toss it on the floor of his passenger side.

My reputation has been ruined, all from one

lousy phone call and an allegation for a crime that I didn't commit.

I'd sooner put my life on the line and walk in front of a speeding bus than let anything happen to Zayn.

How could Charlotte not realize that about me?

I head on up to the address that my lawyer gave me. It turns out it's his condo, not his office. He lets me in, and we have a brief discussion on the following steps to get Zayn and how the process works.

"I need you in front of the cameras after your hockey game."

"Why?" I ask. I hate the media. Everything about it makes my skin crawl. There's also zero chance the interview questions will be about the hockey game. They're going to bombard me with the arrest, the allegations, and the fact that I have a kid and haven't been around for him, never mind the fact that I didn't know he existed.

It will inevitably be my fault because that's the way the news works.

"Are you telling me that Grant isn't going to be spinning this a hundred different ways to make you look bad?"

He's right. That's why I hired him, because he's

the best. It doesn't mean I'm happy with his advice. "Fine."

"And do me a favor, look happy about it. You want people to like you, because that judge will see and hear things that can't be forgotten. Even if they swear not to rule based on media information, everyone's biased, even when they don't intend to be."

"Wonderful," I say and force a smile.

"Just think, Noah, you're doing this for Zayn."

———

After I get home from the lawyer, I need to unwind. My mind is racing, my heart won't stop pounding, and I'm desperate for a shower after spending time in that prison cell.

Did that murderer, the Russian, get out of prison?

I'm not worried that he'll find me. I've got no issue with him, but somehow, I'm the center of the news story when he's the one who pretty much admitted to murdering a man.

And I'm the innocent one.

Celebritydom at its finest. This world is fucked up.

I toss my phone on the bed and strip down for a nice, hot shower. It's not as relaxing as I'd like, with my thoughts racing and my anger simmering regarding Charlotte.

I had real feelings for her, and she screwed it all up. Serves me right for thinking I might one day have a girlfriend again.

Women always disappoint.

First, Jasmine, cheating on me and marrying that sinister jackhole, Brass.

The shower water is hot, scalding, and leaving my skin red, but I feel numb as it pounds down over me from head to toe.

And the sweet, adorable Charlotte showing her true cunning colors when the cat claws came out to destroy me.

She's sorry.

Pfft.

I don't buy it. Sorry doesn't excuse or negate what she did. She put my son back into the arms of his abuser.

I wash my hair and soap up my body as the water cools down before it becomes chilled. I shut off the spray and grab a towel to wrap around my waist before stepping from the bathroom into my bedroom.

I'm not the least bit tired, but I need to sleep if I'm going to be meeting with Malone in the morning, which reminds me that I need to answer his text.

Heading toward my dresser, I grab a pair of boxers and then slip them on after towel-drying myself the rest of the way down.

I grab my phone from the bed, and my messages have blown up. There are dozens of texts from my teammates. It seems they've all heard about the arrest by now.

I reply to Malone, letting him know that I'll be there bright and early, just for him.

Collapsing on the mattress, my phone in hand, I stare at the ceiling before going through the messages. Practically every teammate on the Ice Dragons texted me along with the main group chat that Kyler formed with a few of the guys he's closest with.

Kyler: Did she seriously call the cops and have you arrested?

Jasper: Arrested?!? Who was arrested?

Parker: Surprisingly, not you!

Jasper: Not funny. WHO WAS ARRESTED?

Kyler: Stop the caps!

Asher: Well, you didn't answer him.

Jasper: THANK YOU.

Asher: Okay, now it's getting annoying.

Parker: Chase?

Kyler: You would think that, but nope.

Aiden: Are you going to make us guess?

Parker: Who is in the chat but hasn't responded yet?

Jasper: Noah!

Asher: Noah

Aiden: Owen

Kyler: Two out of three ain't bad.

Jasper: This is me giving you my middle finger, bro.

Parker: Why was he arrested?

The guys are messaging each other as I stare at the screen and finally add my two cents.

Noah: Because my ex-girlfriend is an idiot.

Kyler: Jasmine?

Jasper: I never did like her.

Parker: Why would Jasmine have you arrested?

I run my fingers frustratingly through my hair. I don't want to get into it with the guys about what happened, at least not over text, but they don't let it go.

Owen: Pass the popcorn.

Asher: You're an ass.

Owen: Me?

Chase: Sorry, girlfriend was giving me a BJ. Noah got arrested?

Asher: Go, Chase!

Jasper: OMG

Kyler: No comment.

Jasper: That is precisely you commenting.

These guys, I swear, will be the death of me. I can't help but laugh, even after the shitty day that I've had, and rub my eyes. They burn from laughing so hard. I swear they're trying to make me cry.

Noah: Quit blowing up my phone, asses.

Kyler: Quit leaving out the juicy details. Arrestee.

Noah: Fine. Charlotte called the cops. She had me arrested.

Asher: Burn.

Jasper: Holy crap. I need to call Amber.

Noah leaves the chat.

I can't deal with their antics tonight. Thankfully, none of the guys add me back into the chat, and if they're discussing my lack of a love life and the arrest, then I don't have to read about it. I shut off the lights and attempt to get a few hours of sleep.

We play the Wolverines tomorrow at home, and I need to give my best performance, especially if I have to talk to Coach Malone about putting me on press detail after the game.

Half the night, I toss and turn, worried about Zayn. The other half I spend trying to imagine what I'm going to say in front of the press, how to convince them this is all a misunderstanding and that I'm not the abusive brute they think that I am.

———

"Noah, come have a seat," Malone says as he meets me bright and early in his office.

I'm running on about three hours of sleep and two cups of coffee already. I've played on less sleep, but there's more going on that makes my head spin, mainly, that being Zayn.

My lawyer doesn't have an update yet. He's contacting Jasmine's attorney to find out if she did award sole custody to me and if there's been an order of protection placed against Grant Brass. Doubtful.

"You look like you're running on fumes."

"Is it that obvious?" I ask. I run my fingers through my hair, trying to maintain some semblance of control. "It was a long night."

Malone nods. "I'll say. I've got six different reporters asking for a story on your arrest. It's all over the news that you allegedly assaulted your son. I didn't even know you had a kid!"

I grimace. I suppose I've been keeping a few things from Coach. "It's all pretty new. I only learned about Zayn recently, and the paternity test came back as a match last week."

He stares at me. "That's what you and the boys were going on about the other day," he says as if it suddenly clicks for him.

"Next time, you come to me," Malone says. "Let me deal with the boys, the media, all of it. You've made a mess of things, kid."

I refrain from telling him I'm not a kid but bite my tongue instead. Coach Malone always means well. He's a good guy and tries to look out for the team as much as he can, but sometimes his hands are tied.

"Yes, sir," I say, giving him the respect that he's undoubtedly looking for from me.

"I assume this abuse scandal is just that, a scandal," Malone says, staring at me pointedly.

"I swear to you that I never hit Zayn. Jasmine showed up at my door, both of them with a black eye."

He purses his lips, and his gaze tightens. "And your girlfriend's allegations?"

"She didn't see anything. She showed up and saw a kid with a black eye crying. And for the record, sir, she's not my girlfriend," I say, quick to end that title before it gets out in the news. She's nothing to me.

"Ex-girlfriend," Malone says and clears his throat, correcting himself. "Good. So, I can assume that she won't continue to be a problem."

FIFTEEN

CHARLOTTE

I royally screwed up. After what happened the night of the arrest, Noah won't take my calls or answer my texts.

I got a new phone, the same phone number, so he knows who it is. And I've apologized repeatedly via voice mail and text. I can only assume he's blocked me by now.

I sent him an apology card. It came back returned to sender. He didn't even bother opening it.

Sure, if the situation were reversed, I would not want to forgive him, either, but I made a mistake.

I'm not sure what else to do.

Move on?

Easier said than done.

"You're coming out with me tonight," Amber says. "I'm tired of all this moping around, and we didn't celebrate my birthday together."

"I'm pretty sure I was uninvited to your birthday party," I say, staring at her.

Amber grimaces. "Noah did ask you not to come, and I couldn't not invite my boyfriend and sister. I'm sorry. Am I a terrible friend?"

I shake my head. I can't stay mad at Amber. I could have gone out, just the two of us, to celebrate, but our schedules have been crazy the past few weeks. "No, I did this to myself."

Plus, it's not as though I can hang out at her place. She lives with Jasper, and I feel uninvited by their crowd. Not that he's said anything outright. I feel guilty about what I did to Noah, even though it was unintended. I hate knowing I hurt him.

The only thing worse than hurting him is that I handed over his son to a child abuser.

"Come on, we'll go out tonight. Have fun. Forget all the craziness that's happened lately. You might even find a hot guy to hook up with if you're lucky."

"I am not interested in hookups right now."

Amber stares at me, unconvinced. "Sure, right. Whatever you say."

"I'm not!"

"Because you still have the hots for Noah?" Amber asks, wagging her eyebrows at me.

I roll my lips together, contemplating how to answer. "I don't deserve to be happy until Noah and his son are reunited."

Amber exhales heavily and comes to sit beside me on the sofa. "That's a tall order. I mean, he's doing everything that he can, legally, to gain custody, but it isn't an overnight process. It turns out the mother, Jasmine, doesn't want to relinquish custody of her son anymore. Something about her husband promising never to hit them again. And she's fighting for full custody."

"That's bullshit!" I stand, pacing the length of my apartment, which doesn't give me much room. "She can't do that to him."

"Yeah, I know. She's a real bitch," Amber says. "I mean, the woman kept the fact Noah was a father a secret from him, then dropped the bombshell and doesn't want his involvement. What kind of person does that?"

Amber seems to know more about Jasmine than I do.

She pulls her legs up beside her on the sofa, watching me diligently pace the room. "You're going to destroy your hardwood floor if you keep that up."

"It's laminate," I say and force a smile. "What do you know about Jasmine?" Noah told me nothing. The man is full of secrets.

He's been all over the news, with the press interviewing him about the arrest, the allegations, and his performance during the most recent games that he's played. He's always smiling and polite and manages to subdue the press with a laugh.

But there's more behind the surface and the superficial grin he gives them.

He's made it clear that the topic of his son is off-limits. That he's in an ongoing custody battle and can't comment further on the matter.

"Jasmine is his ex-girlfriend. That's all I know from Jasper. I heard that she cheated on him and eloped with her current husband, Grant Brass. I don't know if that's fact, though." Amber climbs off the sofa and grabs my arm. "Enough about Noah. We're going out."

Forty minutes later, a half a bottle of hairspray, and six outfit changes, we're finally ready to hit the clubs. Amber insisted on doing my makeup and picking out my clothes for tonight.

I'm sporting a black leather skirt and a red shirt that barely covers my midriff. It's cute as sin, but I haven't worn it in ages.

She also insisted I wear the *sex boots,* which she calls my leather boots that lace up to my knees. They are sexy, but I wasn't feeling it or the outfit until I put both on.

I swear she's got it in her mind to get me laid tonight.

I glance in the mirror as I swipe the fiery red lipstick across my lips. Damn, I look hot, but I'm not sure a random hookup will fix a broken heart.

"Let's go!" Amber shouts, practically dragging me out of the apartment. That's usually my doing, insisting she come with me to college parties or bars for a fun night out.

Tonight, I want to stay in, lounge in my pajamas, and eat a bowl of Rocky Road ice cream, which feels fitting because that describes my current love life.

We walk to the nearest subway together.

"Do you mind if we hit the club near my place?" Amber asks.

I honestly don't have a preference tonight. "Whatever you want. It's your birthday we're celebrating." I force a smile, doing my best to get in the mood for a night of dancing and drinking.

"Perfect. There's a new bar. It's super cute and stylish. I've wanted to check it out with Jasper, but he's been so busy this season that we haven't gone out as much as we'd like."

"I always took you more for a homebody."

"Oh, I am, but Jasper likes taking me out, and I don't mind being his arm candy," Amber says.

We head across town together, and there's a line already beginning to form for the bar that Amber wants to get into. We stand at the back of the line, the cold air assaulting my thighs. Everything north of my boots is frigid.

The line moves slowly, and I glance at my phone.

"Expecting a call or text?" Amber quips. She sees right through me.

I shake my head and shove my phone into my purse. "No chance of Noah accepting my apology, is there?"

Amber rolls her lips together and stares at me. "Truth?"

"I know. He hates me for what I did. But I had no idea he had a son! It's not like he told me he's a father. How was I supposed to know what was going on?"

"You talk. Communicate," Amber says. "I get it. If I came home and Jasper had a kid with a black eye, I'd probably punch Jasper myself and then call the cops, assuming he kidnapped the child."

I laugh under my breath. "Well, the kid did call him Daddy."

"Did he?" Amber asks, staring at me pointedly. "Or is that what you thought you heard?"

We step forward as the line moves ever so slowly.

I open my mouth and close it. "The boy said his father hit him." That much, I remember. It's ingrained in my mind.

"And I'm pretty sure Noah told me he was his father."

"Pretty sure?"

"He did," I say, reaffirming my position. "Not that it matters. He won't answer my calls or texts. I even wrote him an apology note, and he returned it in the mail. He didn't even open it. I'd send him flowers, but I doubt he cares about that kind of thing."

"You got him arrested," Amber says, staring at me pointedly. "And then you sent his son back into the hands of the man who abused him."

"I know!" I grimace. "I feel like shit. Okay?"

Amber nods and rests a hand on my arm. "It'll be okay. He's fighting for full custody."

"I heard that on the news," I say. "About the custody battle. I didn't know it was for full custody, but it makes sense."

"Enough about your ex," Amber says as we shuffle toward the front of the line. I pull out my I.D. as we're next up to enter the club. "We're here to have a good time. Can you imagine this place after nine o'clock?"

Music pours in from the open door while the bouncer only lets a few people inside. I'm antsy to get off the street, drink, dance, and forget about all the crap happening right now, which includes the upcoming charity gala.

After freezing our butts off outside, we're ushered into the club. It's loud, and the music pulsates, making the floor vibrate.

"Let's grab drinks. My treat," I shout at Amber and point at the bar. I grab her hand, making sure that we don't get separated in the chaos of the club.

She's right on my heel, and we order four shots between us, tossing them back in seconds before sauntering onto the dance floor.

I don't have to convince her to dance. She joins me, the two of us throwing our heads back and enjoying the beat. We dance and sway, the music electrifying. "Follow me," she says, grabbing my hand and dragging me deeper into the crowd. "Sorry, thought I saw someone."

"Your boyfriend?" I'm teasing her. The Ice

Dragons aren't playing tonight, but I don't know what Jasper and the team are up to now.

"My sister."

"Are we hiding or moving toward her?" I ask. Amber and Emerson have a tenacious sibling relationship. They don't seem particularly close, according to what I've seen and how Amber speaks about her older sister.

Amber laughs, glancing over her shoulder at me. "I don't have to hide from her anymore. I'm twenty-one," she says proudly.

There's no sign of Emerson, but the place is mobbed. It'd be hard to find anyone in the crowd.

We continue dancing for a while before I point at the bar. "Drinks?" I ask, the slight buzz already wearing off.

"Yes!" Amber shouts and follows me back toward the bar, where I order six shots for us. "Are you trying to get me drunk?"

"That's the plan," I say, wanting to momentarily forget all the crap that's been going on lately.

"Yes!" Amber squeals with giddiness, and we grab our shot glasses and clang them together before tossing them back simultaneously.

We stand by the bar for a few minutes, Amber sliding onto the barstool while I stand beside her.

"Any hotties out there?" she asks, grinning at me.

"You tell me."

"I have a boyfriend. You need to get laid!"

She's loud, but the music drowns out most of the conversation. I grumble. "I don't want just any dick."

Amber's eyes widen, and she giggles profusely. "You want Noah's dick," she says with a cheeky grin.

"But he won't even listen to my apology."

"You should come over tonight. Have a sleepover. Jasper and Noah are hanging out. We can make popcorn and watch a chick flick."

I pull my phone from my clutch.

"What are you doing?" Amber asks, leaning forward to watch me.

"Calling him."

"He won't pick up."

She's right. Noah won't pick up, but I don't have to call Noah to reach him. "I'm calling your boyfriend," I laugh. "What's Jasper's number?"

"You are not hooking up with my boyfriend." The smile vanishes from her face as she sizes me up. The girl could never play poker because she has far too many tells.

"Relax. We need to get them to come out here. Jasper will pick you up if we lie and say you're wasted. Right? Then he'll take us back to your place to sober up and Noah is there."

"I am wasted," Amber says.

"Good. Like that, be convincing."

Amber topples off the barstool onto me, giggling as I push her back onto the seat before someone else snatches it.

"Do that when he gets here. That's good."

"Do what?" Amber asks, staring at me, laughing. "The stool is spinning."

I smile at her. "It's not."

"Yes, it is! It's like one of those spinning rides at the carnival. And Noah isn't going to like it if you come over. He already hates you."

I ignore her remark about Noah. He's mad at me. He doesn't hate me. There's a difference. I fucked up and the sooner he realizes that I'm sorry, the sooner we can at least get back to being friends.

"Give me your phone," I say, putting mine back into my purse. I'm not sure if Jasper will pick up for me if I call him.

Amber shoves her entire purse at me. I retrieve her phone, unlock it with her birth year as the passcode, and find Jasper's number.

I hit call, and he picks up after two rings.

"Are you done already at the club?" Jasper asks

as he picks up the phone, recognizing Amber's number. There's not even a standard greeting of *hello*.

"Your girlfriend thinks the bar stool is a merry-go-round."

"No!" Amber shrieks with laughter over the music and shoves her lips near the phone. "It's like one of those tilt-a-whirls."

"I'm on my way. Where are you?"

I give him the information and bite my tongue. "I hope I'm not interrupting your plans for this evening," I say.

"Just don't let her do anything stupid. Okay?" Jasper hangs up, and I drop Amber's phone back into her purse, handing it to her.

"Do you want to dance until the boys come?" I ask.

Amber shakes her head and grimaces. "I don't think I can," she says and makes a face. "The room needs to stop spinning."

I forgot how much of a lightweight my bestie is. "Are you going to be sick? Do you want me to take you to the bathroom?" I ask, worried about her.

"Gosh, I hope not," she mumbles. "Birthdays are supposed to be fun." She grumbles under her breath.

I rest a hand on her shoulder. "Are you okay?"

"Fine, but it's Atlas Storm."

I don't have to ask who to know Atlas. He's in one of my classes, and it seems Amber also knows him. He's the younger brother to Island Bruisers' star player, Knox Storm.

"Hey, ladies," Atlas says, stalking over, beer in hand. He glances us over like he's deciding whether or not he's interested based on our appearance. If his gaze raking us over isn't objectifying, the whistle and wicked wolf grin sure as hell makes my skin crawl.

"Not interested," I say, making it clear that nothing is going to happen. He might as well move on to the next woman he wants to chase.

Atlas smiles, his gaze locked on me. "Are you sure, princess? I heard you and Noah Reece broke up. I promise you I'm a much better ride in bed than he ever was, and you won't disappoint your daddy."

I shift uncomfortably on my feet. "My father doesn't choose my dates, and trust me, there is zero chemistry here." I gesture between us. "I have more heat with a pet rock."

He chuckles and sips his beer. "That's a shame."

"Get lost, Atlas." I know what he's trying to do. He said it himself, wanting to get in good with my father, the head of the Island Bruisers. He's probably enlisting in the NHL draft and wants a guaranteed spot.

"Come on," he says, stepping closer. He places his hand on my arm, his fingers firm but not painful. "I've seen the way you look at me in class. We could be something great."

In class, he hits on every girl in a skirt.

He's not using me to get a draft pick. "Ask Knox for help. I'm not your girl. And get your hands off me, Atlas." I attempt to shrug out of his grip, but his hold tightens, and his other hand comes around my hip.

"I'm not in it for the draft pick," he leans in and whispers.

I don't believe him.

"Get your hands off her," Noah's voice rings behind me.

"We're going," Jasper says, coming around my side and helping Amber to her feet.

Atlas releases his grip and throws his arms up in mock surrender. "Sorry, man. I didn't realize you two were still dating," he says, giving in like I'm Noah's property and belong to him.

"Let's go," Noah growls into my ear. Grabbing my arm, he pulls me out of the bar along with Jasper and Amber in tow.

Stepping out into the cold air, he relinquishes his grip on me. "Do you always have to find trouble everywhere you are?" Noah asks, his tone sharp, and I roll my lips together.

I don't think he's looking for an answer.

"Where's the car?" Amber asks, swaying as she walks. Jasper wraps an arm around her waist to help steady her.

"We're only a couple of blocks from home. I wouldn't have been able to park much closer," he says.

Calling Jasper was a bad idea.

The heat of Noah's stare makes my stomach ache, or maybe it's the shots finally getting to me. I can't be sure which one is making me feel worse. He doesn't want to be around me. Why did I think interrupting their night would be a good idea?

"I'll grab the subway home," I say cowardly, and head in the opposite direction.

Noah huffs under his breath. "You're not walking there alone." His strides match mine, even as I pick up the pace. He doesn't touch me. His hands remain at his sides.

We approach the subway station, but a sign warns us of a long delay.

He sighs and runs a hand through his hair. "Just come back with me," he says.

I know that's not what he wants. It's the last thing in the world, and even if he's offering, it's strictly out of pity.

"You can go home. I'll wait. It's fine."

"And chance that you fall onto the tracks because you're drunk?" His laugh is dark, his eyes wide. "No. That's the last thing I need the press getting wind of. You're coming home with me."

I don't argue. There's no point.

While I want time to explain and talk to him, this isn't how I envisioned it going.

We walk back up the subway stairs to the street. It isn't too far of a walk, a couple of blocks in the dark before we enter his fancy building.

I can feel the doorman's eyes and the concierge staring at me. Were they on shift the night of Noah's arrest?

I feel like I'm being taken back to the scene of the crime.

My stomach is in knots.

The silence stretches on between us. I can't fathom why he's brought me home, even though he says it's because he's worried about me falling onto the tracks. He could just put me in a cab. There's so much that's unsaid between us. The air is thick, and my heart rate increases as I sway on my feet.

Noah wraps an arm around my waist as he ushers me into the elevator. "Upstairs." It's a command. There's no arguing with him tonight. He has his mind made up that he's taking me back to his place.

We ride up in the elevator together, and I've never felt so claustrophobic in my life. The walls are dancing, caving in on me. Each breath is more pronounced as I gasp for air, but there isn't enough.

I'm suffocating.

Spots pepper my vision before everything goes black.

SIXTEEN

NOAH

I never should have gone with Jasper to the bar, but hearing that Amber and Charlotte needed a ride because they were drinking, I didn't want to leave it for Jasper to handle both girls. Amber is his girlfriend.

Charlotte, well, she's not exactly my girlfriend. But I would have liked to have considered us friends before what transpired recently.

And a small part of me wants revenge.

Maybe I showed up because I wanted to see her drunk off her ass and miserable for screwing up my life. Does that make me the bad guy? It's not like I drove her to drink.

But I also needed to make sure that she made it home all right.

I'm pissed at her, but I'm not an asshole. I don't want to see anything terrible or tragic happen to Charlotte. I couldn't live with myself if she stepped out into traffic and got hit by a car or ordered a ride-share and wandered into the wrong vehicle.

Somehow, I've found myself bringing the cute and adorable Charlotte Grace home with me. For the record, what she did to my personal and professional life far outweighs the cuteness that she exudes.

I ought to hate her.

But all I feel is concern as I'm standing beside her in the elevator, and she collapses to the ground.

I didn't see it coming.

Turns out, there's a lot that I can't seem to anticipate when it comes to Charlotte. The girl has my life easily turned upside down.

Or maybe it's women in general. It's not like I had even an inkling that I was a father.

"Charlotte?" I say, bending down to check on her. She has a steady pulse, and I lift her with ease into my arms, the elevator doors dinging open on the penthouse floor.

I carry her inside my place, walk her into my bedroom, and lay her down on the mattress.

"Noah?" her sleepy voice murmurs my name, and it sends my cock stirring.

I hate how she still has a hold on my heart and my body. I want nothing more than to write her off and never see her again, like I said to her the night she got me thrown behind bars, but something is holding me back.

Anger.

Desire.

Lust.

They swirl together and burn inside me. I'd love to forget about her and slam another door shut on whatever it is that we shared, but I need answers, like why she betrayed me. Because every word that she said the night of the incident, all of it vanished in the heat of rage that consumed me.

I should feel nothing for her, but there's a sadness, a loss for something that never was, that consumes me. And maybe those emotions and feelings are getting tangled with my son, whom I haven't gotten to raise or know from the beginning.

Hatred at Charlotte for that is unwarranted. It isn't her fault Jasmine kept Zayn from me. And maybe it's my grief of that loss that consumes me as much as what she did that night.

"Rest," I say, standing at the edge of the bed, refusing to sit or lie beside her. I grab a trashcan and bring it beside the bed.

I head out of the bedroom, wanting to grab a water bottle from the fridge and a couple of aspirin. Plus, I need a minute to clear my head.

She's just a girl. My feelings for her are dead. Well, they should be, but they're not exactly flat lining. Anger brews at the surface, bubbling with disgust.

On the way back to the living room, her purse is abandoned on the floor, and I pick it up to keep from tripping over it.

Her phone vibrates inside.

It's probably Amber checking up on her. I should leave it well enough alone, but the compartment isn't zipped, and I let the phone "accidentally" fall onto the kitchen counter as I place her purse on there as well.

The screen lights up with a dozen messages, but none are from her friend. They're all from her father.

If we were dating, I'd feel like this is highly

inappropriate to read her texts, but she's being bombarded with messages from her dad.

Is this why she went out with Amber tonight and got drunk? Jasper had mentioned Amber's twenty-first birthday, but I'm not sure that Charlotte didn't have an ulterior motive.

I read the beginning of one of the texts from the screen, but I unlock the phone to read the entire thread, which isn't hard to guess her password. I've seen her type it into her phone, her birth month, repeated.

Well, if she wanted to keep her phone secure, she probably should have chosen a better passcode.

I scroll through the texts from her father, not so much as looking at her other threads or who the messages are from. It should be none of my business. I know I'm invading her privacy, breaking every boundary she'd set if we were dating—but we're not together.

Not that it makes what I'm doing okay. I know I'm being a bit of a shit going through her phone. But I'm only reading the messages from her dad.

What if they were important? What if she had plans and forgot, and now he's worried that she's lying dead in a ditch or calling the cops to send out an APB on a missing person?

Okay, so that isn't what any of the texts are about, but they're heated and all one-sided. Charlotte hasn't answered any of his messages in the past week, but the brunt of them have arrived today.

Dad: You better be attending the charity event alone. You're not bringing that sloth Reece to MY party.

Dad: I don't need Ice Dragon drama happening on my turf.

Dad: At least have the decency to answer your father!

Dad: I don't care that you don't want to go. You will do as I say.

Dad: Not going to answer me? If you don't show up, I'm cutting you off. No tuition. No apartment. No money.

The texts continue, but I pause over the one with my name on it. She had told her dad she had a boyfriend and had asked me to attend. That was before the arrest. Had she told her father I was her boyfriend, or had he put it together based on the news reports, because anyone in New York City who had a television or walked past a newsstand wasn't oblivious to the drama that had recently unfolded?

I scroll up farther, wanting to see what else she may have told him about me.

Charlotte: I'll go to your stupid event under one condition: you don't make me a prize for the auction.

Dad: I've already put your name on all the flyers. It'll be great for the charity.

Charlotte: You go and do it. I have a boyfriend.

I glance at the date that the text was sent. It was the day before the arrest. Her father's response is two days later.

Dad: Noah Reece? I taught you better than to date a hockey player.

Charlotte didn't answer him after that, probably because she didn't think I'd still attend the event. And I shouldn't. I'd be doing her a favor while she screwed me over. But the truth is any opportunity to fuck over another team, especially the Island Bruisers, I'll take it.

I purse my lips and know I'm screwing with Charlotte, but damn if she doesn't have to get a little bit of payback for what she did to me. I text her father back from her phone.

Charlotte: I'm coming to your stupid event. The boyfriend is coming too. Be prepared to meet Noah.

I turn off her phone, hoping that satisfies her father while also letting her continue to receive her tuition money. I don't want to screw up her future or her education. I grab my phone charger and plug it into her cell phone, leaving it in the kitchen with her purse as I bring back the bottle of water and aspirin as intended.

She grumbles and rubs at her forehead. "I don't remember getting into bed," she says, seeing me enter the bedroom.

"You passed out in the elevator." I've seen grown men black out from drinking, but I've never witnessed any of them faint. "How's your head?" I should have caught her. I had my arm at her waist, steadying her, and she slipped from my grasp.

Guilt weighs on me.

"Fine," she whispers, staring up at me. Her gaze glances around the room, taking in the surroundings.

More silence ensues.

"Should I take you to the hospital?" I'm not sure what to do after her fainting spell. Is it from alcohol poisoning?

I'm relieved I brought her back to my place and didn't put her into a cab to go home alone.

Wordlessly, she shakes her head.

"There's a bottle of water and some aspirin on the bedside table if you can stomach it."

"Thanks," she mumbles and sits up, taking a sip of water along with the pills.

I watch her cautiously, wanting to make sure that

she doesn't choke or vomit on the water and pills. "Are you sure I shouldn't take you to the ER?"

"I feel fine." She sits up in bed, and I help guide the pillows behind her while she sips from the bottle of water. "The elevator was a bit stuffy, and I think I just needed more water." She gently shakes the bottle at me.

She quietly sips the water, finishing the bottle as I stare at her, unwilling to let anything else happen to her on my watch.

"Do you faint a lot while drinking?"

"Always a first time for everything," she whispers before shuffling back on the mattress and climbing under the covers. "I'm sorry about everything."

I don't ask her which time, for tonight, ruining the evening with Jasper, or the arrest. Maybe she's apologizing because she had my son sent back to the monster who abused him and his mother.

"Sorry doesn't negate what happened." I'm still fuming, even when I don't want to be angry.

She rolls her lips together and nods, a somber expression on her face. "You have every right to hate me."

"Damn straight."

"If you need me to write a letter to the judge or

take the stand and tell him that I had you falsely arrested—how it was a misunderstanding—"

"I don't need your help," I seethe. Does she honestly think I'd trust her to help me after the mess that she made? She's the reason my son isn't living under my roof.

"I truly am sorry. If there's anything I can do to help the mess that I've created, ask."

She's right about that, it is a mess, and it's entirely her doing. Now that Jasmine is home with Grant, they both want full custody.

The only saving grace is the letter Jasmine had written with her lawyer about giving me full custody, which I had picked up the following day as soon as the law firm opened, before Jasmine had time to request the letter be destroyed.

It's now in evidence for our upcoming custody hearing. My little ray of hope that the judge will grant me full custody, given her written request, which she had notarized.

In the meantime, DCFS is investigating Zayn's current living situation with Grant and Jasmine. They are scheduled to also report on their findings at the custody hearing.

She takes my silence as an answer. "Again, I'm

sorry. You can lie on the bed. I can keep my hands to myself," Charlotte says.

It's a bad idea. I should let her sleep it off while I crash in the guest room. But leaving her by herself also seems like a bad idea.

I'm torn.

What if she passes out and vomits in her sleep? She could choke to death.

SEVENTEEN

CHARLOTTE

I roll over and rub the sleep from my eyes, my vision coming into focus in the unfamiliar bedroom.

I'm not home.

The night comes flooding back to me with flashes of Noah walking me back to his place. I glance at the warmth beside me and the sleeping figure.

Noah Reece.

He's out cold.

It's still early, the sun just peaked, and I'm quietly trying to escape his bedroom before he wakes up.

Do we need to talk?

Yes, but I don't feel quite up to it this morning.

Besides, all the apologizing in the world isn't going to fix this mess. Do I grovel? Beg for his forgiveness?

Noah is stubborn, and it isn't like I made a tiny mistake.

I had him arrested.

My stomach knots just remembering him being taken away in handcuffs.

I tiptoe out of his bedroom and down the hallway, finding my purse and phone connected to a charger on the kitchen counter. I unplug my phone and shove it in my purse before high-tailing it out of his place.

Either he's a heavy sleeper, or he pretended to stay asleep so I could escape.

———

"You still haven't spoken with him?" Amber asks, watching me try on the umpteenth gown for the charity event.

"Who? Noah?" I haven't mentioned the drama with my father. Which is weird that he stopped texting me. Apparently, in my drunken haze, I texted him that I'd be bringing Noah to the event.

Dad will be relieved when Noah doesn't show up

because there's zero chance that I can convince Noah to do me any favors.

I don't even bother asking him. I mentioned the event to him before the catastrophe between us, and I don't dare consider reminding him of his promised date.

It would be a disaster, the two of us attending together. For starters, the charity auction is a fundraiser for the local children's hospital. The majority of the special guests are Island Bruisers players.

"Yes," Amber says, staring at me as I show her the black gown that is too form-fitting for my liking. She gestures for me to spin around for her to make a full judgment on the dress.

"This dress might split in half if I sit."

Amber giggles at my response and gestures for me to wander back into the dressing room to try a different gown.

"I meant Noah," she says, and I'm relieved that the curtain is hiding my expression as I stare at my reflection in the mirror.

"Noah?" I squeak. "There is zero chance that he's going to attend. He hates me." I unzip the gown and slide it off.

"He doesn't hate you," Amber quips. "He's just...

reserved, and you know it's complicated. This week, he goes to court for custody of his son."

"He does?" I peek my head out of the side of the curtain. "He didn't tell me that."

For the record, he hasn't told me anything about Zayn since the night I royally mucked things up for him and his son.

"He doesn't want to get his hopes up and get disappointed, but his lawyer thinks he has a solid case. You're right, though. He'll probably be too busy for the charity event if he's got a son at home."

There's something in Amber's voice that has me on edge. I slip into another dress. "I need you to zip the back of this one."

"Ooh," Amber coos excitedly and helps fasten the zipper.

The dress is black, like all the other ones I've tried on for the black-tie affair.

But this one flows out at my hips, leaving me more room to dance and move. Plus, the design has intricate stitching in the bodice which reveals an ample amount of cleavage. Just enough to piss Daddy off. It's cute, fancy, and looks flattering on my figure.

"This is *the* one," Amber says, already loving the dress on me before I've fully modeled it for her.

"I wish you could be my date for the charity event."

"And deal with your father?" She shakes her head, her eyes wide like a doe. "I'd sooner walk across hot coals."

"I don't think that's supposed to be that painful. I mean, don't they do that at, like, spa retreats or something?" I ask.

"Have you ever tried it?" Amber asks.

"Well, no," I say, and I can't recall knowing anyone who has, either.

"Exactly. They may say it's no big deal, but it's hot coals! No, thank you." Amber purses her lips together. "That's the dress. Buy it."

"Do you think so?" I twirl for her, and she smiles, tilting her head.

"Yes, please. I don't think I can stand here another minute and watch you try on another black dress unless it's for your funeral."

I stick my tongue out at her. "Savage."

EIGHTEEN

NOAH

My head hasn't been in the game, not in practice, and certainly not while we were playing the Wolverines.

I'm surprised Coach Malone hasn't benched me, but it seems the entire morale of the team has been down this week. I know why I'm a mess, but the rest of the guys, I can't fathom what their excuse is for being distracted.

I can't stop thinking about Zayn. The custody hearing is this week. I've tried to avoid the news because one of the guys mentioned Brass was giving an interview and laying it on thick about how he could lose his only son, the little boy he's raised since birth.

My son.

He had years with Zayn when it should have been me.

I'm grateful that we aren't scheduled to play the Island Bruisers until after the hearing next week. Right now, I'm not sure that I wouldn't pound the shit out of Grant Brass if I saw him, and it wouldn't be good if he doesn't at least have the puck.

Keep my anger in check.

That had been the advice given to me by the lawyer.

DCFS is scrutinizing Zayn's current home, but they also want to ensure that if I'm granted custody, I'm a fit parent. I can't fault them for wanting that for my son. And it could easily be twisted in court that I have "anger issues" if the hockey fights were taken out of context.

Again, my lawyer's sage advice.

Avoid as many fights as I can and keep gameplay clean as much as possible. Those tend to be Coach Malone's rules too, but it doesn't mean skirmishes don't happen on the ice.

I've never played in a game where someone didn't end up in the penalty box at some point. It's a hazard of the job.

But right now, I'm under a microscope along

with Grant Brass. I've been watching his game footage late at night, recording his games to see where he's screwed up and what aggression he's shown on the ice.

And he's fallen repeatedly into the trap of brutality first. The game comes second.

I refuse to do the same.

"I need a favor." I pull Kyler aside after the Wolverines game, my helmet in hand. We took a hell of a beating out there on the ice, and while we lost, it was a close game.

"Name it," Kyler says, nodding as he strips out of his hockey gear.

"If I get custody of Zayn—"

"When," Kyler corrects me. He's had no doubt that my son will be reunited with me, and this is just a bump along the road. I wish I had his vote of confidence right now.

"When," I say and suck in a sharp breath. Later this week is the court hearing. It's been difficult to keep my head entirely in the game. "When I get custody of Zayn, I might need someone I trust to watch him."

"Oh, of course." Kyler's eyes light up. "You're going to need a nanny for when you have games and practice. You can't have my nanny, but I can help give you some names."

"That's appreciated, but I was thinking more of a sitter. I may want to go out one evening. Specifically, to a charity event."

Jasper spins around, overhearing the conversation. "Is this the gala that Amber has been talking my ear off about, the one where Charlotte is attending, and her father is involved in the event?"

"That's the one," I grunt. I'm not a fan of her old man, although based on the interactions I read and have heard about, neither is she. "If I gain custody of Zayn this week, I'll need help watching him for a night."

"I'm sure Em won't mind watching the kids. You can bring Zayn over, and he can have a sleepover at our place," Kyler says. "What night?"

"Saturday. And I'm hoping I can request one more favor."

"You are running out of favors, Reece," Kyler says. "Go on." He gestures for me to continue.

"The charity event is for the Island Bruisers. I want to shake things up."

"Shake things up?" Jasper quips with a wicked grin. "Count me in."

"Me too," Kyler adds. "If it involves screwing with the Bruisers, you know I'm game."

———

I swear I'm coming down with the stomach flu, the way the nausea sweeps over me and my skin is clammy, but I'm pretty sure I'm healthy.

It's fear edging into my veins, making me sick with worry.

"Are you ready?" Deon asks. He's my lawyer, and I'm paying him top dollar to help me win the custody case.

Although, I'm guessing that Grant is financing Jasmine's custody lawyers because Deon seems to know the opposing counsel. He's been chatting with him while I've been standing outside the courtroom, waiting for our hearing.

I don't want to step inside. Then, it'll be all too real.

"Yeah," I say with a heavy sigh.

He nods and carries his briefcase with him into the courtroom.

Sweat trickles my brow. I wasn't able to eat anything all morning. I couldn't even stomach coffee, and right now, I'm glad for fasting because, otherwise, I'm sure it'd be all over the floor.

Jasper is seated with Amber in the courtroom. He's there for moral support, so is Kyler, Owen, and a couple of the other guys from the team. I inhale sharply when I lay eyes on Charlotte.

What's she doing here? I glance at my attorney, wondering if he's planning on using her as a witness or something, when the door behind us opens, and Jasmine enters with her lawyer and my little boy.

Grant is nowhere in sight, which is a relief, but he's probably not too far behind. I doubt he lets Jasmine out of his sight after the last time, when she left Zayn with me and handed over custody.

I follow my lawyer's lead, doing as he instructs. The entire process takes more time than it should as the judge reads over the findings from DCFS, the letter that Jasmine originally had notarized, along with the police reports. A child psychologist that Zayn recently started seeing since the custody issues began comments that he's been seeing my son and believes he should continue with counseling sessions, but at this point, he can't come to any conclusions other than the child has some behavioral issues that are often found in violent homes.

It feels like stone against stone, neither of us budging. If there weren't issues of abuse, no doubt the judge would allow for joint custody, but I can see his mind ticking, trying to determine who the actual abuser is and isn't.

And that's when my lawyer, Gregory Deon, calls Charlotte Grace to the stand, wanting to hear her account of the events leading up to my arrest.

I try not to scowl, my hands balling into fists, and the courtroom door squeaks open.

If it's not one travesty, it's another, as Grant Brass stalks into the courtroom and sits beside his wife, Jasmine Brass.

NINETEEN

CHARLOTTE

72 hours earlier

"Tell me what I need to do to get Noah to forgive me?" I ask, staring up at Jasper. He's Noah's best friend. He must know what it will take to earn Noah's forgiveness.

"I don't think there's anything you can do. Trust me. You royally screwed him."

I scoff at his remark. "I had him arrested, but the charges were dropped."

"Do you think the other lawyer cares about that? He was arrested. Grant, meanwhile, hasn't been behind bars. It makes Noah look like an unfit parent."

"That's not fair! Grant isn't even the biological

father," I say. I sip my coffee as Jasper holds his between his hands.

I managed to convince Jasper to meet up with me for coffee so that we could discuss Noah, and he was more on board with the arrangement than I expected.

I thought that I'd have to convince his girlfriend and my best friend to drag him to the coffee shop, and I'd have to ambush him. Jasper seems like a pretty cool guy and a decent friend.

"As long as Jasmine remains married to Grant, he's in the picture." Jasper exhales a heavy sigh. "I wish I had a better solution. You asked me to meet you. What did you have in mind?" His gaze tightens as he tries to figure out what I want.

And he's right. I didn't just call him to come for coffee out of the blue.

Noah's custody hearing is this week.

"Grant ought to be behind bars. I can't believe Jasmine won't press charges against him."

"I know. But there isn't anything we can do about that," Jasper says. "Trust me, I've already asked around. And we can rough up Grant on the ice, but he's still a douche when he goes home to Jasmine and Zayn."

"I need the name of Noah's attorney."

"What? Why?" Jasper slides his chair back several inches, the metal scraping over concrete. "What are you planning to do?"

"Nothing bad."

He's staring at me, studying me. Is Jasper trying to determine if I'm lying to him or if I'm just downright crazy?

"I need more than *nothing bad*," he says.

"I want to testify on Noah's behalf. I probably can't testify as a character witness, but I'm why he was arrested. If I explain what happened to the judge, how it was a misunderstanding, and how Grant is the perpetrator, maybe I can help."

Jasper places his hands on the table and then turns them face up. "Or maybe you screw things up even worse for him."

Noah's gaze burns through me, making my stomach clamp, and I bite down on my tongue to keep the sweeping nausea at bay.

I'm doing this for him, to help him gain custody of his son.

If it doesn't work, he will hate me, along with his

entire team. I'm not even sure Amber will still want to be friends with me. It's not like I told her my plan, and Jasper hadn't either, since she admitted to being surprised to see me when we ran into each other at the courthouse entrance.

As I'm called up to the stand, I step past Noah and exhale a shaky breath. He might hate me forever for blindsiding him.

He leans toward his attorney and whispers something into his ear as I'm sworn in and take the stand.

All eyes are on me, but the only ones that matter are Noah's, and he can't seem to meet my stare. His focus is on the table in front of him. Is he worried what I'll say?

I recant my story, the night of Noah's arrest, and in great detail, I explain how I didn't know that Noah was a father because he hadn't told me up until I met his son, whom he was newly acquainted with at the time.

I explain about the 9-1-1 call, what Zayn said at the house, and what I had witnessed when his mother came to pick him up from the police station and her matching black eye, poorly hidden with concealer.

The judge holds up a hand, interrupting Jasmine's attorney, who steps forward in preparation to question my testimony.

"Will we be hearing testimony from Jasmine Brass?" the judge asks pointedly.

"Yes, Your Honor," Jasmine's attorney says.

Jasmine looks flustered as her husband sits beside her, a smug grin covering his face. I'm not sure that Jasmine intended on testifying, but it's clear that the judge wants to hear her side of what happened.

There's no way that Jasmine is going to admit that Grant beats her in front of her abuser. Doesn't the judge realize that? She'll have to perjure herself if he remains in the courtroom.

"Do you have any other questions for Ms. Grace?" the judge asks Jasmine's attorney, "If not, I'd suggest that we break for lunch and reconvene after."

"Just one, Your Honor." Jasmine's attorney steps forward, coming to stand in front of me. He's taller than Noah but lanky. His suit is professionally tailored as he glances at his notes. "Are you sleeping with Noah Reece?"

"Objection, Your Honor. Relevance," Noah's attorney interrupts.

"I'll allow it," the judge says.

Seriously? I try not to blanch at the thought of having to answer Jasmine's attorney's question. My face remains stoic as I answer with an even tone.

"No, we aren't currently sleeping together."

"But you have slept with him," Jasmine's attorney presses.

"Yes, before I found out he had a son, we slept together."

"And what about more recently?"

"Objection, your honor. Relevance," Noah's attorney interrupts.

"Get to the point, Counselor," the judge says, giving Jasmine's attorney a pointed look. "We're not here to discuss Ms. Grace's sex life."

"I'll reframe the question," her attorney says, offering a forced smile. "Ms. Grace, were you in a committed relationship with Noah Reece when you discovered he had a son?"

"Objection, Your Honor. Relevance," Noah's attorney interrupts.

I swear, at this point, the man is a parrot.

"I'm going to have to agree with Counselor Deon. Her relationship status with Noah Reece isn't relevant."

"Mr. Reece has a reputation as a playboy, and I'm

just trying to determine if that's fact with Ms. Grace's testimony. And if it is fact, then does that make him an adequate father?"

The judge shakes her head. "I will not turn my courtroom into a three-ring circus. The issue has never been about Mr. Reece's reputation or promiscuity. From what I can tell, he wants to be in his son's life, and there's no evidence standing in his way. The arrest was a misunderstanding, and I commend Ms. Grace for her actions, doing what she believed was in the child's best interests. With that said, the only lingering question I have is whether he should be given full custody. After lunch, I'd also like Mr. Reece to take the stand. I have a few questions for him," the judge says.

———

"I still can't believe that asshole lawyer kept asking about my sex life," I say, taking a bite of my sandwich. I'm seated across from Amber, and Jasper is beside her. Kyler is seated next to me.

"Pervy lawyer," Amber says, sipping her hot chocolate.

We're seated at a picnic table outside, a block

from the courthouse. The air is brisk, but there aren't too many places to grab lunch nearby. A hotdog cart across the street and a sandwich vendor the next block over near the park.

"He was just doing his job, trying to make Noah look bad," Kyler says. "But he'll be a better father than Grant."

"That really puts the bar up there," Jasper says and laughs.

"What do you think the judge wants to ask Noah?" I ask, taking another bite. We don't have too much time and I want to make sure that we're back before the judge returns from lunch.

"Probably a list of his recent conquests," Jasper jokes. "Maybe she wants his phone number?"

Amber smacks his arm. "Quit being a jerk. She probably wants to know how he will raise a son with a full-time hockey career. I mean, that would be my first question."

I inhale sharply. "Has Noah thought about that? Has he discussed hiring a nanny, or does he have family who can help him?"

Kyler shifts on the bench, facing me. "I spoke with him about a nanny, but it's not like he has anything lined up already. We all would be willing to help, but for travel and game nights, he'll need someone else there with Zayn until he hires a nanny."

"His family isn't an option," Jasper says. "He's not close with his mom, she's got some mental health issues, and his parents are still married. His dad's a narcissist and will expect something in return. I don't think Noah would trust them with Zayn. No siblings, either."

I can't recall Noah ever speaking about his parents, but it's not a topic that I've broached.

"I could do it," I say and grab my soda, taking a swig. "He might not want me around, but my schedule has evenings and weekends off. I can always bring Zayn with me to work. It's just during class that someone else might have to watch him."

"What do you do that would allow you to bring a little kid to work with you? Do they have daycare or something available?" Kyler asks.

"I work for the park district. There is a daycare center at the rec center. I didn't even consider that, but I usually spend my afternoons teaching little kids to ice skate or play hockey."

"Wait, you actually like hockey?" Kyler's eyes widen. "Can you convince Em that it's not so bad and a fun sport?"

Jasper grins. "Maybe some of that hockey love can rub off on Amber too."

"Hey, I'm right here!" Amber pinches Jasper's arm. "Be nice."

"I am nice. You're the one pinching my arm," he grumbles.

———

After lunch, we head back inside the courthouse. Noah is standing beside his lawyer in the hallway.

Slowly, I walk up to him, my hands threaded together, filled with nervous energy. "Hey," I say, offering a warm smile.

Noah emits a soft sigh.

"I'll give you two a moment, but make it quick. We need to be back inside in five," his lawyer says.

"We won't be long," Noah says, staring at me, and I'm waiting for him to cut me off or yell at me, but he does neither.

"I'm sorry about the ambush this morning," I say. I shift my weight from one leg to the other, uncomfortable under his heated stare.

Noah looks hot, dressed sharply in his black suit. It's probably one of the outfits that he wears after a game when he's forced on camera. I know he doesn't like the spotlight, but he's dealt with it recently because of me.

"We'll see if it worked," he says. His eyes are tight, his jaw terse.

"It sounded like good news before lunch."

"Anything can change. I'm not getting my hopes up," Noah says. He glances at his watch. "I should head back inside."

"Wait," I say, expelling a nervous breath. "I know I'm the last person in the world whose help you want, but I'm there for you and Zayn. If you need help until you find a nanny, consider it. Okay?"

He opens his mouth, and I think he's about to argue with me when he nods. "Yeah, okay. I need to get back inside."

I let him go, watch him walk away. He's only a few feet from me, but it hurts. It's like he's turned his back on me, not that I deserve anything less.

His teammates and Amber have already disappeared from the hallway. I quietly follow into the courtroom and sit next to Amber again. Whatever happens, all of us want to be there for Noah.

Noah takes the stand, and sure enough, the judge's first question is, "How do you intend to manage your son and a professional hockey career? You're in the middle of your season. I can't imagine the timing is ideal."

"He is my son. I will always put him first. I wouldn't be managing my son, Your Honor. I'd be raising him. Other professional hockey players have children and families that support them. My teammates have offered to help while I hire a nanny, and I have friends who have offered to step up if I need assistance in the beginning," Noah says, his gaze locking on mine.

And for a moment, it gives me hope. Maybe all isn't entirely lost.

"I have it handled. I assure you, this isn't a spur-of-the-moment decision," Noah says. "I've already purchased a bed and toys. I've turned what was my guest room into Zayn's bedroom. I want to take him home with me, Your Honor, and protect him like a father should protect his son."

"I've heard enough. I'd like to call Mrs. Jasmine Brass to the stand," the judge says.

Noah steps down and Jasmine's eyes widen as she whispers something to her lawyer.

"Your Honor, may I have a word with you in chambers?"

Both lawyers and the judge momentarily leave the courtroom.

I'm stunned, unsure what is going on.

Ten minutes later, the lawyers return to their tables and the judge follows inside the courtroom.

"I've made my decision," the judge says.

TWENTY

NOAH

It's hard not to stare at her across the room. She hasn't seen me and doesn't know I'm here, but it was easy for me to get into the charity event.

Everyone recognizes me.

That's why I hate these kinds of functions. They all expect me to open my wallet and contribute a month's salary without flinching, which I wouldn't mind doing if I wasn't knee-deep in a million other things. One of those includes paying the final bill to my lawyer for the legal fees regarding the custody hearing.

Not cheap.

And that's not the worst of it. I don't have time to

attend tonight's gala, but I owe her. To say I've been busy is an understatement.

But I made Charlotte Grace a promise, and I always keep my promises.

Not that she knows I'm attending. She hasn't seen me yet. She's hiding by the bar, a glass of champagne in hand. She's sipping her bubbly and glancing around the room, probably for a familiar face.

I'm halfway across the room and behind her. She hasn't so much as spun around entirely for me to admire her dress or the way that she wears the gown, which is sexy as hell.

I'm in two minds about Charlotte. I hate her for getting me arrested, but I appreciate what she did in the courtroom. She put herself out there and admitted her flaws and mishaps.

I truly believe it was Charlotte's testimony that helped the judge understand my arrest and see through the lies that Jasmine's attorney kept attempting to spin. I don't know why Jasmine got out of testifying, but it doesn't matter. Anything she said would have been a lie. She'd have protected Grant at the expense of our son.

Watching her relinquish custody and say goodbye all over again was heartbreaking.

Zayn cried.

Jasmine cried.

I forced the tears away, but my heart ached, and it still does any time I think about the afternoon that Zayn became mine.

It should have been a happy memory. It was a win, but why does it feel like such a loss?

Emerson, Kyler's fiancé, agreed to babysit Zayn tonight while I'm at the charity event Charlotte's father is hosting for the Island Bruisers. When I dropped Zayn off this afternoon, Amber was also there, and she offered to spend the night at Emerson's to help out with the kids.

Zayn isn't that much of a handful, but he's got his issues.

What kid doesn't?

I'm sure I was a beast for my parents, and somehow, I turned out okay. But don't ask them. I'm not sure they'd agree.

Charlotte sips her bubbly drink and turns to lean against the bar counter. Her gaze catches mine, and she raises an inquisitive eye.

I've been caught staring.

I smile and stroll over to her, ordering a beer for myself.

"I didn't think you'd come," Charlotte says,

glancing me over. The smile on her face tells me she approves of my tuxedo. Her eyes sparkle, and I swear my jaw hits the floor as I fully admire the view of her dress, including the ample cleavage that she's showing off.

"You asked for my help, and I wanted to support you." I take the beer from the bartender, toss a twenty into the tip jar, and take a swig.

The smile grows as she pulls me in for a hug. "Thank you!" Her excitement makes her glow, and I can't help but feel proud that I've put that grin on her face.

"Don't thank me yet. We haven't done the introductions with your father."

Charlotte rolls her eyes at his mention. "Can I tell him we're getting engaged? Really screw with him."

I cough on my beer at her suggestion. "I'll play your fake boyfriend. That's it." Engaged? That's a line I'm not crossing. There are likely reporters and cameras all over the venue. That's the last kind of attention I need right now, but at least the custody battle is over.

"Thanks, I'll consider that a win," Charlotte says and winks at me. She links her arm between mine, places her half-consumed champagne glass on the bar top, and drags me onto the dance floor. "Better make it look convincing."

"For whom?" I ask, not seeing her father around. Had I not known that she was Charlotte Grace, I wouldn't have had any inkling who her father is, but now that I do, I'd prefer to stay out of his sights.

"All the other guests," she says. "We have to make them jealous, like I'm a hot commodity, if I'm going to be auctioned off for a date night."

I lean in, pulling her against me as I lead her out onto the dance floor. "Maybe I'll buy that hot date with you," I whisper into her ear.

A natural smile adorns her face. "Maybe?" she teases, staring up at me. "A fake boyfriend has to at least start the bidding."

It feels natural, holding her in my arms as I keep her against me, swaying to the music. There aren't too many couples dancing, but we're not the only ones.

She rests her head on my shoulder, letting out a soft sigh. "I didn't think you'd come, and I wasn't sure how I would survive tonight alone."

"You're not alone."

Charlotte pulls her head back, staring up at me. "Well, I know that. I mean there are hundreds of people here, but I feel alone. I hate these extravagant types of events with guests that I don't know or care little about."

"You're not the only one," I whisper into her ear. What I hate even more is that her father is using Charlotte for his own benefit.

A blush crosses her cheeks when she pulls back and smiles up at me. "You're something else."

"So I've been told." My hand rests on her lower back, holding her against me. She's warm and her body melts into my touch. "Listen, I never got to thank you at the courthouse—"

"No thanks are necessary. I don't deserve it after what I've done."

"You helped me gain full custody of Zayn. If you hadn't reached out to my lawyer, I don't know what would have happened."

"That was all you," Charlotte says. "I just caused a few speed bumps along the way."

That's putting it mildly. "I think I get why you did what you did that night, with the police, having me arrested. I'm not happy about it, but I understand your motivations, protecting my son."

"I was always trying to do the right thing. I'm sorry Zayn was returned to his mother when you were arrested." The smile vanishes from her face, and there's a heaviness behind her sullen sapphire gaze. "If I had realized what I was doing, I don't think I can forgive myself for that. I don't expect you to ever forgive me for it, either."

"I'm willing to move on, look forward," I say. What she did still hurts, there's no denying there were consequences, but I don't want to hold a grudge indefinitely. My hand cups her face, bringing her gaze to meet mine.

"How about we work on trusting each other?" she asks, smiling weakly into my hand. "We start anew."

My thumb grazes her bottom lip.

She has no idea what I've done, what I've planned for tonight. I'm not sure she'll trust me after this evening. But the cogs are in motion. There's no stopping it.

"We don't have to date. I mean, I get it. I'm probably the last person in the world you want to be romantically entangled with," Charlotte says, "but for just tonight, can we pretend to be happy and in love?"

Her lips are red and luscious. They're close enough for me to brush mine against hers and kiss her. My mind screams at me to back away, but her scent is intoxicating, and it's as though I'm under her spell. "I can do that," I whisper, leaning in, taking a taste of the ripe forbidden fruit.

The kiss lasts seconds, but it feels like minutes, exploring each other's mouths, the pressure perfect as it starts slow, and we hungrily explore one another with our tongues.

My fingers dig into her hip, refraining from tangling in her hair. I want to unclip the updo, make her shake her red curls out, and bend her over the bar. I'd enjoy fucking her from behind, letting my cock fill her tight pussy as she screams my name for everyone to hear.

But that's a mere fantasy.

And one that I'm not willing to explore and put my career and future on the line over because there are reporters and guests with phones who, on a whim, will record anything that looks remotely juicy to upload to their social media for two minutes of fame.

"Reece," a rough male voice pulls me from my kiss with Charlotte. My stomach churns, already knowing who that voice belongs to without even having to look. Grant Brass.

Of course, he'd be attending tonight's event. He's one of the star players for the Island Bruisers.

He has impeccable timing.

"What are you doing here?" Grant asks, sharp-tongued as he sizes me up. "This is by invitation only, and you're ruining the ambiance."

Two of his teammates, Knox Storm and Mack Conrad, stroll up behind Grant. Does he think that he needs backup at a charity function?

"My girlfriend invited me," I say, wrapping an arm around Charlotte's waist.

"Took you two no time at all to shack up again," Grant says, glancing Charlotte over. "Lucky for me, Char is auctioning herself off for a night." He waggles his eyebrows suggestively.

I step forward, blocking Grant from going anywhere near Charlotte. "You place one bid, and I swear I'll—"

"You'll what?" Knox asks, tilting his head and stepping around Grant. "The way I see it, there's one of you and the entire Island Bruisers team here. You don't have a shot in hell of escaping us, Reece."

"You're going to fight me?" I laugh at his suggestion. "Your entire team against one guy? How the hell is that fair?"

"Never said we had to play fair," Mack says. "You're on our turf, messing with one of our own."

"One of your own who beats women and

children?" I say, staring Mack in the face. "Real noble of you, Conrad."

"He's lying," Grant says and runs a hand through his hair. The accusation has him flustered.

"Your wife has a matching black eye to the one you gave *my* kid," I seethe. "Do you want court transcripts to remind you of what happened?"

"There are no transcripts. She didn't press charges against me," Grant boasts. "A wife knows better than to betray her husband."

Mack takes a step back. "You mean that shit in the papers about the kid, that's for real?" He looks awestruck like he hadn't realized Grant had been lying to him all this time.

"It's hogwash!" Grant shouts, his voice bellowing out, gaining a few stray glances from attendees looking in our direction.

"Take it outside," Charlie Hayes says. He's in his rookie season for the Island Bruisers, young talented blood. At least he has the sense to keep the gala professional and the spat between rivals.

"We're not going anywhere," Charlotte says. "I invited Noah to attend this event. You boys will have to deal with his presence. Grow up!"

A few of his teammates laugh nervously; they

don't seem thrilled with taking orders from a girl, but they straighten up and clear their throats.

"Drinks?" Storm says to the other guys on his team as Charlotte's father is approaching.

The rest of them scatter like roaches, and I inhale a nervous breath, having to meet the man who will undoubtedly hate me before the night is over, especially with what I have planned with my teammates.

"Reece." Mr. Grace's features are hard, his eyes tight and his lips narrow. He stares at me like he's studying me for an exam, and I'm the course material.

"Mr. Grace," I say, trying to be as formal and polite as possible. If he believes that I'm dating Charlotte, then I need it to appear convincing. I hold out my hand, introducing myself.

He doesn't take my hand. He ignores it like I'm not holding it out awkwardly and having just been rejected. "Charlotte, would you mind giving us a moment?" Mr. Grace asks his daughter.

She forces a smile. "Of course. I'll grab us fresh drinks at the bar," she says, her hand coming to rest on my arm for a moment before giving it a tentative squeeze just before walking off.

"Charlotte is my baby girl," he says, his eyes boring into mine.

I refrain from reminding him that she's not a baby or that if she were, he wouldn't be sending her out on a charity auction date.

"She's important to me," I say. It's easier if I don't have to lie and there is truth in my words. I've never been great at lying. As a kid, I'd get tripped up in my little tales and end up with a blistered bottom.

"Charlotte is more important to me and the team." Mr. Grace tilts his head slightly, his graying hair peeking through the bright lights mixed with dark brown.

She must have her mother's coloring, with her blue eyes and red locks, because she looks nothing like her father. I'm assuming that she's not adopted.

"Whatever you think you have going on with my daughter, it's a fling. She'll snuff it out in due time. She's smart enough to know her future belongs with the Island Bruisers when she comes and works for me. Don't make it any harder on her. If you have any integrity, you'll end this tryst before you break her heart."

———

We're served hors d'oeuvres, an elaborate meal, and then, finally, the auction begins. I'm grateful for the distraction because speaking with her father was pure torture.

Maybe I shouldn't be surprised that Daddy Dearest wants his daughter to follow in his footsteps, but Charlotte hasn't mentioned anything to me either way about it. Not that we've talked recently about our careers, or much of anything.

But I have heard her discuss working for the park district, which puts a career with the Island Bruisers on the right path.

It's not like we're dating.

Tonight is all fun and games, at least with pretending to be a couple. That's not the only entertainment laid out for this evening at the charity auction.

"I'll be right back," I whisper, giving Charlotte a quick kiss on the cheek before excusing myself from the auction and heading for the back door. I'm quiet as I sneak in the Ice Dragons teammates. I convinced every player on our roster to join us for the main event because it's for a good cause.

At least, that's what I told the newbies. It is, after all, a charity that we're helping.

Kyler, Jasper, Owen, Chase, and a couple of the

other guys already know the truth. They're the ones who supported me with Zayn at the courthouse and would do anything to screw over the Bruisers, especially when it comes to Grant Brass.

When I came up with the plan, I was still pissed at Charlotte and wanted to get even with her. Hopefully, she'll find some humor in what we have planned.

If not, our fake romance is over.

TWENTY-ONE

CHARLOTTE

I glance at my watch. Noah has been gone for a little while. I'm seated in the second row at the auction, and pretty soon, they'll switch from auctioning off cruises and fancy trips to a date night with me.

I had hoped that Noah might be able to talk some sense into my father, but the look on Noah's face when I went to fetch us drinks was abysmal. I think my father gave Noah the speech that no man wants to ever have with his girlfriend's dad. The *if you hurt her, I'll kill you* speech. At least that's what I'm assuming was said between them because neither fessed up to their discussion.

Father is seated next to me as the auctioneer lists

off the prize and then does the bidding for each item. He talks so fast, it's any wonder that the auction isn't over in minutes. But there are hundreds of items that were donated from different organizations for tonight's event. Everything from signed jerseys donated by the Island Bruisers to dinner with yours truly, me.

Although I didn't technically donate myself for a dinner date, my father decided to do that for me. He likes to think that he can control my life and my future. He's wrong.

"Next up," the auctioneer says, "is an autographed Mack Conrad jersey. Come up here, Mack." The auctioneer cheers him on.

He climbs up the steps for a welcoming applause and takes the jersey, opening it and signing it for everyone to see. "I'll even sign a heart next to my name," Mack says. "One of a kind." He winks, and I swear all the women gasp excitedly.

I don't see the appeal, but Mack Conrad is easy on the eyes. He's also a friend of Grant's, which automatically puts him into asshole territory. Anyone who associates with Grant Brass falls under dickhood.

"We will start the bidding at one thousand dollars," the auctioneer says.

And that's when I see a glimpse of Noah at the edge of the stage. He's waiting to come out, but I'm not sure why.

What the hell is he up to?

The bidding for Mack's jersey goes up to thirty-three hundred dollars before I finally get my answer.

Noah shuffles onto the side stage, comes over to the auctioneer and whispers something to him. "Have at it," the auctioneer says, handing Noah the microphone.

"Ladies and gentlemen, this evening, we have a real special treat for you guys."

My stomach sinks, and I'm worried about what Noah has planned. Is he telling them outright that the date with me is canceled, and he's buying my evening up before anyone else has an opportunity?

That wouldn't be so bad, would it?

I mean, there's a chance one of the Island Bruisers might bid on a date with me. And if it's Grant Brass, I might physically have to murder the man before we get to dinner.

"What's this?" my dad asks, glancing from the stage at Noah to me, expecting an answer.

My mouth is agape as I try to form a few words so as not to let my father interrupt Noah. "Just watch. It'll be good."

I hope I'm right. I mean, Noah wouldn't steer me wrong. We're on good terms.

"It better be. Your ass is on the line if he embarrasses me."

I exhale a shaky breath as Noah steps out onto the center of the stage with the microphone in hand. "Ladies and gentlemen, I have a real special treat for you this evening."

My hands are sweaty, and I wipe them on the skirt of my gown, trying to calm my breathing. That pit in my stomach is growing like a boulder, and I have this strange sense that it's about to be launched downhill at full speed.

From the side of the stage, Chase is doing something with his phone. A minute later, music billows into the auditorium, pumping and upbeat.

Noah smiles, not the least bit surprised by the onset of audio. "Our next item up for auction isn't just a jersey from an NHL player. It's a hot date with the goalie at a four-star restaurant."

Aiden struts out onto the stage wearing a suit and tie. He's not exactly in black tie elegance for the event, but the man did dress up.

He spins around at the center of the stage while Noah takes a step to the side to let Aiden have the spotlight.

"Your date includes dinner with the hottest goalie in New York City. He plays for the Ice Dragons. He's rough. Tough. But easy on the eyes. This auction is for a date night with Aiden Blake, where he'll wine and dine you. If you're one lucky lady, he might even walk you to your front door." Noah winks at the crowd.

The ladies are all captivated by his presence and the date with the goalie.

"Ten thousand dollars!" one lady shouts.

Noah grins. "Okay, we'll start the bidding at ten thousand dollars."

Aiden looks surprised, but hearing that has him flashing his muscles, and then he spins around and wiggles his butt for all the girls to ogle.

I shouldn't do it, but I glance at my father, who is stewing in his seat. He hasn't interrupted Noah, probably because the ladies are going wild for Aiden and helping the charity in the process.

"You have some explaining to do later," my father seethes, glaring at me. I swear the man is about to blow steam through his nostrils like one of those dragon cartoons.

Noah continues auctioning off individual players from the Ice Dragons for date night. Everything from a four-course meal to, let's skip straight to dessert, which is intended as a sweet date at the ice cream parlor. But the ladies are opening their wallets like it's Christmas and they're buying presents for all their children and, some of them, their grandchildren.

"And last but not least, the ultimate hockey date with three Ice Dragons players. You'll fly to your destination of choice via our private jet, where we'll wine and dine you."

"Does that include the mile-high club?" one guest quips.

Several other ladies giggle at the question.

Noah clears his throat and tries to regain his composure. "While these three men aren't quite bachelors, they know how to spoil a girl and make her feel like no one else exists. Let's hear it for Jasper Greyson, Kyler Greyson, and myself, Noah Reece."

The Greyson brothers are the only two without a suit coat on. Jasper and Kyler give each other a wink before ripping their shirts open for all the girls to see their bare abs. They toss their shirts into the audience and gyrate to the music as they wiggle their asses at the ladies.

The rest of the Ice Dragons join them on stage, doing the same, giving the ladies an exciting treat and getting the bidding higher.

"Twenty-five thousand," a woman shouts from the back, lifting her number up high as she leaps to her feet.

"Fifty-thousand," another woman stands, holding her number up, making it clear that she wants to win the prize.

The ladies aren't done bidding or fighting over the three of them.

Noah glances at me, a smug look on his face, pleased with the outcome.

My father begins to lean forward to get up, and I grab his arm, stopping him from standing and ending this before the bidding is done. "Think about the kids. They have cancer," I say, imploring him to keep his ass glued to the chair.

He glares at me, shaking his head. "What have you done?"

TWENTY-TWO

NOAH

It's any wonder that we aren't kicked out of the venue, but the older ladies opening their wallets and writing massive checks certainly helps.

The guests are more excited about us in attendance than the Island Bruisers. I want to think it's because we're the better team, but it isn't like they are auctioning off a date night, dessert, or a trip via private jet.

And we aren't doing it as part of our publicity agreement per our contract. It was all to screw with the Bruisers. Well, that and to keep Charlotte from having to auction herself off as a date because I am not okay with that happening.

Perhaps if she had wanted to offer herself as a prize for a night—

No.

I still wouldn't have wanted her to do that, either. Some gropy guy might get the wrong idea after paying a boatload of money for dinner and drinks with her.

My teammates, we can handle ourselves with the ladies. Most of them are older than we are. Some could have been grandmas. Honestly, it's a bit hard to see past Charlotte sitting beside her father.

His terse stare will probably give me a few nightmares, but it's not as though I'm actually dating his daughter. It's just for fun. Fake.

I should probably find Charlotte and make sure that I didn't get her into too much trouble with our little prank. But it did help a good cause. How long can she stay mad at me for helping her out of trouble? She made it clear that she didn't want to participate in the auction, so I offered up something else in exchange.

Her fiery red hair is the first thing that I notice. It matches her skin tone as she's high-tailing it toward me.

Oh, crap.

She's mad.

Furious.

I can see the heat radiating off her tiny little form, and I have half a mind to run in the opposite direction, screaming to my teammates to *abort* and for all of us to flee the back exit, the same way that I let those guys inside.

"That was something," Charlotte says, staring right through me.

She's small but mighty.

I don't so much as move from the spot where I'm standing. The guys are hanging out behind me. Jasper and Kyler have their suitcoats on, but their shirts have long since been discarded. I'm pretty sure they popped a few buttons when they tore their dress shirts off to entice the ladies to bid.

That had been my suggestion.

All the guys should have done that earlier, but Kyler made a good point. If we go out there to strip, we'd have one shot and be done. We could bring in more money for the charity if we dragged out the auction and offered multiple date nights and prizes.

Really screw with the Bruisers.

It doesn't hurt that the press was there snapping pictures. I caught a few guests with their phones out. I'm unsure if they were live-streaming or recording, but either way, it'll be all over the internet by morning.

The only person who still doesn't know about it is Coach Malone. It's best he finds out after the fact, so as not to get him into trouble. We're saving his ass.

"It was pretty great, if I may say so myself." I'm beaming, thrilled that the auction went according to plan. I was a little concerned if the auctioneer didn't hand over the microphone, how I'd get control of the stage. Bribing him in front of thousands wouldn't go over well if it was caught on camera.

"My father is pissed, and I'd guess so are the Island Bruisers," Charlotte says.

The guys from the other team are sulking, standing at the opposite end of the room. A few are scrolling through their phones, biding time until the night ends, and they are contractually allowed to leave.

Charlotte doesn't look happy to see me. I knew what I was doing was running a risk of pissing her off. It's not like I hadn't contemplated that, and a small part wanted payback for what she did to me, but not at the expense of hurting anyone else.

As far as I'm concerned, tonight was a success. We helped the charity. The guests were thrilled about our surprise appearance. Maybe we pissed off one old man and his daughter; that's life.

"That's too bad," I say, my tone even. "We managed to get a lot of generous donations, thanks to the boys."

Charlotte rolls her lips together. "You should go, all of you," she says forcefully, her cheeks reddening as she fails to meet my stare.

"Does that include me as well?" I ask, bringing my hand to her chin to lift her gaze.

"Yes." Her tongue pokes at the corner of her lips. She's holding something back.

"Are we fake breaking up?" I ask.

"I don't see another choice. After what you did with the guys." She steps back from my reach and folds her arms across her chest. "I can't be seen dating someone who crashes parties."

My jaw tenses. "That isn't what happened." She knows we didn't crash the charity event. We made it better.

"You need to go before the media gets inside, and knowing my father, he'll do everything in his power to destroy your reputation and the team's as well."

Paparazzi and the press were waiting outside the front entrance when we arrived. Did they stick around and are waiting for the Island Bruisers to leave?

She shuffles us toward the back exit.

"Come with us," I say and brush a loose strand of hair behind her ear. Her updo is falling apart, unraveling, which is about how I feel right now.

"I can't. I have to clean up your mess."

I don't force her. If I did, it would mean carrying her over my shoulder and dragging her out. Her dad would call the cops and have me arrested for kidnapping his daughter. I don't expect him to like me, but after what I did today, undoubtedly, he despises me.

I lean in, press a chaste kiss to Charlotte's cheek before stepping backward through the open door as I exit last and join the guys outside.

Most of my teammates have scrambled like they came, piling together in vehicles. I didn't ride with them. I came here on my own.

Jasper and Kyler are waiting for me outside. They are the two who don't seem the least bit frenzied, probably because they have promising careers, at least Kyler does. Jasper is still fairly new on the team, like me, but he's got his older brother looking out for him.

"Meet back at my place?" Kyler asks.

"You bet." His fiancé is watching my son, and as much as I'd love Zayn to experience his first sleepover with friends, it won't be tonight.

———

"How did the auction go?" Emerson asks. She's in the living room with the kids.

Bristol, Kyler's daughter, is wide awake, lying on top of her princess sleeping bag, munching on popcorn while watching a Disney film.

My little tiger, Zayn, is sound asleep in his pint-sized sleeping bag, snoring softly.

We take our adult party into the hallway, keeping an eye on the kids but not wanting to wake Zayn, either.

"Perfect," Kyler says proudly. "We raised well over half a million dollars between all of our prizes."

"How much did the date for the three of you raise?" Em asks. It had been her idea to include Kyler's private jet to take one lucky guest anywhere with three of the hottest NHL players.

"Seventy-five thousand dollars," Kyler says.

Em's mouth drops. "Who was the winner?"

All of us glance around at one another, shaking

our heads. "Some lady with a very generous checkbook?" I quip.

Kyler wraps his arms around Em's waist, pulling her against him. "I missed you, M&M."

She wrinkles her nose and growls playfully at him.

He captures her lips with his, one hand on her hip, the other coming up to tangle in her hair as he deepens the kiss, probing her with his tongue.

"I swear, you two get a room!" Amber says. "That's my sister you're tongue-fucking."

"At least someone's getting some," I mutter, leaning against the doorjamb. My bachelor days are over, especially now that I've got a kid.

Jasper comes up from behind, wrapping his arms around Amber's waist. She leans into him, tilting her head back for a sweet kiss.

I glance away, awkward. When did I become the guy who doesn't have a chick? I've always found it easy to get girls and get laid, but Zayn complicates things.

Not that I'd do anything differently with him. I'm glad that I won sole custody. I'm grateful that he's in my life and my focus. But I do miss that warmth, that sizzle between the sheets, the feel of a warm female body beneath me as I kiss and ravish her.

And in that fantasy, I see a flash of fiery hair.

Crisp blue eyes.

It's one hundred percent Charlotte Grace.

Even when I don't want to have feelings for her, she's still in the back of my mind, still pushing her way past the barrier.

"I ought to take Zayn home and get him to bed," I say, heading into the living room.

"He's welcome to crash here. You know we have enough beds for guests," Kyler offers.

"Thanks." While I appreciate his offer, I'm trying to get Zayn into a routine and want his new home with me to feel like home.

———

It's been a week since the charity event. I haven't heard a word from Charlotte. I sent her flowers to try to smooth things over between us.

I texted her, which meant unblocking her number. However, I'm not sure she doesn't have me blocked.

I haven't heard a word from her since the event.

She's probably pissed at me. Coach Malone wasn't too thrilled when he found out what I'd orchestrated, and the reason behind it had seemed to tick him off even further.

But he's over it. He knows benching me isn't good for the team, and as long as I perform up to my usual standards, he lets shit slide with me.

He's like the easy parent, the one you go to when you want to stay out late or need money. The parent who doesn't ground you for your fuck ups, and I've had my share of them.

Although looking back, I'm not sure, at home, I ever had an easy parent. That's probably why I like Coach Malone so much. He's a decent father figure, unlike my old man.

"I expect you to play your best and keep it clean because we all know they won't, after the stunt you boys pulled last week on them." Malone doesn't have to remind us about the charity event.

We're playing against the Island Bruisers tonight on their home turf, and I'm not looking forward to it. I love hockey, the game, the atmosphere, the excitement when the puck is dropped—all of it. But knowing that Grant Brass is still out there and an idol to young kids has me wrenched inside.

"They'll want their revenge," Aiden says with a laugh. "Let them *try* and have it."

"Don't be cocky, Blake," Coach Malone shoots

Aiden a look. "That's what gets our asses handed to us. Go out there and show them that you're the best. That the city loves you because of your talent."

"You mean it's not because of our swagger?" Owen jokes.

"I thought it was because Jasper and Kyler ripped their shirts off that the ladies loved them," Chase jokes.

The guys chuckle and laugh, nodding in agreement. The team grows more rowdy by the second.

"That could be it," Jasper says. "The ladies want a real man in bed."

"That's enough, boys!" Malone scolds us like we're teenagers, although, for the record, some of us still act like it. "Get your gear on, your head in the game, and kick some Island Bruisers ass."

"How's the new nanny working out for you?" Kyler asks as we head out of the locker room together.

"Good. She's with Zayn at home." I had contemplated bringing the kid to a game, but I thought better of it with Grant playing opposite us. The last thing I want is to traumatize the kid.

Truthfully, I was just as much concerned he'd see Grant, feel more familiar and connected with that monster, and all the time that we've built moving forward would be like two steps back.

I'm a little uneasy when it comes to raising a kid. I'm sure it's like a bike, I'll fall off and have to get back on to try again. I'll make mistakes, it's inevitable, but I don't want any of those screwups involving Brass.

"I'm glad one of my recommendations worked out for you."

"Yeah, she's good with Zayn. Seems to know what he needs before I do." However, she spends much more time with him than I do now. It's tough with the hockey season, and I can't take a break from practice or games to raise my kid. I need the money.

"You'll figure it out. She's just there to help you, more so right now. It'll get easier in the off-season."

I hope Kyler is right. He's been a single father forever. Right now, he has his fiancé who helps with Bristol, but they also have a nanny.

It doesn't feel like there's much of an off-season. Even when we're not in the middle of hockey season, we're still lifting weights, training, practicing, and making sure that we remain focused.

"I don't know how you do it," I say. It feels like a struggle, but I'm getting by. It helps that I have a solid job that pays handsomely. I don't have to worry about finances for my son or affording a full-time nanny as long as I'm employed by the team.

"Same way that you do." Kyler pats me on the back as we head out onto the ice. "You got this. You're doing great. Don't let seeing Brass get under your skin."

My teammate knows me too well. I always was closest to Jasper, but now that Kyler and I are both fathers, we've grown closer because of that connection. He's been like a mentor, helping me figure out how to wind the legal system for custody and now raising my son.

Jasper skates right up to me and gestures toward the glass. "Looks like you have a hot date in the stands."

What is he talking about?

We skate on the ice before the game for a few minutes to warm up, make sure our blades are ready, and we stretch it out so that we don't pull a muscle when we start.

I glance in the direction Jasper had gestured when I catch her red curls. She's seated in the front row next to the other team's box. Her father probably got her those seats so that she could support the Island Bruisers.

She's wearing a coat, so I can't see whose jersey she has on underneath.

Is what he said true? That she'll be working for them after graduation. My stomach coils just thinking about her being in Grant's proximity. I don't want him anywhere near her.

"We take Brass out of the game," I say to Owen, keeping my voice low. He plays left wing up against Grant Brass, unless Grant manages to steal the puck and comes in my direction.

"I know you've got beef with the guy, and anyone who messes with my buddies deserves a beat down..." Owen lets the words trail off, "... but I can't get ejected from the game."

I bite my tongue. "You won't. We won't. Worst case, we get sent to the sin bin."

Owen doesn't even have to think about it. "I don't usually like to play dirty, but sometimes you have to do what's best for the sport."

"What's best for humanity," I say. Although I don't intend on killing him, I'm not a brute. I would like to see his face slammed against the wall a couple of times, maybe a bloody nose, and if I'm lucky, a broken leg or something that might keep him out of the game for a while.

But intentionally injuring a player isn't how I

play. I protect myself, my teammates, and go after the puck. If someone gets hurt, then so be it.

I've been good.

My lawyer wanted me to keep things clean, and I've played a little too nice over the past couple of months. I've followed his rules, his instruction down to the letter, to make sure I gained custody of Zayn.

There's a fight brewing inside of me, building up and boiling to come out.

I'm scorching with the ice under my blades.

The game starts. I'm left defenseman, that's my position, but I tackle it with grace, stealing the puck as often as possible, keeping the Bruisers from scoring.

Aiden is a fantastic goalie, but he's our last defense to the goal. If Chase and I can keep the puck from coming near him, there's less chance of scoring.

I check Conrad against the glass. As much as I want it to be Grant, he's several feet from me.

He returns the favor, my back landing against the boards, but I keep playing, vying for the puck as we fight it out fairly on the ice.

"If you and your boys needed dates that badly, we could have loaned you some of our bunnies," Conrad taunts.

I ignore his remark, stealing the puck and sending it to Owen as we move forward, attempting to score.

It's a dauntless battle, the other team checking Owen into the boards. Kyler manages to steal the puck and sends it to Jasper.

I can't hear what's being said, but the Island Bruisers are throwing insults at us every chance they get. They're trying to rile us up, but Jasper knows to keep a level head.

He's used to the trash talk from other teams we all are accustomed to. It's nothing new.

The only difference is that this time, we've rightfully pissed them off prior to the game. It's not just about the battle on the ice. They're trying to regain their pride. We made them look foolish in front of the press, especially when the news channels got wind of our surprise visit.

The puck slides back to Owen, and Grant is right on it. He pulls back his stick and swings high, landing a blow to Owen's face, striking his nose.

Blood droplets fall onto the ice.

Kyler and I race across the rink for Grant, refusing to let him get away with it. Kyler slams him against the boards, and I join in. We're not the only ones. Jasper is right behind us. The other team's players do the same, racing toward Grant to protect or defend him.

Telling Owen to go after Grant for me was a mistake. He shouldn't be fighting my battles. Not that what I said mattered. Grant was clearly out for blood. That's nothing new, whether at home or on the ice.

I pound blow after blow into Grant's ribcage when Conrad yanks me backward on the ice. "Give it a rest," Conrad says, holding me back.

Charlie Hayes joins in the fight, attacking Kyler along with another one of the Island Bruiser's players. It's hard to see who is fighting whom with my back turned to the scuffle.

The referees blow their whistle, attempting to break the fight apart. Grant gets sent to the penalty box. He's not the only one. Kyler and I do as well. Not that I mind, except they have an advantage with one more player than we do.

———

Kyler and I are released from the penalty box, but we're down by a score. I don't let it bother me. We still have plenty of time to kick some Bruiser ass.

Intermission gives us another little break while

we are shuffled into the locker room. There's no pep talk from the coach. He shakes his head, glaring at us in disappointment.

"They're out there slinging insults to get you to start fights. They want you ejected from the game or, at the very least, off the ice," Malone says. He's not oblivious to what's been going on.

"We still have two more periods. The game isn't over yet," Chase adds. He's trying to bring up morale. We're only down by one score, but it was a point that should never have happened. Thanks to the sin bin, they managed to get on the scoreboard.

Somehow, Owen's nose isn't broken. He's got a couple of steri-strips on from the assault, but when he puts the helmet back on, he'll look good as new. A little blood on his uniform, and it's just like another day at the ice rink.

Coach gives us some advice and things to work on before sending us out of the locker room.

I follow the guys back to our bench and sit while we wait for intermission to end. I can't help but glance in Charlotte's direction. If I could run over there and talk with her, I would. But that's not allowed. I can't abandon the team.

Malone is the last one out of the locker room. "What is it?" he asks.

He must have caught me staring. It's not like I can tear my gaze away from her. "Charlotte Grace."

"I thought you two were done. She's a liability, son."

I open my mouth to object to his description of her, but he cuts me off.

"She's a distraction. Is there something you need to say to her to get off your chest?"

I nod vigorously. Malone snaps at one of our hockey equipment interns.

"Yes, sir," the intern asks with bright eyes.

"Go fetch the redhead," Malone points at Charlotte Grace. "Have her come over to our bench. We need a word with her."

"Yes, of course." He tears off in pursuit of her and doesn't ask questions; he does as he's told.

"Get your head back in the game, Reece." Malone doesn't want to let it go. Aren't there other guys for him to harp on? I'm not the only one who is distracted.

TWENTY-THREE

CHARLOTTE

Coming to the Island Bruisers game wasn't my idea of fun. Yes, I love hockey, but I'm here strictly as a favor to one of the foster parents at the park district. Their daughter has never been to a game, so I offered to take her.

And seeing as how I get free tickets to the Island Bruisers games, it made sense for me to bring her. I wish that we could have sat anywhere else.

Behind the glass is fantastic, the best seats in the house as far as I'm concerned, but it's also the worst because my father is shouting at his players, harassing them for missing a shot or failing to make a goal.

Abbi looks horrified. It doesn't help that every other word out of the coach's mouth is a swear word. My father should have been a sailor.

I tried covering her ears initially, but I've since given up. It's pointless. I'd have to put earplugs in her ears for her not to hear the remarks coming from his mouth.

It's intermission which at least means no cursing. Or rather, if he is swearing up a storm, he's doing it in the locker room with the guys. Abbi and I don't have to hear it.

"Do you think they'll sign my jersey?" Abbi asks, staring up at me with bright eyes.

I love the kid. She's my favorite student I teach hockey to, not that we're supposed to have favorites. But the kid is not only a natural in terms of athletic ability, but she's cheeky.

Abbi is wearing an Ice Dragons jersey, specifically Kyler Greyson's number. There's zero chance she's getting a Bruiser's autograph on that jersey. My father kept throwing me death daggers when he saw the little girl with me.

He probably assumed it was for work or some volunteer youth program. He's not crazy enough to worry that I hid an eight-year-old kid from him.

"I don't think they look too kindly on the rival team," I say.

"No, I meant the cool team. The Ice Dragons," she says and points at their bench. Their players are slowly coming back from the locker room, and I lock eyes with Noah.

Well, I notice him. He's staring in this direction, but I'm not sure he knows I'm at the game. It's foolish for me to think that he can spot me in the crowd.

A young boy, who at first glance might be in high school, but I realize he works for the Ice Dragons, approaches us. He's wearing their logo on his collared shirt and has black slacks on. He's much more professionally dressed than the fans tend to be.

"Hey, the boss wants to speak with you."

"And what if I don't want to talk to him?" I ask.

He grimaces and shuffles his feet. I've made him uncomfortable. "I'm just an intern trying to do my job. Please, come with me."

Abbi's brow furrows as she folds her arms across her chest. "We don't go with strangers," Abbi says.

I rest an arm on her shoulder. "That's right, and I'm sorry, but I'm not going anywhere without my protégé."

"That sounds fancy," Abbi says, grinning up at me.

"She can come too, but you guys better hurry. The game is going to start soon."

I grab my bag, and we follow him through the stands and around until we reach the team.

"Who's this young lady?" Kyler asks.

Abbi's eyes widen and she spins around, showing him her Greyson jersey.

"The girl knows talent," he quips, grinning and proud that she's a fan of his.

"This is Abbi," I say, introducing her to the team. "She's one of the kids in the hockey camp where I coach."

"You coach hockey?" Malone asks, clearly surprised.

"I like hockey, sometimes I'm not fond of the player, but I like the game."

"Burn!" Abbi says and snaps her fingers.

Noah smiles at her. "I bet someone around here has a marker. Coach, can we get a permanent marker for the kid's jersey?" Noah quips.

"I want Kyler Greyson to sign my jersey," Abbi announces.

"I was going to suggest all of us sign it," Noah

says and throws his hands up in the air, "but if you just want Greyson's signature—"

"All of you?" the squeal of delight comes out with a fit of giggles as she has trouble holding herself still. "For real?" She relents and begins jumping up and down.

The other guys nod in agreement and shrug nonchalantly. "Yeah, sure. We can sign your jersey, kid."

"It's Abbi," Kyler says, and I swear the girl is about to faint. The fact he knows and remembers her name is enough to make her cheeks flame.

Someone is crushing hard.

I won't break her heart and tell her that he's engaged or that she's much too young to like a man three times her age.

"Is that why you called us over?" I ask, glancing at Noah, suspecting he has something to do with it. "Did you see Abbi in her Ice Dragons jersey?"

Noah's ears redden, his helmet on the bench. "I wanted us to talk," he says, nodding for me to follow him away from Abbi, giving us a few feet of privacy away from her listening ears and his teammates.

I fold my arms across my chest. "So, talk." I wait for him to tell me why he dragged me from our seats, although I'm grateful his teammates are indulging Abbi and signing the back of her jersey.

"It's Abbi with an I," she says, making sure they spell her name right. "And I like hearts and hockey."

The guys are chuckling, all trying to sign or draw little characters on her back and sleeves. She's got a plethora of different permanent colors being signed onto the jersey.

"Can we start over?" Noah asks.

I press my lips together. That doesn't seem like a realistic option. "I don't see how," I say. We've already caused enough drama between us.

"I forgave you for getting me arrested. What I did at the charity event wasn't that big of a deal. I mean, in comparison, it was literally nothing. I helped out sick kids."

"Is that what you're telling yourself?" I seethe. "Because you embarrassed my father, your rival team, and me."

"How were you embarrassed?" Noah asks, taking a step closer toward me.

"I vouched for you, invited you as my fake boyfriend, which I know is on me, but then you went and made a mockery of what my father had planned. It was humiliating."

"To him, or you?" Noah asks.

I bite my tongue. I wasn't that embarrassed about the whole thing that happened. If anything, I had defended Noah and his teammates for their actions to my father.

"You should have told me. I could have helped."

"There's no way that you would have gone through with it."

"You don't know that," I say. "I might have been onboard, but instead, you disrespected the entire event and, worst of all, me."

Noah shuts his eyes for a second, and exhales a deep breath as he regains his composure before staring at me. His gaze sends butterflies straight into my stomach. "Quit making this about you. Everyone had a good time. The charity received more contributions than they otherwise would have received. It was a win for everyone."

"The Island Bruisers aren't in agreement. Quit being selfish."

His jaw drops. "So, we've resorted to name-calling, is that it?"

"I said you were being selfish. That's not calling you a name. It's a fact. You were in it for the glory. The recognition. You wanted to be front and center, and you got your opportunity at the expense of the rival team."

"That's not fair," Noah says. His brow tightens and he drags me away from the player's bench and into the hallway toward their locker room. "What I did was intended to help you, to keep your ass from having to go on a date with some douche canoe who wants to get in your pants."

"Do you think I can't handle myself?"

Noah's jaw is tight. "You're putting words into my mouth. I never said that or implied it."

"You did if you think some random date will get lucky. Just because I slept with you on the first date doesn't mean I do that with every guy I meet." I shift my weight on my feet, uncomfortable with this conversation.

"You told me that your father was forcing you to offer yourself up as a date for the auction. I was doing you a favor, trying to help bring in more money to the charity, keep your father off your back, and have a little fun."

"It's the little fun part where you screwed up," I say. "Everything was fine until your boys decided to start doing a strip show at the charity auction. Those older ladies could have had a heart attack!"

The laughter that bubbles from his chest is too much. He bends over, trying to catch his breath as he's laughing from the image that I've put into his head. "Stop it. You're going to kill me!" More laughter vibrates through him.

"It's not funny," I say.

"It kind of is," Noah claims, standing up straighter. "Maybe we shouldn't have had some of my teammates do a little strip tease, but that's all that it was—their boxers never came off.

"Right, because that makes it so much better! Do you hear yourself?"

"Do you hear yourself?" Noah retorts. "I knew you might not thank me for what I did, but I thought you'd realize how much help I was and be appreciative." He steps closer, invading my personal space, as we stand toe-to-toe.

"That doesn't make any sense!"

"Neither do you!" Noah shouts and the next thing I feel is his lips are on mine as he walks me back up against the wall and his tongue sweeps across my lips and my mouth parts hungrily for him.

With one hand tangled in my hair, the other strokes my cheek and moves down my neck, caressing my breasts.

Heat floods my body. No doubt he feels it too.

He tastes like chestnut and oak. His touch sets fire to my core, sending tingling sensations flooding through me. He's awakened all of my senses, putting them on heightened alert.

I push him away after our intense kiss. "You can't just kiss me and expect me to fall limp into your arms, and we live happily ever after."

Noah's gaze flinches. "I was expecting it to shut you up."

"Ha!" I say and point at him. "Well, you're wrong, again."

TWENTY-FOUR

NOAH

Charlotte Grace is the most frustrating woman I know.

Correction.

Charlotte Grace is the most frustrating person on this planet. And probably any other planet in existence in this universe or any other universe.

I swear she enjoys complicating matters just to toy with me.

I'm seated on the bench, and the coach makes me sit the game out because I showed up late after intermission. There's a chance he'll put me in, but I'm paying the penalty.

Yes, kissing Charlotte may have had something to do with it. That wasn't the only thing. It was also the hard-on that she had me sport that made me rush off into the locker room to recover before going out on the ice.

I wasn't chancing anything happening to my best man.

And while I blamed it on a muscle spasm in my calf, the coach didn't buy my story. He told me if my muscles are spasming that much, then I ought to sit my ass on the bench and rest them.

I didn't think that little lie through.

Malone's not an idiot. I'm sure he knew what we were doing. I'm just not sure what he's doing.

Abbi and Charlotte are seated on the bench in the back with the players. Why didn't he have them return to their seats after the game started?

"Do you still have stuff to work out?" Malone asks, glancing at me before returning his attention to his players on the ice.

"No, sir."

He doesn't appear convinced, but I'm trying my damnest to make it believable. "I'm good. I'm ready to be put back in."

"Your spasms may be better, but your head isn't in the game."

It's another five minutes before he lets me in and takes Cole Stephens out. I make up for my mistake, ensuring that the puck doesn't come anywhere near the goal when the Bruisers head down to our side of the rink.

———

We win by one, which is all that matters. The close game may have been brutal, but at least we were the victors tonight.

Coming off the ice, the guys are heading for the locker room.

Charlotte and Abbi are standing, waiting for the guys to clear out.

"That was so much fun!" Abbi shouts over the noise of the arena. The fans are still celebrating the win.

I don't expect to see Charlotte tonight at the bar to celebrate, given that she's got a kid with her, which is probably for the best. I've got to head home to Zayn anyhow.

I'm starting to understand why Kyler and Em don't hang out with us after the games when we win. Priorities. Sure, I realized he put his kid and family before partying, but the feeling of doing what's right makes my chest swell with pride.

"Thanks for supporting us tonight," I say, my gaze on Abbi.

"Of course!" she squeals, delighted that an Ice Dragons player is talking with her.

I'm not sure which team Charlotte was cheering on tonight. Maybe it shouldn't matter, but it does to me. I want her to wear my jersey and support me.

I exhale a heavy breath. "I've got to hit the showers."

"Good game, Reece," Charlotte says and tugs her bottom lip between her teeth.

Is she still thinking about the kiss as much as I am?

I offer her a crooked smile and step closer. "How are you two getting home?" I ask.

"We're going to take the subway," Charlotte says.

"If you can wait twenty minutes, I'll give you girls a ride home."

"Are you sure? I need to swing by and drop Abbi off with her parents," Charlotte says, glancing at her watch. She'd be hard-pressed to get on the train in less than twenty, and I don't want to risk her losing Abbi in the crowd.

"My *foster* parents," she says. "Please, can we?" Abbi grabs Charlotte's hands, her wide eyes pleading up at her.

I like this kid.

"Yes, we'll wait outside the locker room for you."

———

It takes a little longer with Coach yammering on after the game, and I take a quick shower. While I rode the bus to the arena with the guys, one of the requirements for away games, I arranged to have a car service take me home. Not that I don't love traveling back to our turf with the guys, but I wanted to get home to Zayn a little quicker and not be tempted to go out for drinks after.

When I'm finished in the locker room, I say goodbye to my teammates and head out into the hallway to find Charlotte and Abbi waiting patiently.

I like that Charlotte is good with kids. For someone who told me she never wanted any, I thought she'd hate kids.

"Let's get out of here," I say. I lead them through the maze of hallways and pull out my phone, texting the driver that we're on our way.

"You drove?"

"Not quite," I admit.

Landon, my driver, is already waiting at the side

exit. He steps out and opens the back door of the SUV to let us pile inside.

It's three rows of seats, and Abbi climbs into the very back row, leaving me room next to Charlotte.

The kid is a genius.

Charlotte provides the driver with Abbi's address before we head away from the ice rink.

"Great game tonight," Landon says.

He probably listened to the game on the radio while waiting for me. I've offered to get him tickets, but he never accepts any gifts. He works for a company, so I've always assumed it had been against their rules to receive anything other than a tip.

"That was so much fun!" Abbi shouts from the back seat. "First and best hockey game ever."

"You did great out there on the ice tonight," Charlotte says, smiling, her gaze locked on mine.

My breath catches in my throat. The sparkle in her gaze sets my body on fire. She watches me like she wants to devour me, but she hasn't so much as touched me since that fiery kiss.

I have to remember to keep my dick in check. There's a kid in the backseat, and Charlotte and I are still on shaky ground.

I've managed to forgive her. It would be nice if she'd extend the same courtesy.

What I did wasn't nearly as bad as what she did, although Kyler kept me from making things worse at the charity event. I have him to thank later for that, when Charlotte does forgive me because, eventually, she will. She has to. I won't give up until we've set things right between us.

Even if nothing transpires between us again, we will run into each other. She's best friends with Amber, who is dating my best friend.

We make our way to Abbi's home, and Charlotte climbs out, walking Abbi to her front door. She makes sure that she relinquishes Abbi to her foster parents before returning to the vehicle.

"Where to?" the driver asks.

I start to give Landon Charlotte's address when she rests a hand on my arm and stops me. "How about we go to your place? Talk. Plus, I'm sure you're eager to see Zayn," Charlotte says.

"Thanks."

Landon heads toward my place. The air in the back of the vehicle is thick with tension.

She wants to come over to talk. Is that code for sex? Knowing Charlotte and her fiery mouth, probably not. But at least when we're done arguing, hopefully, quiet enough not to wake Zayn, I can go to bed.

"Good game tonight," Charlotte says.

"You said that already." I smile half-heartedly.

She nods and purses her lips. "You unblocked me as a contact. At least, I assume you did since you texted me recently. Thank you for the flowers," Charlotte says and then emits a heavy breath like it took all her energy to say that simple sentence.

"You're welcome. Thank you for being at the custody hearing."

A silence follows, but it's calmer, more serene, and I reach for her hand. Charlotte offers it to me, opening her palm and threading our fingers together.

"Abbi's a sweet kid," I say, surprised that Charlotte took her to a game.

"Yeah, that kid has been through a lot."

"I assumed as much, when she mentioned her foster parents."

Charlotte nods. "Yeah, many of the kids I work with have rough backgrounds. Parents who are addicts or working three jobs to keep a roof over their heads. They're the latchkey kids without an older sibling at home. Most can't even afford the hockey equipment, so we try to provide them with what we can through donations or used gear."

"I could talk to the team and see if we could donate some gear we no longer use," I offer.

She smiles weakly. "Thanks, but I'm pretty sure your feet are too big, and your hockey stick is taller than some of my kids."

"You think my stick is big," I joke, nudging her. She laughs, which I consider a huge win. "So, what do you do with the kids?"

"I run the hockey and beginner's ice-skating classes."

———

When we arrive at my place, Zayn is sleeping on the sofa next to the nanny.

"Sorry, Mr. Reece. I tried to put him into bed, but he kept waking up and asking for you."

"That's fine. I can tuck him in." I bend down and lift a sleeping Zayn into my arms, carrying him across the hall to his bedroom.

Charlotte watches by the kitchen, smiling.

"Is there anything else you need?" the nanny asks, once I return after putting Zayn to bed.

"No, that's all. I'll see you in the morning," I say.

She heads out of the penthouse suite.

"Poor girl has to come back in the morning?"

Charlotte asks, glancing at her watch. It's already after midnight.

"Yes, but she doesn't have to go far. I'm renting her a place a couple of floors down. It's not ideal, but I don't have room here without moving."

"That's really nice," Charlotte says, surprising me. "If I were a nanny, I'd love not to have to wake up in the middle of the night to take care of the kid."

I playfully swat her bottom. "Is that how it's going to be?" I ask, laughing. "You refusing to take care of our kid at night?"

"Our kid?" Charlotte asks, raising an eyebrow. "Are you referring to Zayn or a future kid because, for the record, I am not pregnant. This uterus prefers to be uninhabited."

"I didn't think you were pregnant, but I appreciate the honesty," I say. That was something Jasmine never gave me. "Uninhabited?" She has a funny way of saying things, but I find it endearing and adorable.

"Yeah, because children are little spawn. I'm sure Zayn is an exception, but I'm not putting a little baby inside of me that I have to push out. No freaking way."

My mouth drops. "Wait. Is that why you're against kids?"

"I'm not against them," Charlotte counters. "I don't want to carry them. There's a difference. I like kids. Abbi is great."

"Abbi is, what, ten?"

"She's eight," Charlotte corrects me. "Out of diapers. No baby food or formula. She's like the perfect age before they start talking back and hit those teenage years."

"Let me guess, you were a little rebel in your teens," I say.

"Yes, and I don't want to raise a little hellion. I was out drinking, making out with boys, you name it, I was dipping my toes in it."

TWENTY-FIVE

CHARLOTTE

I've never been much for weddings. I'm happy to celebrate with the couple and share in their day, but vowing to love someone forever, why do you need a ring to prove your loyalty?

Maybe I'm just jaded.

I'm a half-romantic. I love romance movies. Sit me down by the fire, and I'll curl up under a blanket watching two lovers struggle to find their happily ever after.

Books, I'm the same way.

But the minute a relationship is real, and couples start posting save-the-dates and engagement photos, I want to hurl.

Noah invited me as his plus one. My best friend

is also in attendance, since her older sister is getting married, which will make the party a little more fun. And I'll know quite a few guests because they're teammates of Noah's.

I am happy for Emerson and Kyler.

Their wedding is outdoors in their backyard. For a billionaire, who could get married anywhere, he chose home. There's something sweet in its simplicity.

The backyard is gorgeous, with white Christmas lights circling the evergreens. Tiki torches offer enough light for the evening festivities and a tent for guests to dine and dance in after the wedding ceremony. Giant heaters are set up to keep the guests warm since it's a winter wedding.

A light dusting of snow speckles the ground, falling from the sky, making the air feel even chillier.

Bristol walks down the aisle as their flower girl, and she looks like a little princess. She carefully drops one petal at a time, tossing it and waiting until it lands gracefully before throwing another.

When she reaches the end of the aisle, she tosses the rest of the petals straight into the air and lets them rain down on her.

The girl knows how to make an entrance.

There are a few giggles from the audience, and

Kyler glares at her, warning his daughter to behave while he waits for his bride to walk down the aisle.

"Bristol!" Zayn shouts and waves at her as she stands at the front with her father. Noah's face turns as red as Rudolph's nose. I guess he wasn't expecting an outburst from his toddler.

Noah sits beside me with Zayn on his lap, bundled with snow bibs over his little suit. Noah had insisted he didn't want his son to catch a cold since the wedding was outside.

Kyler and Emerson's wedding is perfection. Their ceremony is short, but their vow exchanges even bring tears to my eyes. It's clear that they're madly in love, and I'm happy for them.

After the ceremony, Noah has to hold onto Zayn to keep him from running onto the dance floor and knocking over the cake while we wait for Kyler and Em to cut the cake and then have their first dance.

Zayn is squirmy, and it's clear that it's trying Noah's patience. He's standing, rocking his son, who has no interest in holding still.

"Can I?" I ask, offering to take Zayn from him.

Zayn wiggles out of Noah's arms and into mine. "Good luck," Noah says, but the worried look tells me that he's not sure I'll do any better.

"Do you want to take a walk through the

garden?" I ask Zayn, carrying him away from the guests.

He seems to settle, and I glance back at Noah, who is keeping a close eye on us. We wander over to the flower beds which are empty this time of year. But there are some beautifully lit trees with white twinkling lights behind them.

It's enough to capture Zayn's attention for a few minutes. From the distance, it's hard to see the cake cutting, but I don't mind missing it if it means Noah has a few minutes to himself. He's been trying to hold Zayn since we got to the wedding, and the kid is a minute away from melting down.

Noah's given him snacks and water. He's taken him to the bathroom twice. I'm pretty sure the little one wants to run freely, and hopefully, Noah will let him do that when the guests get up to dance.

Away from the commotion and excitement, Zayn rests his head on my shoulder and closes his eyes. I rub my hand over his back as he settles down for a few minutes.

I appreciate the quiet and stillness of the night. Away from the other guests, it's tranquil and calm.

"Babysitting duty?" Amber jokes as she joins me over near the decorated trees. She's in a sleeveless dress and wraps her arms around herself, clearly chilly.

I'm wearing a long-sleeved dress with lace trim, designed for winter.

"Trying to keep someone preoccupied until dance time," I say.

"Or nap time," Amber adds.

"No nap." Zayn pops his head up, eyes wide.

"Why is it that kids hate naps, but as adults, I'd kill to have one during the week?" I ask.

Amber shrugs and guesses, "You want what you can't have?"

Noah clears his throat from behind. I didn't hear him come up. "What is it that you want but can't have?" he asks me. His voice drips with lust that sends flutters down south. Heat floods my body, and I'm sure I'm blushing, but maybe Noah will chalk it up to the cold.

We've been taking things slow since I stayed over at his house after the game a couple of weeks ago. We platonically shared a bed. Noah slept on his side, me on the opposite side. Sometime during the night, his arm wrapped around my waist, and we cuddled. It was the best feeling to wake up to until Zayn jumped on the bed and proceeded to snuggle between us.

Amber grins and gives us a wave as she heads back under the tent, where it's warm. "Catch you on the dance floor."

"We were talking about a nap," I say with a wry smile.

"Sure, if you say so." Noah offers to take Zayn back, and I relinquish him to his father.

Zayn is all wiggles.

"I think we can probably let him run around on the dance floor for a little while. They moved the cake so at least he won't ruin their wedding." Noah lets Zayn down when we reach the dance floor. He's not the only one running around like a maniac. Bristol is twirling on the floor, mopping it with her dress.

"I don't think even a tipped-over cake would ruin their wedding." Not that I'd want to see that disaster, but I'm pretty sure they'd laugh about it and shrug it off.

"Well, I'm glad I don't have to find out."

————

"Dance with me," Noah says, taking my hand and pulling me out of my seat.

I've had a couple of glasses of wine. I haven't kept

track of what Noah's had, but he's been to the open bar a few times.

Zayn already crashed after an hour of dancing and is asleep on the sofa inside Kyler's home. Maybe having a wedding in the backyard was genius, especially with kids attending.

Bristol is fighting sleep, dancing, and singing to the music, although I don't think she's got any of the words right. No one cares because everyone is having a good time.

Noah strolls with me onto the dance floor, and the song is perfect for a slow dance. "So, I was thinking," he says, and I chuckle.

"Don't hurt yourself."

He scowls playfully and leans in, kissing me.

That's how he's learned to silence me, and I don't mind it. If we weren't in the middle of the dance floor at a wedding, I'd be deepening the kiss. But I'm trying to keep it polite, especially around the kids, like Bristol, who is still awake and watching us dance.

My arms wrap around his neck, my fingers playing in his hair as we sway to the music together. "We'd make beautiful children together," Noah whispers into my ear.

I laugh. "Is that your way of saying you like me?"

"It's my way of saying I want to put a baby in you."

The heat from his words makes my skin burn. I bite down on my bottom lip, glancing away. "You're cheeky." For a man who's been taking things slow with me, those words are rather unexpected.

"And I want to see Zayn with a little brother or sister," Noah whispers. His eyes lock onto mine.

He's serious.

My stomach does a little belly flip. "Someone has baby fever," I say, dropping a kiss to his nose. "It's cute."

"Cute?" He laughs. "Don't tell the guys you called me cute. You'll ruin the tough image that I have going for me."

I lean in toward his ear, as though I'm about to whisper a secret into his ear, when I playfully nip his ear lobe, sucking and tonguing his skin.

He moans, and I'm grateful the music covers up the sound of his desire for me.

"Are you trying to turn me on?" Noah's voice is rough and coarse. He pulls back just slightly, a wicked grin on his face. "Are you sure you want to go there? Because I can make you scream my name without us ever leaving the dance floor."

"I want to see you try."

TWENTY-SIX

NOAH

Watching Charlotte with Zayn tonight has made the sweet feelings that I have for her turn primal.

It's hard not to notice her sexy hip sway as she walks across the dance floor. With my body brushed up against hers, the heat feels combustible.

I want her in a way I haven't wanted anyone in a long time.

She's not just another girl. I don't want her as a fling or a quick romp.

Charlotte Grace holds the key to my heart. I didn't realize it until tonight. Everything about her is perfect.

I mean, sure, she royally screwed me over in terms of my kid when she first met him, but I can see that it was in an effort to protect him. It was a mistake, and both of us are to blame. I kept him a secret from her. Maybe if I hadn't done that, the arrest, the fact that he was returned to his mother, and the custody battle would never have happened.

The past is just that. It can't be undone.

It's time to move forward, and I've slowly been allowing myself to do that with Charlotte. I've been pushing her into the friend zone as much as I can after all that's happened between us.

But at every opportunity, when she's snarky and sassy, I find myself kissing her to shut her up. Whether it's my heart or my dick begging for her, they are one and the same, me wanting Charlotte Grace.

I've just been too blind to see it, too focused on Zayn, which isn't bad. My son deserves the first spot in my life, above my career, which has been a jolting reality, but I've had the support of the nanny to keep me on task with my job. I'm at the games and practices on time.

Watching Charlotte with Zayn, how sweet she is with him and able to manage his little outbursts, has me envious. For a woman who swears she doesn't want kids, the more I hear her talk about it, the more I realize that she's just scared.

Afraid of what comes next.

Terrified of the physical act of childbirth.

Frightened for the unknown.

There are no guarantees. I've learned that lesson along the way. And some of the best surprises are those that come least expected, like Zayn. He definitely was not planned.

Dancing with Charlotte is easy. My hand at her lower back feels natural. We flirt, both of us treading carefully until she does that wicked thing with her tongue on my ear, and fuck it, I can feel my dick responding to her ministrations.

Thankfully, I'm pressed tight against her. I'm sure she feels my cock straining against my trousers, nestled up against her, but she doesn't so much as look down or comment on it.

And that's when I say and do the unthinkable. She makes me moan and I challenge her to screaming my name on the dance floor, without ever leaving our spot.

Charlotte doesn't tell me I'm crazy, which I probably am.

She doesn't suggest I walk away and embarrass myself further when any number of my teammates could see my cock at full attention.

No. Charlotte Grace says that she wants to see me try to arouse her.

Fuck me.

I have to do this without anyone knowing what's happening until her final moment of ecstasy. And there aren't enough couples on the dance floor for me to physically feel her up and turn her on.

I have to get creative.

I pull her closer, tighter. My knee slides between her thighs, and she gives a sharp gasp as I put pressure on her center. "Good girl," I say, pleased at her breathing and soft moans.

Her tongue darts out, tracing the corner of her lips as she tries to regain some semblance of control.

Good luck, *sweetheart*.

With my left hand on her lower back, I stroke her over her dress, my fingers moving back and forth in the way they would if they were buried between her thighs. My fingers inch lower, but they're still teasing her, still on her back, dipping lower toward her bottom.

Charlotte emits a soft hum from the back of her throat. Her cheeks are red, her eyes slightly glazed over.

My breath tickles her ear and neck. If I can't

finger fuck her or drive my cock inside of her, then I'll have to get creative to get her off another way.

"I want to rip that dress right off your body," I whisper into her ear.

She takes in a sharp breath and raises an eyebrow. Silence follows. She doesn't speak, so I take it as a sign to continue.

"I've been thinking about what you'd taste like against my tongue. I want to guide your hand between your pussy lips and let you feel your wetness coat your fingers. Then I'd guide them to my lips."

She sighs softly as we sway to the music, my cock nudging her as I feel her hips rock against me. She tangles her fingers in my hair, pulling me closer, tighter, her lips descending on mine for a searing kiss.

I open my lips, let her taste me, have me, but all she gets is a kiss on the dance floor.

We're at my teammate's wedding. We can't fuck here for everyone to see us. Her touch as she runs her fingers through my scalp is tantalizing.

I swore I'd make her come undone and scream my name, and I'm pretty sure she's returning the favor. I'm unsure whether I should be pleased or annoyed that she's trying to upend my challenge.

Charlotte is undoubtedly distracting me, but I don't think it's intentional, the more I study her rosy lips, her fiery cheeks, and her sunset-glazed eyes. I should put her out of her misery, let her come and reach her peak as she chases her orgasm.

"I want to fuck you, Charlotte," I whisper into her ear, and she moans and thrusts her hips against me. I take it as encouragement and tease her, my fingers inching her dress higher.

Her lips part, her eyelids struggling to stay open. She's already teetering on the edge, and at best, it's a mediocre orgasm.

Fucking her, she'd scream so much louder. I've heard the blissful sounds she's made in bed with me. The slight whimpers and moans she's making now are pale in comparison, but I refuse to lose this little challenge.

She grabs my hand and drags me off the dance floor, through the backyard, and inside the house, where it's quieter.

My mouth is on hers, latched on as I fumble with the zipper on her dress while walking her backward down the hallway.

The guest rooms are too far away, upstairs, to finish what's been started. I drag her into the nearest closed door. There's a desk in the center of the room with a computer and several screens attached to the wall.

I hike up Charlotte's dress while her fingers undo my belt buckle.

"Condom?" she asks.

I pull one out of my wallet and tear the foil packet. Within seconds, it's on, and I have her bent across the desk.

Charlotte spreads her legs, and I guide my fingers over her warmth, spreading her wetness, making sure that she's ready before entering her.

With one hand, I grab her hair clip, unclasping and fingering her locks. With my other hand, I position my cock inside her entrance, teasing her.

"Fuck, Noah. Deeper." She wiggles her hips back at me, trying to match my slow thrust with her more intense need.

My hands move to her hips, steadying her as I drive my cock inside of her, doing exactly what she begs for until she's sated.

Her moans aren't the least bit silent, but they're drowned out by the loud pulsating of music from the band just outside the house.

"Fuck," I curse. Already, she's clenching onto my cock, making it difficult for me to hold out much longer. "Don't you dare chase that orgasm yet," I growl at her.

Charlotte whimpers and I slide out of her and spin her around to face me. She's gasping for breath. Her cheeks are flushed, and I find the zipper on her dress, bringing the whole thing down to the floor with a smirk.

There's something much more intimate about seeing the person you're fucking. I want to dominate her, to see her stare back at me while I make her come, naked and quivering beneath me.

Anyone could walk in. Neither of us bothered to lock the door, but the party is outside, and hopefully, it stays that way.

"Climb on the desk," I command.

She lifts her hips and sits at the edge of wooden desk. Charlotte spreads her legs, flashing me her pussy. "See something you like?"

I throw one leg over my shoulder and bend down, sweeping my tongue over her sex. Her fingers tangle in my hair as she drags me back up her body.

"We can do that another night," Charlotte says. "Right now, I want you to fuck me. Hard."

Just hearing her talk dirty makes my cock twitch with anticipation. She wraps her legs around me as I drive my cock inside her. Every stroke, she matches with her hips gyrating, begging me to let her have her sweet release.

I reach down between us, circling her clit, and I feel her shudder and listen to her breaths as she gasps for air. She's not the only one close to the edge of oblivion.

"Come for me," I whisper into her ear, nibbling on her neck as she trembles in my arms. Her pussy walls clench onto my cock, sending me over the edge with her.

Panting hard, gasping for breath, my heart pounds wildly against my chest as I pull away, disposing of the condom in the nearby wastebasket.

I retrieve Charlotte's dress from the floor and help her put the gown back on before we quietly tiptoe out of the office, only to get caught by Jasper, wearing a huge grin on his face.

"What?" I growl at him.

He flashes me his phone and I swear if he got video of our festivities, I'll murder him. *Grant Brass has been arrested on charges of assault and rape.*

"Jasmine?"

Jasper shakes his head. "A college girl, someone at NYU. Allegedly, he chatted up a redhead at the bar who wasn't interested, and he wouldn't take no for an answer."

"Sick bastard," I mutter. Had he thought the redhead was Charlotte, or was it just a coincidence?

"The league is already setting a press conference for tomorrow. Think he'll be kicked out of the NHL?"

"Yeah. He can't play if he's in prison."

EPILOGUE

CHARLOTTE

Noah and I have been dating for the past several weeks. Everything has been perfect, which has me on edge.

I'm bound to screw up. I've done it once before, but this time, there's so much more to lose.

I actually love him, not that I've said those three words. I'm too afraid to be the first one to voice them.

What if I push him away?

What if he feels I'm moving too fast?

A thousand thoughts race through my head when I even consider saying *I love you*, all of them strangling me with crippling anxiety.

Dating and hookups were so much easier. But

finding love and keeping it, that's the hard part. But the truth is that I don't want anyone else.

My father called to ask if I'm still dating Noah Reece. He was trying to offer an olive branch, inviting him and Zayn for Christmas dinner with the family. It'll be awkward if Noah accepts the invitation, but honestly, all I care about is spending it with Noah and Zayn.

I carry my skates with me to the park district's ice rink. NYU classes are done for the winter semester, and today's the last skate class with the kids until after the new year.

"Charlotte!" Abbi waves to me excitedly, like I didn't know she was in my next hockey drills and thrills class. She's been taking skating classes with me since she was four, when I taught her to ice skate in my beginners' on-ice class.

"Have you been practicing your drills?" I ask. She's got a natural talent on the ice. It's why her foster parents have been talking about pulling her out of the park district and putting her in a more intense program.

I respect their decision, but I'm going to miss her.

"Yes," Abbi says and skates over to the wall, waiting for me to finish lacing up my skates and join her and the other kids. "We have a surprise for you, Ms. Grace."

It's that sweet sing-song voice and her use of my last name that has me raising an eyebrow. "What are you kids up to?" I ask.

Abbi and the other kids whistle, giving off some type of weird vibe.

Turns out, they're signaling Santa.

I laugh, seeing a man wearing a Santa costume as he steps onto the ice rink. "Santa can ice skate?" I say with a laugh.

Was this part of the park district plans they forgot to tell me about, or some prank set up by one of the kid's parents?

As Santa skates closer, I get a better look at him, and he's definitely not the *real* Santa Claus.

My mouth drops when I see who is behind the beard and hat.

Noah Reece.

"Don't forget your sled!" Abbi shouts.

"Or the presents!" Lotti cheers, gaining a lot of laughs from the other kids.

Noah pulls a sled onto the ice. In the front is Zayn, wearing an elf costume, while there are heaps of presents in the back. "I thought I'd bring you some holiday cheer."

My mouth drops, surprised by the grand gesture. "Wow, you shouldn't have."

"Don't say that. He brought us presents!" Georgia skates over to the sled, her blonde pigtails coming slightly undone. She sizes Santa up, folding her arms across her chest. "Oh my gosh!" The squeal from her high-pitched eight-year-old lips is almost too much.

Noah waits for her to finish because we're sure Georgia has something else to add.

"You're not Santa! It's Noah Reece." Her mouth drops, and she stares up at him in awe. "You play hockey."

He bends down and places his finger to his lips. "You can't tell anyone. It has to be our secret."

The other kids all giggle and skate forward, heading for Noah and the giant sled of presents that he brought for the kids.

"I can't believe you did all this," I say, dumbfounded by the surprise. I didn't see it coming.

"I love you. Of course, I'd want to make their holidays extra special," Noah says.

"I love you," I whisper, yanking on his Santa coat and tugging his beard out of the way as I pull him down for a kiss.

"Not into the beard, huh?"

"That white scruffy fluff? No, thank you."

––––––––

Thank you for reading *Arresting the Hockey Player*. I hope you enjoyed Noah and Charlotte's story.

Looking for your next hot read right now? Want a spicy billionaire romance featuring a grumpy single dad? Check out Billionaire Grump!

I am Levi Luxenberg. Forty-year-old billionaire. CEO of Luxenberg Enterprises. And apparently, father of one.

A week ago, having kids wasn't even in my ten-year plan.

Now, I have a five-year-old daughter who will hardly look in my direction.

I am aware that Amelia is grieving her mother's death, and I swear I'm not a complete jerk, but I jumped on a private jet to Chicago at a moment's notice, and the kid won't even say a word to me.

As if that wasn't bad enough, our pilot just got sick and I have to fly commercial for the first time in years.

You'd think that would be the end of it, but no.

The cherry on top?

Amelia would rather interact with Clare, the divorced, jobless, tipsy woman sitting right in front of us, than me.

She chats with her, she smiles at her—she even draws her a freaking picture.

I would be really mad if I didn't actually need a nanny. Urgently.

Since my assistant screwed my wanted ad over and made me look like a grumpy billionaire desperately looking for a wife, Clare suddenly seems perfect for the job.

She has no place to live, no idea who I am, and no qualms about being my live-in nanny on a trial basis.

The problem is, I think I might want to keep her around longer...

Here's a sneak peek of Billionaire Grump.

––––––––

Chapter One
   Levi

.   .   .

"Grumpy Billionaire desperately seeks a nanny for his five-year-old daughter. Expect to work late nights, have no social life, lots of tears, and absolutely no alcohol, drugs, parties, or fun."

That was the ad that went out this morning. My assistant, fed up with my shenanigans, decided to give me a taste of my own medicine. I can't believe Nancy thought that's what I wanted the ad to say, that I'm a billionaire. Is she trying to attract every gold digger?

I'll admit that I haven't always been kind to my assistant. She's been required to field calls from previous dates, forced to tell them I'm not interested.

Is this her idea of payback?

"What?" I answer my phone. It's my assistant.

"Did you get the text that your flight home has been canceled?"

"No," I growl, and put Nancy on speakerphone while I open up my messages. There are dozens of messages and even more emails that have been ignored.

I'm a busy man, and I haven't had time over the past forty-eight hours to deal with work.

I just discovered I'm a father, and the little girl was whisked into a temporary foster home after her mother died in an automobile accident.

My attorney handled a comparative DNA test and requested Amelia's DNA. I saw the truth for myself on paper. Although after staring at the young girl, her eyes as blue as the depths of the ocean, I know the kid is undoubtedly mine. She has Katelyn's blonde hair and build. She's small for her age, but Amelia's birth certificate indeed has my name as the father. And the kid's date of birth matches up to when Katelyn and I had been together.

Amelia hasn't said a word since I met her. I'm sure the kid talks, but the silence is heavier than anything I could have imagined.

I'm sure it's because she's grieving.

Me too.

But for different reasons.

I'm not ready to be a father.

I glance down at the little girl seated across from me. She hasn't touched her breakfast, and I practically ordered one of everything on the menu because she refused to give the waitress her order.

"I can book you two first-class tickets direct from O'Hare to JFK."

"Inform Douglas of the travel situation and that we'll need to be picked up from JFK."

"I'm on it," Nancy says. "I'll text you the flight details."

"I hate flying commercial," I grumble.

"I'm sorry, Mr. Luxenberg."

"Yeah, me too." I end the call and shove my phone into my jacket pocket.

Amelia stares at me, her pancakes untouched. Just like the strawberry milkshake, with whipped cream that dribbles down the side of the glass.

I steal a piece of her bacon, and her eyes narrow at me like it's hers and I shouldn't touch it. But she doesn't scold me.

I'm only met with further silence. I'd almost rather her yell, scream, cry, and throw a temper tantrum. Not that I'd be good with handling that type of outburst, but the silence hurts my heart so damn much.

I'm in over my head, and I desperately need a nanny, someone who is good with kids.

My phone pings in my pocket, and I grab it, glancing at the text from Nancy confirming the seat assignments. We're both on the same flight, but Amelia is assigned to the row in front of me.

The seats aren't together.

"Fuck!"

Amelia's eyes widen, and her jaw drops as she stares at me.

"Don't say that word," I scold before she can repeat it.

We finish at the restaurant and head straight for the airport. I don't have any checked baggage, only the carry-on suitcase and backpack. The kid didn't come with many clothes, only a small knapsack with a handful of outfits.

Last night and again this morning, Amelia refused to change out of the bright-pink frilly tutu, white tights, and white T-shirt. It's amazing her white shirt is still clean after sleeping at the hotel.

Stubborn.

Another reason I need a nanny. I'm not the most patient person.

We board the plane early, and I explain to the stewardess about our seating arrangement. It's a full flight, but the woman seated next to me offers to switch. She's cute, with long blonde hair and a full figure that makes my cock twitch admiring her curves.

"Hi, I'm Clare," the blonde says, smiling at Amelia.

Amelia squeezes her stuffed unicorn tighter. Its mane is rainbow and sparkly, and it's the only toy the kid brought with her.

"She's shy," I say, not wanting to elaborate on the recent trauma in her life to this stranger.

"I was shy when I was her age, too," Clare says, her eyes entirely on Amelia. It's as though I don't exist. "What's your friend's name?" she asks, pointing at the unicorn.

Clare shuffles into her new row in front of us on the airplane. She doesn't sit. She hovers, leaning on the headrest, trying to engage with Amelia.

Amelia doesn't respond, but I do. And it's more of a bite.

"That's enough questions for today," I say, my temper short. I gesture for her to turn around in her seat.

"You don't have to be rude," Clare says, and spins around, sitting in her seat.

Amelia's nose scrunches, and I can't tell what she's thinking. She brings the unicorn to her face, and her mouth moves ever so quietly, but I can't hear what she's saying. It's like a secret between her and her fluffy friend.

I don't apologize to the girl seated in the row in front of us. Maybe I should since she is doing me a favor, switching seats.

"Have you ever been on an airplane?" I ask Amelia.

She doesn't answer me. Her mother didn't always live in Chicago. I met her in New York. We were a short romance that burned bright and hot early on.

At take-off, Amelia grips the chair handle. I rest my hand over hers. "It's okay. Just a little bumpy. It's supposed to be like this," I assure her.

There's no sign of her nodding or saying anything to indicate that she understands me. Her mother, Katelyn, didn't speak any other languages, as far as I'm aware.

After we've reached cruising altitude, the stewardess asks us for our drink orders. I refrain from having any alcohol. I'd love a stiff drink right now, but it's not going to help me forget why I was in Chicago.

I retrieve a few children's menus and crayons from the backpack. One side has drawings to color along with the menu, and the opposite side is blank. Thankfully, the restaurant gave us extra for the flight. Pulling down the tray table in front of Amelia, I put the items down, letting her color.

She stares at them and then glances back at me.

"Go ahead. You can color," I say.

I don't know much about kids, let alone raising one. My younger brother, Connor, is a dipshit, and thank god he hasn't procreated.

I've tried to look out for him. Hell, I gave him a job in management at the New York hotel. But he has a knack for either firing decent employees or making them want to quit. But I'm not going to just hand him a paycheck and not make him get his ass into work five days a week. Where else can I put him?

I may have inherited the company, but I also turned this place around. It was barely profitable when I took over after our father's death. I had no choice but to shake things up and make it better, because otherwise, who would take care of Mom?

Dad left me the business, which meant taking care of my mother and handling my younger brother. I'm not a complete dick. I didn't put either of them out on the street, though it was tempting with Connor.

The seatbelt fasten light is turned off, and the girl in the row in front of us turns around, watching Amelia.

"What are you drawing?" Clare asks.

Amelia scrunches her nose. The paper is completely blank.

"How about you draw a picture of your balding dad?" Clare grins.

"I'm not balding," I snarl. Why can't she turn around and mind her own business?

"Right," Clare says, and snaps. "What's that called again with the hair that's spikey?" She gestures above her own head like her hair is sticking up two feet high.

Amelia chuckles and points at my head. "Troll hair," Amelia says with a giggle.

I suppose it's better than being called balding at my age. "Do you think I've got troll hair?" I force a smile, grateful to have heard little Amelia's voice.

Amelia shrugs, the smile vanishing, and my heart aches.

I want to hear her laugh and be carefree. She's five. She should be over the moon with curiosity and talkative. This quiet side is frustrating to deal with.

Clare stares at us, and before I have time to comprehend what she's doing, her fingers are running through my hair. She's making my hair spiky and stand on end.

Amelia giggles and smiles the biggest grin, pointing at my head. "Troll hair."

"Can you draw me a troll?" Clare asks.

Amelia nods and reaches for the purple crayon, gripping it tight as she begins coloring on the blank white paper.

I breathe a sigh of relief and run my hand through my unkempt hair, trying to fix the mess before our plane lands. There's enough press in New York to spot me the minute I step off the plane, and I don't need ridiculous pictures in the newspaper and on social media of me with troll hair.

As it is, I'll have to put out a press release and make a public announcement about Amelia before I'm bludgeoned with accusations.

Clare gives me a thousand-watt smile, but it's clearly forced. She turns around and heads toward the stewardess, saying something quietly to her.

Both of their eyes latch on me before looking away.

I'm used to the stares and curiosity. She must have realized that I'm billionaire Levi Luxenberg. I've been on magazine covers and interviewed by celebrities. I'm used to the attention. Usually, I ignore it.

But now I'm not just looking after myself. I have Amelia, and I can't keep my daughter a secret. I just have to ask everyone to respect our privacy.

I keep an eye on the stewardess once Clare is back in her seat, making sure no one is snapping photos of Amelia and me on the plane together.

Thirty minutes later, Clare turns around to check on Amelia. "How's the drawing?"

Amelia is still very hard at work on her troll drawing. I didn't expect much, but the kid has a knack for artwork. She doesn't answer Clare, but that's okay because I know that she can, and eventually, she'll speak when she's ready.

The stewardess brings Clare a mini bottle of vodka, and she mixes it with orange juice, holding it while talking. I haven't been paying attention to how much she's been drinking in front of us, but this isn't the first drink that she's been served.

I opted to get Amelia an apple juice, which she's sipped a few times.

Clare's cheeks are red and her lips glossy. "I wish we could stay in the air forever, just keep flying."

"Why?" Amelia asks, glancing up from her crayons.

My kid seems to be enthralled with the tipsy woman seated in the row in front of us. Great.

"I don't want to face New York. After a loveless marriage and finally growing the balls to leave my narcissistic and emotionally abusive ex, I have to find a job and a home with nothing lined up. I spent six years as a preschool teacher, and I loved every minute of it. But the minute we got married, *he* made me leave my job. He didn't like that I wasn't home when he wasn't home. Afraid that I'd have a life outside of him. Jealous douch—" She slaps a hand over her mouth and looks at Amelia. "Oops, I meant jealous guy."

Mostly unfazed, she continues to ramble, not the least bit done with her overshare.

"My best friend let me stay in Chicago with her during the divorce, but I've worn out my welcome. Newlyweds," she says with a laugh. "See why I'd rather just stay in the air and fly free?"

"And you thought spending money on a first-class plane ticket would be smart?"

"Not that it's any of your business, but I stole these airline miles from my ex."

I offer a wayward smile. "Good for you."

Amelia stares up at Clare, perplexed. I imagine that most of that went right over the kid's head.

"What are your plans when you land in New York?" I ask.

She sips the orange juice and vodka from the clear plastic cup. "I don't know. I've been in survival mode for the past eight months. My ex bled me dry with the divorce. I'll probably flip burgers or something and sleep in a cardboard box."

Amelia hands the troll drawing to Clare.

"Is this for me?" Clare asks with wide eyes. Amelia nods. "Why don't you give it to your dad? I'll bet he'd like to hang it on the fridge."

"I don't have a dad," Amelia whispers, staring up at Clare.

My stomach clenches at her remark. "I'm her father," I say, clearing my throat.

Clare stares pointedly at me like she doesn't believe me. "The kid obviously doesn't think you are. Maybe I should sit with her."

"Excuse me?" I'm appalled by her suggestion.

"Would you like me to sit with you, sweetie?" Clare asks Amelia.

Amelia glances from me to Clare. The kid doesn't know what the hell is going on, and neither does the woman sitting one row in front of us.

Amelia unlatches her seatbelt and wiggles around me to get out of the aisle. I grab her waist, not letting her run around like a maniac on an airplane. Now isn't the time or place for her to run free.

"Sir, I'm going to have to ask you to remove your hands from the little girl," the stewardess says, exchanging a brief glance with Clare.

"For fuck's sake, I'm her father!"

"You need to calm down, sir," the flight attendant

says.

Amelia's eyes widen, and she scurries away from me after I lash out at the stewardess. She climbs into Clare's lap, which is not helping matters.

"She's my daughter," I say.

The stewardess bends down to Amelia's level. "Is that man your father?" she asks the little girl.

Amelia's eyes widen, and she glances from me back to the stewardess. We're all met with silence.

Fuck.

"Amelia, come back to your seat," I seethe, trying my best not to raise my voice, but my jaw is tight, and my hands are bunched into fists.

I don't blame Amelia. It's the stewardess and the nosey blonde who have decided to muck into other people's business.

Amelia doesn't respond to me, and why would she? We barely know each other. Doesn't she get that if she leaves me, she'll be back in foster care? She had to be put in emergency placement with a family until I arrived. Does she want to go back?

"Sir, sit down in your seat," the stewardess says.

"Is this how you treat your first-class passengers? You kidnap their children?"

"You're right, sir. I apologize. How about you show us photos of your daughter on your phone?

Then we can clear up this entire misunderstanding before having to get the authorities involved."

Amelia has been in my custody for less than a day. I don't have pictures of her on my phone.

"I can't do that," I say.

There are no emails from the social worker regarding Amelia, either. Everything was handled by phone or by my assistant.

"That's what I thought," the stewardess says.

"You don't know what the hell you're talking about." I stand to explain the situation without Amelia overhearing it all over again.

"Sir, you're going to have to sit down. We're going to be landing soon."

Not soon enough.

I grumble and plop back down into my seat. I swear I'll never fly commercial again.

The young gentleman who was in seat 1A climbs into the row beside me, trading seats with Amelia while Clare buckles her seatbelt.

I should be the one fastening her seatbelt and looking after her. She's *my* daughter.

As we land, the flight crew announces that no one is to get up from their seats because there's been a hiccup, and the authorities need to be brought onto the plane.

Fuck.

Could this week get any worse?

Read Billionaire Grump now!

SHOP EXCLUSIVE MERCHANDISE & SIGNED BOOKS

THANK you so much for reading Arresting the Hockey Player! I hope you enjoyed the novel. I absolutely loved writing it.

If you love signed paperbacks and exclusive content, be sure to check out my website: https://shopwillowfox.com and sign up to be notified of sales, new release news, and exclusive content!

ABOUT THE AUTHOR

Willow Fox has loved writing since she was in high school (many ages ago). Her small town romances are reflective of living in a small town in rural America.

Whether she's writing romance or sitting outside by the bonfire reading a good book, Willow loves the magic of the written word.

Visit her website at:

https://shopwillowfox.com

ALSO BY WILLOW FOX

Dangerous Boss

Bossy Single Dad Series

Billionaire Grump

Mountain Grump

Bachelor Grump

Ice Dragons Hockey Romance

Faking it with the Billionaire

Daring the Hockey Player

Arresting the Hockey Player

Looking for kinkier books? Try these spicy stories written under the name Allison West.

Gem Apocalypse Series

Emerald Rebellion

Amber Voyeur

Sapphire Sacrifice

Scarlet Assassin

Crimson Crown

Royally Claimed Series

Palace Secrets

Maiden Claimed

Grave Misfortune

Prefer a sweeter romance with action and adventure?
Check out these titles under the name Ruth Silver.

Aberrant Series

Love Forbidden

Secrets Forbidden

Magic Forbidden

Escape Forbidden

Refuge Forbidden

Boxsets

Nightblood

Royal Reaper

Reaper Academy: Alt Spicy Edition

Standalones

Stolen Art